MW00344576

Sax

Desert Rebels MC, Volume 4

Tory Richards

Published by Tory Richards, 2020.

This is a work of fiction. Similarities to real people, places, or events are entirely coincidental.

SAX

First edition. July 15, 2020.

Copyright © 2020 Tory Richards.

ISBN: 978-1393926924

Written by Tory Richards.

Table of Contents

Chapter 1

H olly

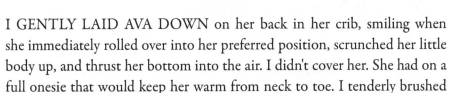

I GENTLY LAID AVA DOWN on her back in her crib, smiling when she immediately rolled over into her preferred position, scrunched her little body up, and thrust her bottom into the air. I didn't cover her. She had on a full onesie that would keep her warm from neck to toe. I tenderly brushed my hand over her baby-soft curls and felt my heart swell at how much I loved her. The intense feeling was akin to how strongly I still felt about Sax.

I didn't dwell on the question of who her father might be, accepting the fact that it was any one of five men, four of whom had raped me when Raven, Bobbie, and I had been kidnapped the year before. After I'd been rescued by Sax and his brothers, I'd tried to move on with my life. But six weeks later, when I'd found out that I was pregnant, the whole ordeal of the rape, combined with the fact that Sax did not want children, had forced me to make a decision that I'd felt was best for everyone involved.

At a little over three months along, I'd officially broken it off with Sax and left the Las Vegas area to have my baby. Breaking up with the only man that I'd ever loved—the man that I still loved—had nearly destroyed me. But I'd known that he would never accept the baby, even if it were his. He'd been patient and understanding with me after the attack, but I'd taken the coward's way out, letting him believe that the reason I was breaking up with him had to do with the assault and my inability to cope with it, rather than my pregnancy that he knew nothing about.

I was going to go to Hell for that, and for the terrible secret that I'd kept from everyone.

My intentions had been good. I'd wanted Sax to hate me, to move on with his life and find someone else so that by the time I returned with a

1

baby he wouldn't question it or give a damn. I may have stayed away forever if it hadn't been for the old ladies in the club, and my best friend, Bailey. A mother of four, her advice and wisdom had come in handy during my pregnancy and over the months that followed. It would have been scary going through all of that completely alone.

Now I was back in Nevada, and it felt good. This was where I belonged, where I wanted my daughter to grow up. It had taken me a couple of months to make all of the arrangements for the move once I'd made up my mind that it was time to go back. Moving with an infant wasn't easy, but Bailey, Raven, and Jolene had helped me out in a big way. And even though I was no longer an old lady to one of the Desert Rebels, I was welcomed back by them as family.

Bailey had provided me with an extra crib that she'd had available after her triplets had outgrown theirs, along with a playpen and a baby swing. Bobbie and Jolene had scoured the outskirts of Las Vegas and found the perfect little Southwestern-style casita for us. It only had three rooms: a bedroom for Ava and I to share, a bathroom, and the main room was broken up into a small living area and kitchen. The casita had been vacant for a long time, but the walls had a fresh coat of paint, and the windows, kitchen, and bathroom had been scrubbed down. The floors had been covered with beautiful throw rugs. By the time I'd arrived, Bobbie and Jolene had even furnished the place for me.

I'd decided to stay in the Vegas area for work, but deep down I wondered if I'd chosen to work away from the home base of the Desert Rebels in order to put distance between me and Sax. He'd gone nomad after I'd left, but I knew the day would come when he would return. Desert Rebels was in his blood. He would never leave them for good.

If only things could have worked out between us. Leaving Sax had been the hardest thing I'd ever had to do, and it was all on me. Finding out that I was pregnant had devastated me. As much as I'd wanted a baby, I'd wanted *Sax's* baby. But I did not know whose baby I was carrying, and even if I had, Sax had no interest in being a father. Breaking it off with him had seemed like the best solution at the time, because there was no way I was going to get rid of my baby. My plan had been simple, if not a little naïve, and I'd prayed that time apart would be my friend. Time could heal a lot of things.

I crept out of the bedroom and closed the door behind me, releasing a long sigh.

"She should stay asleep until morning now." I walked back to the sofa where Bailey was sitting and texting. "I owe Moody for letting you come and stay with me for a couple of days. I didn't realize I'd need the help." I'd had a few boxes to unpack and the kitchen to set up.

Bailey glanced up from her phone, setting it off to the side. "Honey, we women never think we need help because we try to do it all. And Moody encouraged me to come. He said I needed time away from the kids." She reached for her glass of water. "He was right. I can't remember a time when I wasn't up to my elbows in bottles and diapers."

I couldn't help laughing. "What about Moody?"

"He gets plenty of time away from the kids. He still has his bar to run, and he takes on the occasional job."

Neither of us delved further into the type of "job" Moody might be taking, because Moody was a nomad, and like the Desert Rebels, he never discussed business. After the triplets had arrived he'd stopped accepting work so that he could stay home, but now that they were older, he'd gradually started taking on jobs again.

"Speaking of jobs—did you hear from Crickets?"

Crickets was a new restaurant opening up close to the Las Vegas strip. "Yes!" I got excited just thinking about it. "They called me in for an interview the day after I dropped off my application and offered me the hostess position. Demon is letting me work at Grinders until they open."

"When do you start there?"

"Not until Monday night, so I have the next four days to enjoy. Bobbie has invited us to spend the weekend with her and Demon. The club is having a kind of welcome home for me and a celebration for Jolene and LD at the same time. He's officially claiming her."

"What about when you start work? What are you going to do with Ava?

"Annabelle is going to take her for me until I find a permanent sitter. Hey, did you hear that she and Jolene's brother, Danny, are a thing?"

Bailey nodded. "I'm happy for her, and he seems like a nice guy."

"He's always been a nice guy, just not very reliable or smart with his decision-making. LD got him out of some big trouble not too long ago, and now Danny is working it off for the club."

"So I heard. Honey, I wish I was close enough to help out with Ava."

"As if you don't have enough kids to worry about. What's one more, right?" We laughed together, and then a funny look came over Bailey's face that made me narrow my eyes at her. She didn't have to say anything—the truth was right there on her face. "Oh, my God! You're pregnant right now, aren't you?" No wonder she'd refused the wine I'd offered earlier.

She nodded with a glowing smile. "Moody's going to flip when I tell him. He's always said that he was going to put five babies in my belly, and you know how our men are—possessive, sexual beasts." As if she'd just realized what she'd said, her face fell and her hand covered her runaway mouth. "God, honey, I'm sorry—"

I don't know how I kept the smile on my face, even while knowing that Bailey would see right through it. We'd practically grown up together, and had been besties long before Moody and Sax had come into our lives. I took a deep breath to calm the emotion threatening to spill over.

"Don't fret, honey. Sax is my cross to bear, and now that I'm back we're probably going to cross paths. I don't want anyone being uncomfortable with saying his name or talking about him in my presence." I'd already had that same conversation with Raven and Bobbie, and they'd promised to pass it on to the other ladies in the club. "So, how far along do you think you are?"

"Almost three-and-a-half months."

My eyes grew big. "And you haven't told Moody?"

She shook her head. "He's been gone on one of his mysterious jobs," she joked, holding up air quotes. I remember now, she'd already told me that her friend, Emily, was staying with the kids. She and Tommy, the bartender at Moody's bar, Naked Lady, were expecting their first, and Bailey had thought that it would be a good experience for her. "And I'm not going to tell him he's going to be a daddy for the fifth time over the phone."

"I can't believe this is number five," I said in awe. "I guess I'm lucky that I have one." There was a wistful note in my tone. I thanked God every day for giving me Ava. I'd wanted a baby so badly when I'd been with Sax, but he'd been adamant that we not raise any children in the club. It hadn't mattered to him that his brothers were doing it, and doing it happily.

Bailey reached over and took my hand. "Maybe you and Sax—"

I shook my head before she could finish. "I can't see that happening. The only fighting we ever did was over the subject of having kids. Once he sees Ava that will be all he needs to move on, if he hasn't already."

"Well, then maybe we should work on finding you someone who wants a family."

I returned Bailey's smile. "It's much too soon for that. I'd have to stop loving Sax first, and that's going to take some time." I met the hopefulness in her eyes. "I've loved having you here the last two days, honey. It's been nice catching up."

"It has. Let's do this again soon. Next time you and Ava come to my place. Now that the renovations are done, we have a beautiful, spacious guest room." She and Moody lived in a huge adobe-style house in the desert, but the layout hadn't been conducive to their growing family.

"I'd like that." I sighed heavily. "Do you really have to go in the morning?" I already knew the answer. Of course she did. The woman had four kids and she missed them like crazy.

"Afraid so. Emily has already had to call in reinforcements to help manage." We both laughed. "And you have a welcome home party to go to."

"Yeah." I was looking forward to seeing and catching up with everyone that I hadn't yet had a chance to. Knowing that Sax wouldn't be there had made it an easy decision for me to make. I wasn't sure that I'd ever be ready to face him again.

And if he'd moved on?

I'd have to deal with it.

Chapter 2

S ax

I was ready to return home. I'd been away from my club for far too long. Missed my brothers, missed what was happening. Keeping in touch hadn't been on my agenda when I'd gone nomad. I hadn't wanted to know what was going on, and I sure as hell hadn't wanted any news about Holly. Demon had known that I'd needed to distance myself from shit until I could figure out what the fuck had gone wrong in my life.

And why the woman I loved had torn out my fucking heart.

I still couldn't get her last words to me out of my head. They haunted me even in my sleep. How easily she'd broken it off with me, and then just left. For a long time, I'd blamed what had happened to her, the incident still too raw and fresh on her mind for her to deal with anything else in her life. That she hadn't been able to cope. I'd given her time, been understanding when she'd asked me to move into the guest room. But fuck if it hadn't hurt when she pushed me away.

I'd thought we were stronger than that. The fuckers who'd kidnapped our women and assaulted Holly were dead, but I knew that there was something else that had happened to her, something she'd kept from me that had eventually worn her down. I'd probably never know what that something was. Once she'd taken off for parts unknown it had hit me like a fucking ton of bricks. We were really done. She was gone, and no one knew if she was coming back.

We. Were. Done.

Christ, accepting that hurt like a bitch. I'd spent the last few months just roaming the country, sleeping beneath the stars. Keeping to the back roads to suck in the undeveloped countryside. The kind of peace and quiet where a man could reflect on shit. After a while though, the peace and quiet had become too fucking much, and I'd started hitting the bars. Not looking for companionship, just the familiar sounds of bottles clinking and inaudible

6

conversations that filled the room with so much noise that you couldn't think.

The women who approached me were immediately shot down. I wasn't interested in strange pussy. Holly was the only woman I wanted beneath me. That was made glaringly obvious when a striper at one of the bars that I'd stopped in invited me into the alley in the back of the bar for a quick fuck. I'd blamed my inability to get it up on too much fucking alcohol. Not even her painted mouth had been able to get a rise out of me. Every time I'd looked down at her and seen a face other than Holly's, it had killed my libido.

The bartender was welcomed, though, and he kept my fucking glass filled. Usually a beer man, somewhere along the way I'd switched to tequila. I drank as much as I could and still handle my bike, and then I'd go find a tree to sleep it off under. Come morning, I'd wake up stiff and sore and with a hangover that lingered all damned day. Still, I'd move on, determined to outride my demons, and the woman's face that haunted me day and night.

During the months that I was on the road I'd had to work my way through a gamut of emotions ranging from hurt and loss to anger, and then, finally, hate. I berated myself for my fucking weakness. I was a one percenter, for Christ's sake, a member of the Desert Rebels; letting my emotions play with me wasn't something I'd ever done before. My brothers and I were strong, fierce warriors, and we ruled our MC that way. I thanked fuck that they weren't around to see me break over a woman.

Over Holly.

My woman.

We'd had a good run, and I sure as shit had never seen the end coming. Hell, we'd only ever fought over the subject of having kids. She couldn't understand why I didn't want any, and, looking back now, I could see where my reasoning had been weak. A lot of my brothers had families. The kids in the club were happy and well-protected. Maybe if I'd been able to tell Holly the truth about what lay behind my decision she would have accepted it better.

Jesus, I should have told her the truth.

Would it have made a difference? I wondered. She hadn't left because I didn't want kids, she'd gone because of what happened to her after she had been abducted. Had she thought that I'd blamed her in some way? Looked at her differently? Had I treated her differently? Fuck. I had. But not for the reasons she probably thought. I was giving her time, time I thought any woman would need after being violated. No man wanted to think of another man touching his woman, and knowing what she'd suffered had fucking destroyed me, but I'd never thought that any of it was her fault.

I'd blamed myself for not keeping her safe, for not protecting her.

That had been my job, and I'd fucking failed.

I ran my hands through my long hair and gave my head a shake. I had to stop thinking about this shit. What's done is done, and no amount of stewing over it was going to change anything. I'd leave Holly alone as she'd asked me to do. I'd pretend that we hadn't meant anything to each other when and if I ran into her again. Forget about the fucking years we'd been inseparable and happy. Forget about how we'd talked about our future together. I had to get a grip and move on as she'd begged me to do.

Yeah. Move on. Like LD. The poor brother had finally moved on with his life after his wife and kid had been murdered, but it had taken him years to get there. I couldn't imagine ever getting over something like that. I was happy that he'd found Jolene. I'd met her, but didn't really know her, but if she made LD whole again I was already half in love with her. The last time I'd contacted Demon, he'd filled me in that LD was planning to claim her officially on the day that I returned.

That brought me back to the memory of the day that I'd claimed Holly. Damn, that girl had been a little wildcat! So soft and sweet to the world on the outside, but a sexual, demanding nymph in the bedroom. She'd owned my balls as well as my dick, making the sex between us memorable every fucking time. The day I'd made her officially mine had been no different—even knowing that we had an audience she'd shamelessly given herself to me.

I'd taken her out to Sunrise Heights, the official spot for where my brothers went to claim their old ladies. The rules had been set in place by the founding members of the MC, and were simple—fuck her in front of one or more brothers, and they returned to the clubhouse to confirm the official claiming. Most of my brothers didn't tell their women beforehand that they were being watched, which made for a very steamy, no-holds-barred fuck session.

8

SAX

Holly and I had been together for a couple of months at that point, but I'd known long before then that she was the one for me. The day arrived, and I'd taken her out to the location, harder than fucking stone the whole ride there. She'd teased me until it was all I could do to stay on the road, and I'd almost come in my fucking pants. By the time I turned off my bike I'd forgotten all about the reasons why I'd taken her there. I'd swung around on my seat and attacked her.

"I need you, Sax!" she'd whispered in my ear, right before sticking her tongue inside.

Her hands were already pulling and tugging at my cut and t-shirt to get them off. Growling with need, I'd helped her and then slammed my mouth down on her parted lips. As I devoured her lips and fucked the inside of her mouth with my tongue, her little claws had raked over my exposed flesh, mercilessly scraping over my nipples before tweaking them hard. Holly's sexual hunger had always matched mine, maybe even surpassed it at times when I was at my weakest. She thrived on attacking me when I was in the grips of coming hard inside her.

Why would this time be any different? Keeping my mouth locked onto hers, I'd tore at the delicate blouse she was wearing, ripping the thin material easily off her body, pleased to find that she wasn't wearing a bra. When my girl thought there might be sex involved between us, she'd dressed appropriately. And I was right—when my finger crawled up the inside of her thigh, beneath her skirt I found her bare, wet cunt.

"Fuck, Baby," I'd muttered against her swollen mouth. The thought that someone may have caught a peek of her pretty pussy on the way there and seen what was mine turned my blood hotter. "Love that you're ready for me."

"Always, Sax," she'd whispered with feeling. She'd sucked my bottom lip into her mouth, her hands trying to undo my pants, she was so eager. "I need your cock in me, Baby. Fill me with your hot cum."

Shit! I'd shuddered. This was the only time Holly had lost control and talked dirty to me, and I loved every word out of her mouth. She'd pulled my dick out and wasted no time taking what she wanted. Scooting into position, she'd guided my hard cock toward the glistening opening of her bare pussy lips, wrapped her legs around me tightly, and pulled herself sharply against my body, impaling herself. Sinking fully inside her, I'd rolled my head back on my shoulders and closed my eyes with indescribable pleasure.

When I opened them again it was to see that she'd leaned back on the seat, her head back, eyes closed, hair blowing in the breeze against her shoulders, leaving the top half of herself beautifully exposed to me in an erotic pose that sucked the breath from me. Her tits were thrusting forward, nipples hard little crowns just begging for my mouth. Growling, I leaned in to her and took the tasty flesh between my lips.

Her eyes flew open, and a sexy, knowing smile had spread across her face. Our lower bodies hadn't yet moved, taking time to relish the feeling of first entering her that we both loved so much. As I'd run my mouth back and forth between her tits, she buried her hands into my hair and held me to her. But once I'd felt her tight pussy clamp down on my dick, I hadn't cared about anything else but fucking her, and filling her with my cum

Holly knew what she liked, and she demanded it. It was the only time I let her have control, because she was wild with her needs. I began to move my dick in and out, groaning each time my flesh was swallowed up and held tight in her greedy little pussy. I kept my hands wrapped around her fleshy tits, pinching her nipples and enjoying the sounds of the breathless whimpers that rushed out between her parted lips. She'd moved her hips in response, meeting my thrusts, nails biting as she ran her open mouth along the side of my neck and shoulder.

When her teeth sank into me, I'd grunted and lost control, as she'd known I would. I grabbed her by the hair and snapped her neck back so that I had access to her throat. "Turnabout is fair play, Babe," I rasped between sharp nibbles. It had turned me on, marking my woman, and I sucked hard enough to leave the telltale mark. I'd wanted everyone who looked at Holly to know that she was claimed.

"Feels so good, Sax. I love your cock."

"I love you," I'd growled, saying the words for the first time.

Holly had drawn back and looked into my eyes, hers instantly filling with tears. "Really?"

I'd paused from thrusting. "Fuck yeah, Babe." I'd reached up and cupped her cheeks, taking in her flushed loveliness. "You're it for me." I wasn't moving, but I could feel my dick pulsing deep inside her.

"Oh, God! I love you, too!" she'd cried, wrapping her arms around my neck and kissing me. "I've been afraid to say it, afraid it would scare you," she confessed.

She hadn't been wrong to think that way. When a man hears those words too soon it can send him running. But I'd known long before that moment that I loved this woman. Feeling her muscles clench around me caused me to begin thrusting again. We kept our eyes locked, watching the pleasure we were experiencing filter across our faces and fill our eyes.

"I want to watch you come on my dick," I'd rasped, picking up speed. At the same time I reached down to her clit, finding it swollen and sensitive. She'd quivered when I touched it.

"Yes!" she'd gasped, her lips parting as she sucked in air.

Tiny moans escaped her as I'd rubbed the little nub in the way I knew Holly liked. I sank my finger in her pussy with my dick to gather up more cream. Her nostrils flared, revealing how turned on she was. I'd shifted into a position that would allow my dick to hit her G-spot, and that was like striking a match. She'd cried out and fucked herself on my dick, clenching it tightly.

"Sax!" There was excitement in her voice, and I knew that she was getting ready to explode.

"Come on my dick, Baby," I'd grated, thrusting hard and fast. "As soon as you come, I'm going to fill you with my cum. I'm going to pump so much inside you that you'll be leaking for a week. Everyone will smell my mark on you and know you're my old lady!"

Her eyes had grown big at my last words, and she'd screamed her release, clutching onto me as if afraid she'd fall off my bike. My dick was drowning in her sweet release, and I couldn't hold back. The tingle at the base of my spine, the tightening of my balls, warned me not to fight it any longer. With a long groan and a series of shudders, I'd emptied my balls inside Holly until we'd collapsed against each other, spent and satisfied.

A memory I'd never forget.

Jesus Christ. I looked down at myself, where my hand was still gripping my deflated dick, cum all over the front of my fucking jeans. I'd lost myself in the memory of making Holly my old lady, seeking release that I hadn't felt in a while. As I lay there panting beneath the tree that I'd spent the night under,

11

a noise and a movement drew my attention to the right of me, and I laughed out loud.

Several cows were standing close to the fence, watching me.

Chapter 3

H olly
  I sat at the table with the rest of the old ladies, telling myself again that coming home had been the right decision. I looked around, taking in the men in leather and cuts, looking every bit the scary outlaws they were, the scene softened by the sight of their women and children in the room. I'd missed this—the gatherings, the parties, and the cookouts the MC held on a regular basis. The men fought hard, but they played even harder. And they were very protective of what they had.

Today was meant as a welcome home gathering for me and a celebration for LD and Jolene. They'd just returned from Sunrise Heights, looking well sated and surprisingly happy. I'd never seen that look on LD before, and I'd have sworn that it was love I was seeing. It softened his harsh features, making him look less menacing. The biker was the scariest looking man I'd ever seen, and I gave kudos to Jolene for taming him.

With the rite of passage complete and witnessed by Bull, she was now LD's old lady. He hadn't wasted any time spreading the news when he'd returned. Flashes of my own claiming by Sax at Sunrise Heights filtered through my mind, but I quickly brushed them away. Thoughts of Sax and what I'd thrown away brought me down. Instead I focused on Ava as she was being passed around by the old ladies. JoJo and Ellie had their own little toddlers, but they still fought for their time with my daughter.

"She's beautiful."

Raven's compliment put an instant smile on my face. "Thank you." I turned my head in her direction. "So, when are you and Cole going to announce that you're expecting?"

Her face revealed her surprise that I'd guessed her secret. "Oh, God, is it that obvious?"

I shrugged lightly. "A lucky guess, honey. I noticed that you weren't drinking, and you have that glow about you. Cole's looking pretty pleased

13

with himself, too." We both looked in his direction and found him watching us, a cocky smirk on his handsome face.

She giggled. "We'll announce it soon. We just didn't want to steal Jolene and LD's celebration."

"How far along are you?"

"Just past the first trimester." She took a sip of her water. "Did you enjoy your visit with Bailey?"

I nodded. "I always enjoy my time with her. We've been besties for a long time. I only wish that she lived closer." I leaned in, as if telling a secret. "She's expecting number five."

Raven's beautiful mouth dropped open. "You're kidding! I can't imagine having five children. When do they ever have the time to—?"

Laughter erupted from me, and I cut her off. "To have sex?"

"To do anything," she smiled. "Much less have sex."

"Well, you know the kind of men we're involved with, they're always horny, and apparently they find the time."

Ava began to fidget and I knew that she was getting hungry. I'd pumped several bottles of breast milk earlier that morning, but had then gone off and left them. Thank goodness they were in the fridge and wouldn't go bad. I started work at Grinders that Monday, and Annabelle would need them. I glanced at Annie, who was just handing her back to JoJo, a nervous look on her face when Ava began to fuss. Fussy babies made some people uncomfortable.

I laughed. "I'll take her back now, I need to feed her," I announced.

"You going to do it here?"

I'd told JoJo when I'd arrived that I'd forgotten the prepared bottles. I glanced around. There were too many men and children present, and while no one may have noticed me breast feeding Ava, I'd feel better in a quiet spot somewhere. "I think I'll go inside and do it. She usually falls asleep right after, and that way I can lay her down where it's not as noisy." I rose to my feet and took her out of JoJo's arms. Cuddling Ava to my breast, she instinctively turned her mouth, rooting for a nipple. Laughter followed me as I walked away.

"Want any company?"

Loco's question was way too cheerful, and caused me to glance his way just as I was about to enter the clubhouse. His eyebrows were doing the Groucho Marx thing, and I sensed that he'd guessed where I was going and what I was about to do.

I shook my head with mock disgust at the club man-whore. "You must be desperate if you want to see a fat boob leaking milk." They were so big and swollen they felt like balloons ready to burst.

His laughter caused several heads to turn our way. "All tits are beautiful," he said.

I continued inside to one of the sofas and settled into it. There was no one around, and I prayed that it stayed that way long enough to fill Ava's little belly. I unbuttoned my blouse, unhooked the cup, and pulled it down, baring my breast. As soon as I brought Ava up to it, her little mouth latched on to the nipple and she began to suck with greedy contentment. The relief was instant for me, and I let out a sigh.

My body had changed since I'd had Ava. I'd always had an hour-glass shape, but now my curves were fuller and softer than they'd been before, and a couple of stretch marks lined my stomach. Did I care? No. The old ladies had complimented me on my luscious curves, and the way that some of the men's eyes lingered on me backed up their statements. But more importantly, the changes had brought me Ava.

I smiled down at her as she suckled. Her eyes were already closed, indicating that she was falling asleep. Her little mouth continued to work though, and the noises she made caused my heart to swell with love. I was amazed at how much one little tiny human being could make me feel. Her soft brown curls and brown eyes, the tiny freckle on the tip of her button nose, all captivated me.

As I stared down at her cubby face and rosy cheeks, I tried not to wonder who her father might be, because it didn't matter. I hated those men and what they'd done to me, but I could never hate Ava. She was perfect.

I heard the outside door open, but I kept my gaze lowered to my daughter. My breast was exposed, but her tiny hand rested upon it, and her mouth was still latched on to my nipple. I hoped whoever had stepped inside would keep going. As soon as they were gone I'd take Ava to the old room that I'd once shared with Sax and lay her down in the playpen kept on site for visiting babies.

A woman's giggle accompanied by a man's low murmurs drew my attention to the doorway.

And my heart stopped.

I'd been told that Sax was gone, that he'd turned nomad, but there he stood, stock still in the doorway with shock on his deeply tanned face, and I swear that he wasn't breathing. His eyes darted back and forth between mine and the baby at my breast. It was hard to tell what he was thinking in his frozen state. And when his eyes finally lifted to mine, there was no disguising the emotions simmering in his hard, accusing eyes. The skin stretched tight over his lean jaw, revealed a tic, while his mouth pressed so tight that his lips turned white.

My heart fluttered wildly at the raw anger on his face, and I could barely breathe. I could feel the scorch of his hate and betrayal as if someone had bundled me into an electric blanket and turned it up high. Why wasn't he saying anything? What was he thinking?

That he hadn't been expecting to see me was obvious. It appeared that neither one of us had been warned the other was coming. Maybe no one had known. My gaze shifted to the woman at his side. She was young, eighteen or nineteen I guessed, and much too young for Sax, yet she had the look of an older, experienced woman. The look in her blue eyes had turned curious, and then gradually filled with dawning realization that all women got when they knew they were encroaching on another woman's man.

I recognized the challenge in her smirk and the way she wrapped her arms around Sax's muscular bicep for what it was. She thought I was a threat, and she was staking her claim on him. I don't know how I kept from crumbling with hurt right there in front of them. What had I expected? I knew the day would come when I'd have to face him again, and that when I did I might find that he had moved on. But now that the moment was here, the reality was destroying me inside, because deep down I'd hoped that he loved me too much to look at another woman.

I knew that kind of thinking wasn't fair.

The only thing that prevented me from getting up and leaving the room with as much dignity as I could muster was that my daughter hadn't let go of my nipple yet. I knew from experience that if I pulled away too soon she'd wake up, and I didn't want that to happen. I was trapped, literally, beneath the accusing glare of the man that I loved more than anything. The only thing left for me to do was pull myself together and act as if seeing him with another woman wasn't killing me.

"Hi, Sax." I cringed at the crack in my voice.

"When the fuck did you get back?" he practically snarled.

I hadn't expected a warm welcome from him. "A couple of weeks ago." I cleared my throat. "When did you get back?" I asked, letting him know that I knew he'd gone away, too.

"Today."

Oh. The girl next to him huffed as if to remind us that she was still there, but neither of us looked at her.

"I see you didn't waste any time in getting that baby you wanted."

I flinched at his hurtful words as his eyes narrowed over Ava, and I could see that he was working something out. "You didn't want me to touch you, but you sure as fuck let someone inside else inside that greedy pussy."

A sharp gasp escaped me as the assault that I'd endured instantly flooded my mind. I couldn't believe he'd said that. The Sax that I knew would never have been so cruel or hurtful on purpose. He knew what I'd gone through, how hard I'd fought my attackers. To insinuate that I'd loathed his touch but let another man have me was an insult. I felt the warning sting in my eyes and knew what was coming next. The girl snickered with amusement, her presence making the situation worse.

"Come on, sweetheart, I'll take you up to my room."

His words cut through me like a knife. With the girl clinging to his arm, Sax led her toward the stairs. Words escaped me as I watched them climb the steps, knowing what they would be doing once they reached his room. By the time I remembered about the playpen it was too late and they were out of sight. I sat back against the cushions and slowly regained my breath.

Ava's limp little body revealed that she was done and sound asleep. I knew that she would stay that way for at least a couple of hours. I felt numb, barely noticing when Bobbie came into the room until she was practically standing over me.

"Honey, are you sleeping with your eyes open?"

I managed a small smile. "I must have zoned out," I admitted. "Bobbie, can you do me a favor? Sax just took his girlfriend upstairs and the playpen is in his room." I couldn't believe how normal my voice sounded.

"Say no more, honey, I'll be right back."

She rushed up the stairs, and while she was gone, I fixed my nursing bra back into place. When she came back down the stairs without the playpen, the first thing I thought was that she'd been too late, and that Sax and his friend were already going at it. I tried not to visualize them naked and in bed together, but that was hard to do. Why would he take her to his room if he wasn't going to fuck her?

"I moved the playpen to mine and Demon's apartment," she explained. She held her arms open and down toward me. "Now let me have that little one and I'll take her up for you."

"Are you sure?" I carefully handed Ava over.

"Yes." She cuddled Ava against her chest. "None of us knew Sax was coming home today or we would have never put you there in his room," she explained regretfully.

"No worries. I should probably go home tonight anyway." I'd originally planned to stay the night for the adult party and then return home in the morning, but now that Sax was here I had no desire to stay.

"Oh, no you won't." She pulled the receiving blanket Ava was bundled up in over her bare legs. "Demon and I won't be using the apartment tonight, so it's yours. And you know you can still come to our house."

That had been the original plan, but once I'd been talked into staying for the party I'd had to change it. If I was going to stay up late it just made sense to remain at the club. I smiled at her invitation. "Thanks, but once Ava goes down for the night I don't like to wake her. I appreciate the use of the apartment, though."

"Anytime, honey. I'll be back."

I watched Bobbie for a minute as she carefully walked up the stairs with my most precious cargo. But no sooner had she disappeared around the corner than Sax appeared. His gaze automatically came to me, and I caught my breath and stood up. His expression was still raw and angry, his eyes hard, glittering orbs of burnt sienna that scorched me where I stood. He looked like he wanted to hit something or hurt someone.

He wanted to hurt me.

Like I had hurt him.

I swung around to leave, my heart racing with a fear that I'd never felt before with Sax. I didn't know this man, the one storming down the steps in his haste to reach me before I made it outdoors. His boots stomped loudly behind me, and I knew that he was catching up, and then he was upon me, flipping me around and slamming me up against the wall next to the door. My gaze flew up to the hate in his, my breath coming hard.

"Sax—"

He slammed his fist against the wall next to my head. "I fucking loved you!" he hissed down into my face, his nostrils flaring.

A sob escaped me as I tried to hold back my emotions. His pain was tangible, tearing me apart, because I'd caused it. His face was so close to mine that I felt his breath against me. I felt boxed in, even though his arms weren't trapping me against the wall. I watched his eyes drift over my face and down my neck to where my blouse was still opened. I'd forgotten to do up the buttons after feeding Ava. His eyes lingered on the swell of my breasts above my bra. My whimper drew his gaze back up to mine.

"I fucking loved you," he repeated in a guttural snarl, drawing back when he realized that he was scaring me.

I sucked in air, keeping my back to the wall, trying to calm my racing heart. He'd *loved* me? As in past tense. He'd moved on, just as I'd told him to do. As he continued to stare at me I wiped my tears away and took a trembling breath, determined to get the words out I that needed to. I wanted him to know the truth. Not because I wanted to hurt him more, but because he deserved to know.

"And I still love you."

Chapter 4

S^{ax}

"I still love you."

Son-of-a-bitch!

Hours later, I still couldn't get those fucking words out of my head, or the sight of Holly's tear ravished face. I'd watched her walk away after she'd uttered a comment that had nearly brought me to my fucking knees, too stunned to do anything else until the pain had set in on the damage that I'd done to my knuckles when I'd hit the wall. She had no right saying that shit to me and then walking away as if she hadn't just gutted me.

Walking in and seeing her with a baby had felt like the equivalent of someone ripping my fucking heart out. At first, with her head bent, I hadn't recognized her. She'd let her hair grow long enough to pull it up into a messy bun, and the brown had golden highlights running through it. Plus her curves had filled out some. She'd always been curvy, but in a controlled way that she'd worked hard to keep tight.

Yeah, her tits were definitely bigger, and so was her ass, but in the kind of way that made me want to sink my teeth into it. She'd always been gorgeous to me, but I liked the changes motherhood had obviously gifted her with. The fact that no one had informed me that Holly had a baby, or was even expecting one, had made me question my brother's loyalty until Cole had explained that none of them had known.

I had to ask myself why Holly would keep it a secret, but then reminded myself that I shouldn't care. Except that I fucking did care. I wanted to know who the fucking father was, who had put a baby in her belly that should have been mine. I pounded the bar with the side of my fisted hand, letting the rage fill me as much as the tequila. I'd always told Holly that I didn't want kids. It was the only thing that we'd fought about when we'd been together, but I'd never expected her to go out and get pregnant as soon as she broke it off with me.

Unless she'd broken it off with me because she was already pregnant.

Had she been fucking around on me?

Had it been with one of my brothers? I thought about it for a minute, and even my half-drunk brain didn't believe that for a minute. I trusted my brothers. I'd trusted Holly, too. And maybe in time I would have given her the baby she'd wanted so desperately...

"Another shot, Brother?"

I nodded.

Snake dropped one off and looked to the side of me. "What about you, boss?"

I cut my eyes to where Demon was sitting next to me. I hadn't even noticed that he'd joined me. Maybe because of the woman who was sitting on the other side of the room from me at the old ladies' table. I smirked at Snake's persistence of calling Demon boss while the rest of us called him Prez.

"Whiskey."

"You drinking your troubles away?" Demon snorted.

I smirked. "What troubles?"

He motioned in the direction to where the women were sitting. "Woman troubles."

It sounded as if he was an expert on the subject. Hell, he was. He'd gone through some shit before he'd made Bobbie his old lady.

"I don't have a woman," I corrected him. I stared down at my beer to keep my eyes off Holly.

"What about the woman you brought back with you?"

Frowning, I glared at him. "You know why I brought her here. Hell, I haven't even fucked her."

I'd brought Goldie to the clubhouse to replace Tamara, the club bitch who'd betrayed us and finally met her end a few months ago. Goldie had been hitchhiking on the interstate looking for an adventure when I'd ridden up on her. I didn't normally put bitches on the back of my bike, but when she'd explained that she was on the run and why, I'd decided to help her out.

"So how do you know she's gonna make a good club whore?" Demon questioned gruffly, picking up his glass.

21

I laughed. "You fuck her if you want to know," I suggested, an unwise move.

Instead of decking me, he grinned. "Think Bobbie will have something to say about that."

"There are plenty of brothers around who can test her out," I said, not really giving a fuck.

"So you're not staking a claim? Because it looks like she and Snake are already getting friendly."

I followed Demon's gaze to the end of the bar. "He can have her." Snake was definitely putting the moves on Goldie, though she appeared to be uninterested in his advances. "When did he get his patch?"

"After LD went to Vegas and we had trouble from the Insane Boys we patched in our existing prospects to make room for new ones. Needed to get our numbers up."

I nodded, remembering the night the Insane Boys had attacked Grinders, killing eight of our brothers and four old ladies. We'd taken out some of them, too, and in the end Desert Rebels had gone after the IBMC and destroyed them all. I hadn't been around for any of it, and I still resented Demon for not calling me back. I should have been there.

"What else did I miss while I was gone?"

"Same old shit, Brother. Already know about the IBMC."

We sat quietly for a minute with our own thoughts. Not an easy thing to do with rock booming through the clubhouse. It was a typical Friday night. Hell, like any night really, it was just more crowded on the weekends. The bar was packed, and from what I could see everyone was enjoying themselves, high on booze and weed. There was some fucking going on, but I was oblivious to everything but the woman sitting across the room.

"You get over her yet?"

I glared at Demon, restraining myself from ripping his head off.

He snorted and went back to his drink. "Why don't you talk to her? Work shit out?"

I shrugged, not looking at him. "Nothing to work out, Brother." My gaze went to Holly. "Better off without her." I said the words, but didn't feel them. "Especially now that she has a kid."

"You really hate kids that much?" He frowned. "Fuck, the clubhouse is going to be full of them soon."

"I don't hate kids," I said, surprised that he would think that. "Just don't want them." I had my reasons, though they weren't the ones that I'd given Holly when she'd started talking about babies. I stared at the woman who'd ripped my heart out and stomped on it, wondering once again who the fucking father was to her kid. "Wonder who the baby daddy is," I muttered, for my ears only.

Demon had no trouble hearing me. He motioned for Snake to bring him over another drink. "She hasn't said." He ran his hand through his hair. "I don't think she knows."

That comment sobered me like nothing else, and my head whipped his way. "Come again?"

I watched his shoulders lift in a shrug. "Sometimes you can be a dumb motherfucker, Brother. Think about it. Ava is six months old. By my calculations, Holly was already pregnant when she broke it off with you."

He stared at me expectantly, as if waiting for me to figure it out on my own.

He got tired of waiting. "I'm guessing she left here before she started showing, when she was about three, four months along."

I'd had too much fucking tequila to comprehend what Demon was talking about. I thought back to that time, trying to recall the series of events that had led up to our breakup, staring down into my empty glass as if I'd find the answers there. If memory served me correctly I hadn't touched Holly after her attack. Jesus Christ, had she gotten pregnant by one of the men who'd raped her?

It had killed me to see Holly after what those fuckers had done to her, to watch the shame and regret fill her eyes before she'd lowered them to the ground, the blame she'd placed on herself. The thought of one of them putting a baby in her made me sick. I shook my head to clear it, refusing to go down that path.

Bobbie chose that moment to join us. She stepped up behind Demon quietly and wrapped her arms around his neck, nuzzling the side of his neck. With a grin and a growl he brought her around to the front of him and pulled her down onto his lap.

"I'm tired," she murmured leaning into him.

"You want to go home, Babe?"

She nodded.

"We could always use our room upstairs if you're too tired to ride home."

"No, Holly and Ava are using it." She gave me a speculative look. "Since you moved Goldie into yours." Was she fishing for an explanation? Knowing Bobbie, she wouldn't wait long to get one. "Is she your new girl?"

I snorted, amused that she'd come right out and asked. "Nope." I hadn't moved Goldie into my room either, but that was all I muttered. I didn't have to explain myself to her, even if she was Prez's old lady.

"She's replacing Tamara," Demon grinned, wrapping his powerful arms around Bobbie and pulling her close. "New club pussy."

That got him a huff and a hit in the arm from Bobbie. "You'd better not try her out, or I'll cut your balls off."

He laughed loudly, amusement dancing in his one good eye. He'd lost the other one in a prison riot years before, and now kept it covered with a patch. As he laughed at Bobbie's expense, she leaned in and gave his bottom lip a sharp bite out of frustration. He snapped his head back, surprised that she'd reacted so violently, before he slammed his mouth down over hers. It wasn't a long kiss, but by the time they drew apart they were both flushed and breathing hard.

"Let's go," Demon growled, looking deep into his woman's eyes. Bobbie was forced to her feet when he scooted off the stool. "Glad you're back, Brother." He gave me a pat on the shoulder. "See you at church in the morning."

I gave him a chin lift and then they walked away. Snake came back to my end of the bar, and I made the mistake of catching Goldie's eye. Her smile grew big and she winked at me, but I was glad that she didn't leave her stool to come over, even if she did look damned good in that moment. She was a pretty girl with blonde curls, blue eyes, and a cupid mouth that would look good wrapped around any man's dick, especially with that bright red lipstick she was wearing. She'd cleaned up good, too, rocking the tiny red dress she'd borrowed from Mitzi.

She'd told me that she was twenty-one. Her driver's license backed that up. I hadn't been about to bring an underage girl with a woman's body into the club. We didn't need that kind of trouble. She'd tried her best to get me to fuck her while we'd been on the road, and I honestly didn't know why I hadn't taken her up on it. Fucking out in the open beneath a star-studded night would have been fun, and I would have gotten off. But my dick hadn't been into it.

The fucker wanted one woman only, and that woman was across the room from me, looking sexy in a pair of ripped jeans and a sheer blouse over a black bra. Holly belonged here. She fit in. But I couldn't imagine how the hell we would be able to make it work together. I hadn't questioned Demon about what was going on with her—where she was living or working—because I hadn't wanted to give him reason to think that I cared. My brothers could be like a gaggle of old hens when they caught wind of something to rib another brother about.

I didn't need that shit.

Didn't want it.

Holly and I were done.

And no matter what my dick wanted, he needed to accept that too, and soon. Using my hand for relief was growing old. Sooner or later I was going to turn to one of the club girls.

As if her ears had been burning, Goldie slipped off her stool and made her way toward me, looking all sweet and inviting. Snake shot me a look but remained at the other end of the bar, where he was serving. The club girls were available to any brother who was in the mood, along with any civilians who they were stupid enough to attend one of our wild parties.

I braced myself, because the look in Goldie's blue eyes revealed that she had me in her sights, and she wasn't going to take no for an answer. I let my eyes drink her in because, hell, I was a man, and her little red dress barely covered her pussy. Her smile revealed that she'd noticed my interest, and it gave her the confidence to wrap her arms around me and kiss me on the neck.

"Have I thanked you properly for rescuing me?" she asked when she pulled back. "Let me give you a bonus, Sax. You denied me on the ride here, but I want you." Her hands toyed with the top of my pants.

"Didn't rescue you, honey. Brought you here to do a job." I gave her a cold look. "Do it."

Her laugh was low and sexy. "I'm trying, baby. I want you to be my first."

I jerked my head back. *What the fuck?* It took me a minute to realize that she wasn't implying that she was a virgin, but that she wanted me to be the first brother she fucked. "Sorry, Goldie. Not interested."

My gaze lit on Dancer, who was walking our way. He looked as if he had something on his mind, and wasn't paying attention until I reached out and grabbed him by the arm when he was on his way by. He stopped and looked at me inquisitively, his eyes shooting back and forth between me and Goldie.

I took Goldie by the hand and pulled her around closer to him. "Here, Brother. Break her in."

I knew my words were heartless, but she needed to learn fast what was expected of her, and that I hadn't brought her here because I wanted her for myself. I ignored her slight gasp and the look of disbelief she pinned on me. Dancer's face lit up as he took the smaller hand that I pressed into his.

"Hey, baby, you new here? Come with me, I'll show you a good time."

I didn't watch them walk off. No, my eyes went back to the old ladies' table where Holly was sitting. Fuck, she was sitting there, laughing and talking as if nothing was wrong and everything in the world was fucking fantastic, while I was drowning myself in alcohol and misery. I was pathetic. I should show her I didn't fucking care, too. That I'd moved on, as it appeared that she had. I scanned the room until I found Mitzi and locked eyes with her. A jerk of my head pulled her from her chair to walk towards me.

"What do you need, baby?" she cooed, getting up close and personal.

I grabbed her around the waist and forced her to straddle my lap. She laughed, buried her hands in my hair, and brought my face down to her exposed tits. I grit my teeth, instantly noticing that she smelled good, but it wasn't the warm lavender scent that I was craving. When she began to grind down on my dick I pulled away from the flesh that was suffocating me, meeting the hurt in the brown eyes of the woman who still had the power to gut me.

Holly sat frozen, watching me with Mitzi. Even from across the room I could see the liquid glistening in her eyes. Fuck me, what had she expected? This was my fucking clubhouse, and I wasn't about to feel guilty for having another woman grinding down on my lap with her tits in my face. Then, in the blink of an eye, Holly was smiling and saying something to the others at her table before rising to her feet. It was clear that she was leaving.

I didn't expect her to come to me, but I watched her walk to the stairs and then climb them. I locked my hungry eyes on the delicious sway of her full ass in those tight jeans. Jesus, what had she done to me? I'd remained soft to Mitzi's movements until the sight of Holly's ass teased me into a hard-on. Shit. The way Mitzi was acting, it was clear that she thought she deserved the credit for it.

"Oh, baby, it's so good to have you back. Let's go up to your room."

I pushed her away from where she was nuzzling against me and easily pushed her off my lap. I was going up alright, but it wasn't going to be to my empty room, and not with Mitzi.

Chapter 5

H olly
    I couldn't say how long I'd been asleep when I woke abruptly to a presence in the room, and then the feeling of someone crawling up and over me. As their weight settled against my body fully I opened my mouth to scream, but a hard, callused hand prevented me from crying out. I sank further into the bed and stiffened against the much larger, firmer person on top of me. I knew that whoever it was was a man because he was so close I could feel his facial scruff against my cheek.

"Ssh," came a low warning in the darkness. "Don't want to wake the kid."

Sax. He was fully dressed. His breath laced with alcohol. And he was hard, though I didn't think he was there to fuck me. I'd seen Mitzi grinding on him earlier, the sight causing me to cry myself to sleep.

"Ava," I whispered when he removed his hand. "Her name is Ava." I didn't tell him that she wasn't there, that Annabelle had offered to take her to her room for the night because she hadn't felt like partying.

"Who's the father, Holly?" he growled down at me. "Who the fuck put a baby in you?"

I swallowed hard, frightened by this Sax, because he was a man I'd never seen before. I was conflicted, because while he was a harder, more dangerous version than the man I'd left, the changes in him turned me on. Should I tell him the truth? He should have already guessed it by now.

"I don't know who he is, Sax." I felt him stiffen above me. "I was raped—"

"You expect me to believe that shit?" he snarled. "I fucked you for years and you never got pregnant." He hesitated, as if he were pulling his thoughts together. "Know what I think? I think you fucked around on me. You wanted a baby, and when I wouldn't give you one you found some fuck who would."

His words broke my heart. If he could believe that I'd fucked around on him, then he'd never really known or trusted me. I had loved him with all of

28

my being. I still loved him. I knew that if I told him the truth he would never trust me again, so I kept it buried.

"You were pregnant when you left."

It wasn't a question, but a cold, hard fact that I admitted with a simple, "Yes."

His snort vibrated against my breasts. "I hadn't touched you, Holly. After the attack I didn't lay a fucking finger on you."

I could barely take the anguish in his voice, and I clenched my teeth as the silent tears fell from the corner of my eyes to my pillow. Why did he think it was so implausible that my pregnancy had been the result of rape? Was it easier for him to believe that I'd slept with someone else?

Maybe he couldn't bear to think that Ava might be the product of my assault.

"Which one of my brothers do I kill?"

The coldness of his tone frightened me. He meant it. "I never cheated on you," I whispered hoarsely. A sob escaped me. "I love you."

He pounded the pillow next to my head. "Enough," he snarled impatiently. "I don't want to hear that fucking lie out of your mouth again." Even as he growled the angry words, he kept his voice low.

It wasn't a lie, but his tone revealed that he wouldn't believe that it was anything but. That he'd made up his mind, and he was too filled with hate and rage to contemplate any other possibility. Ava could very well be his, but telling him that wouldn't help at that moment. He was fueled by alcohol and another emotion that I hadn't seen in him before. A kind of desperation.

"I loved you." Again in the past tense. His tortured whisper broke me. "I. Loved. You." His mouth moved against the side of my neck as he spoke, the feel of his firm lips causing little tingles down my spine.

I felt his hands glide down the side of my barely clad body where he gripped my hips brutally hard. I remembered how good we were together. How every time we'd fucked, it had felt as if it were the first time all over again. The excitement, the intense ride to completion, had never waned between us. As the hard ridge of his cock rested against my pelvic bone, I thought how easy it would be for Sax to open his pants and just slip into me.

"Fuck...I missed this," came his quiet voice right before he inhaled deeply. "Missed your fucking smell, your laughter, how good it feels loosing myself in you."

I squeezed my eyes shut tightly, seeing Mitzi on his lap. "I'm sure you haven't gone without since our breakup."

He stiffened against me, his hands clenched my hips. He pulled back far enough so that I could see the glitter of his eyes as he glared down at me. "You're so fucking wrong, Holly. I never considered us over."

His words made my breathing stop. I had only a second of disbelief, because I knew that Sax was an honest man, and I couldn't doubt the ring of truth behind his words.

I believed him. Why couldn't he believe me? As we lay there in silence I began to be aware of his delicious weight against me, his hands slowly caressing my hips where they'd been hurtful before. When his cock jumped against me I couldn't stop the moan that rushed up my throat. God, how I wanted this man, but I was afraid, so afraid, of his rejection. I couldn't take that.

"Fuck, Holly, let me in." His words were so low that I barely heard them.

He didn't wait for my response. He dragged my hands above my head and pinned them with one of his against the bed. His other hand slid around my body and around to my ass, squeezing a cheek while he ground his cock against my pulsing clit. There was hesitation in his movements, as if he were trying to make up his mind if he should continue or stop, waiting for me to deny him. He should have known that I was weak when it came to him, and I'd been too many months without him.

I whimpered at the feel of his mouth against me as it grazed the length of my neck and over my shoulders, and then traveled back toward my mouth. As he neared it I opened mine on a breathless sigh of want, willing him to fill that hunger by claiming my lips. He hovered over them, our breaths mingling, everything inside me coming alive. My nipples were so hard they ached. And when Sax finally lowered his mouth onto mine, it was a tentative brush of our mouths. He moved his lips back and forth over mine, testing, sampling, teasing.

"Sax," I whispered breathlessly, and that was all it took for him to take my mouth like a man who was starved for air.

The gentleness and teasing was gone, replaced by beautiful brutality that revealed his hunger and need for me. And I was right there with him, opening my mouth eagerly for our tongues to mesh and play in a dance that drew ripples of pleasure all the way from my core. I was disintegrating from the inside out, melting into a mindless puddle of bliss. I strained against the hand holding me down. Strained against Sax's powerful body pinning me to the bed. I arched wantonly into the hard, throbbing ridge of his cock, begging for something that I couldn't put into words.

Take me! I wanted to cry out. *Fuck me!* I needed him so badly, needed to feel him inside me again. My body needed a release that it hadn't felt in over a year, and it occurred to me that this was the first time he'd touched me since the attack. I was so ready for him. My pussy was pulsating and wet. As Sax ground his mouth against mine in a kiss that gave pain as well as pleasure, I knew that this was as much a form of a punishment as it was satisfaction.

I bit down on his bottom lip as he pulled away, panting. We were both breathing hard. Our eyes clashed, glittering with emotion in the darkness, our hearts pounding as one. His jaw was taut, nostrils flaring, as I was sure mine were. Would he fuck me now? God, I wanted him to! He knew about Ava now, and the sky hadn't fallen. Maybe, just maybe, we could get through this somehow. Could begin anew.

Even as the unlikely thought flashed through my mind, I remained cautiously optimistic.

"You want me to fuck you now?" he grunted in a cold, hard voice. His softness from before had completely disappeared.

I blinked, startled at his gruff question. This didn't sound like the man I knew and loved. I was seeing a side of Sax that I wasn't familiar with, a rougher version. Had I done this to him? I wanted him, wanted his hands and mouth on me so badly that I knew I was going to make the wrong decision. Knew it because my heart was involved, and part of me was taking responsibility for the way he had changed, acting as if he didn't care one way or another what my answer was. He was hard as steel against my pussy, but I sensed that if he'd wanted to, he could walk away without any problem.

As tears leaked out of the corners of my eyes, I uttered the two words that I knew would devastate me completely. "Fuck me," I whispered. My need for him far outweighed my common sense or survival instinct.

Sax released a low animalistic sound that vibrated through my body. Before I could brace myself, he flipped me over and pulled me to my knees. I gasped at his roughness, and again when his hands ripped my boy shorts from me. He took a minute to put his hands on my ass, clenching his fingers into the fleshy mounds, and then spread my cheeks. My eyes grew big when I felt him move in, and then his mouth was on me, biting and licking me before spearing his tongue inside my anus.

I jerked forward with surprise, but Sax's hands held me tight against him while he thrust a finger inside me and fucked me with it. I whimpered a little at the pain of being stretched. We'd experimented with anal play before, but it wasn't my favorite, although I couldn't deny the unexpected thrill that shot through my body in response to his roughness and take-control-attitude. In the past he had always asked before doing anything with my ass, but now it appeared that he wasn't giving me a choice.

He was taking.

A second finger entered me causing me, to gasp sharply. Was he being rough on purpose? When he began to scissor his fingers I realized what his intentions were. I stiffened. "Sax..." There was no way he could miss the apprehension in my tone.

He leaned over my body, placing his mouth against my ear. "Shut up. I don't have a condom, and I plan on coming inside your body." His tone was so cold, as if he resented what he was doing.

"Damn you!" I whispered.

"We're both damned, Baby."

I felt his hand between us as he undid his pants and pulled his cock out. I felt the scorching heat of it at my entrance, and then the wide head of it as Sax ran it up and down the crack of my ass. I moaned loudly when I felt him tease my clit before running his shaft up and down my slit, gathering up the wetness there. I quivered beneath his administrations, panting hard. His harsh breath was against the nape of my neck. I could feel his muscles trembling as if he were fighting against something.

"Fuck it!" he swore, thrusting forward and sinking his cock inside me as if he couldn't help himself. Sounds of our mutual pleasure echoed throughout the room, the pleasure so intense I had a mini-orgasm around his hot flesh.

"Sax! Oh, God!" I whisper-yelled as he thrust hard and fast a half a dozen times.

His only response was his groans as he pumped in and out, his hands gripping my hips hard enough to leave bruises. Another orgasm bloomed inside me, growing fast and with intensity. Sax's cock hit me everywhere, my body swelled around him like a sponge. I instinctively clenched my muscles, satisfied by his grunt, and then he pulled out. I barely had time to take a breath before he penetrated my anus.

I cried out as the pain of his entry caught me unprepared. Sax didn't go slow, didn't wait for my body to stretch for him, he didn't seem to care that he was causing me discomfort. Thankfully it didn't last long. He replaced his cock in my pussy with his talented fingers. He worked my clit just the way he knew I liked it until I was a quivering, gasping mess again. My G-spot wasn't ignored either, and between that and the pleasure I was now feeling as he fucked my ass, I detonated with a scream.

I wasn't alone. Sax found his own release at the same time, groaning and grunting as he filled me with cum.

"So fucking tight."

It was the only thing he said when he withdrew from me. I collapsed onto the bed, closing my eyes as I gave in to the pleasant fog that enveloped me. My pussy was soaked. I could feel it between my legs, and still buzzing slightly. I was wet between my ass, too, and knew Sax's cum was leaking out of me. I was too tired to move, and too afraid of what was going to happen now between us. I didn't fool myself into thinking that sex with him had solved anything.

I waited for the bomb to drop.

"Don't worry, I know this didn't mean anything," Sax began in a gruff voice. "You scratched an itch, that was all."

"You're a liar," I responded calmly, hiding the hurt his words had caused me. "You could have satisfied your itch with Mitzi if that's all this was."

"I said *your* itch," he snorted. "And what makes you think I didn't fuck her before I came here?"

I stiffened at his cutting words, the vision of them at the bar flashing in my mind.

"You fucking walked away from us. Left me a fucking note when you ran the fuck away to have your kid."

"Her name is Ava," I growled.

"Doesn't matter. What matters is I came back with the intention of moving on without you. You gave me that right, and that's what I intend to do." He laughed and jumped off the bed. "Not going to turn down easy pussy."

What was he saying? That I was easy? As he stood glaring down at me I reached for the covers and brought them up to cover my nakedness.

"You've changed," I murmured with disappointment in my voice.

"Yeah, having the woman you love betray you will do that to a man. And you should know better, Holly. You were my old lady for a long time, long enough to know what we do to fucking traitors. But don't worry, Baby, I'm not going to kill you. Just stay out of my fucking way or suffer the consequences."

I could only lie there quietly and stare up at Sax as he muttered the hateful words in the coldest, most unfeeling voice I'd ever heard him use. The fact that he believed what he was saying tore me up inside. I'd hurt him terribly with my actions, when at the time I'd genuinely thought that I was saving him. I knew now that I'd made a mistake in believing that. I bit the inside of my cheek to keep from crying or making it worse by reacting out of desperation. Now wasn't the time to try and make him understand why I'd done what I'd done.

That was a long way off.

Chapter 6

S^{ax}

I wasn't proud of how I'd used Holly and then walked away, treating her no better than a club whore. My anger and confusion over what had happened to us was turning me into a man that I barely recognized, at least where she was concerned. If her attack had been the reason that she'd left, I would have given her forever to heal and come to grips with it. The rage that I'd felt when it happened had been directed at the fucking bastards and my own inability to protect her, and not at Holly.

Junior, the little fucker, had had us all fooled, and we'd never seen his betrayal coming.

Tamara, who'd been a club whore for years, had fooled us, too. She'd been the bitch who'd betrayed Holly, Raven, and Bobbie on the day they'd been kidnapped, tipping Junior off to their whereabouts. She was the reason they'd been taken from the salon by Junior's hired mercenaries.

I wished that I could kill them both all over again.

Fuck. I wished that none of it had ever happened in the first place.

Annabelle came down the stairs carrying Ava. She was cooing and smiling down at the baby as if the kid were her own. I'd noticed that about her, that she loved children, that she was good with them. I'd heard that she was with Jolene's brother, Danny, now. Apparently, Demon had him on some kind of probation and was watching closely how he treated his sister. If that was true, I doubted that they'd even fucked yet.

The club had gone through some changes while I'd been gone, nothing surprising. Demon had talked about starting up a chapter in Las Vegas when we'd picked up a huge construction contract there, and since I'd been gone he'd put that plan in place. Many of our brothers had relocated there for the work, and LD had been a shoe-in for the new chapter's president. He could be just as ruthless and dangerous as Demon. He'd always been a scary fuck, but the edges were softer now that he had a woman.

My gaze followed Annabelle as she sat at the table where Bobbie and Raven were having breakfast. The women immediately began to do that mushy cooing shit that women did when there was a baby close by. As they passed Ava around, I caught a better glimpse of her than I had when she'd been sucking at Holly's tit the day before. She had a lot of hair and big brown eyes, and right now she had a big smile on her face as she was fussed over. I could see Holly in her pale, chubby, little face, and around her nose and mouth. But there was someone else there, too, in the eyes, something that struck a familiar cord that I couldn't put my finger on.

I wondered which one of my brothers Ava resembled, and then quickly shook the thought away. I trusted my brothers. When had I stopped trusting Holly? Christ, I didn't like the feeling that left in my gut. I'd accused her of fucking around on me. If I hadn't been so fucking blind with hurt over her leaving me, maybe I would have been able to accept the idea that her pregnancy had been the product of rape.

But that only explained how she'd gotten pregnant, not why she'd left, and I couldn't shake the thought that something about the situation didn't add up. In all the years that we'd been together, she'd never gotten pregnant. Why now? No, there was something Holly wasn't telling me. Why the fuck was I sitting here stewing over it? Would the truth change anything?

Ava's happy squeal brought me back to the here and now. Holly was coming down the stairs, and the kid had obviously caught sight of her mother. My eyes ate Holly up, noticing again how motherhood had filled out her luscious curves. Her tits stretched the t-shirt she had on and bounced with every step she made as she came down. Damn, she might not be mine anymore, but that didn't stop my dick from standing up and taking notice of her fine ass.

I recalled the hours before when I'd gone to her room. I'd fucked her good and hard, maybe too roughly. But she wasn't walking like her ass was sore. Her gaze flickered to me, and I smirked when her cheeks turned pink, just like they'd done when she was younger and we'd first got together.

That's right, Baby. I reamed your ass out good and filled it with cum.

I wasn't going to apologize for that. I'd do it again if the opportunity presented itself, that's why I'd warned her to stay away from me. I knew that I couldn't keep my hands off of Holly. Seeing her again after all this time only proved how much I still wanted her.

After her initial stumble at the sight of me, she pulled herself together and reached for her daughter. The kid squealed louder, wrapping her little arms around Holly's neck and giving her an open mouthed kiss on the chin. I had to fight back a grin as Ava sucked Holly's chin into her mouth. Watching Holly's beautiful face soften with love for her daughter did something to me that I couldn't explain, and I had to look away. I was overwhelmed with feelings of loss and regret that I couldn't deal with right now.

I pushed my half-eaten breakfast away and picked up my coffee cup.

"Church, Brother," Loco announced as he continued past me without stopping.

It was then that I noticed that others were already making their way in the direction of the room where we held church. "Coming, man." I noticed Holly glance my way as I was getting up, but the second our eyes met she quickly looked away.

I hoped that she was gone by the time I came back out.

Demon was already at the head of the table when I entered church. I returned welcome home pats on the back as I made my way through the room. Cole took his spot next to Demon on one side, and Oz was seated on the other. Cole motioned for me to sit next to him. I frowned, wondering what was up. That spot was usually saved for the VP, and I realized at that moment that Demon hadn't mentioned if the club had voted in a new vice president to replace LD once he'd become president of the new Las Vegas chapter.

"What's up, Brother?" I sank down into the chair that he pulled out for me.

He shrugged, grinning. "May as well take the VP's chair since we don't have one yet."

"And why is that? Fuck, it's been months." That should have been the first order of business once LD left for Vegas. In fact, I was surprised that Cole hadn't moved into the position.

Demon's sharp, commanding voice kept Cole from responding.

"Listen up, Brothers!"

The room quieted down, and all eyes moved in his direction. He looked my way. "We've been waiting for your ass to come back home, Brother. Hope you beat down whatever demons you were chasing."

I didn't know about that. I hadn't expected to see Holly again, and so soon after getting back. "I can handle them," I said instead. "I'm good, Prez. Demons won't get in the way of my duties."

Demon nodded, satisfied with my answer, even though I suspected that he didn't believe me. "Glad to hear you say that."

He reached for something that I guessed had been sitting on his lap. It was a patch, and even upside down I could see that it was for VP. I didn't think anything of it until he tossed it my way. I caught it, giving him a frown.

"Took a vote while you were gone. Congratulations. You're our new VP."

What the fuck? I blinked, looking back and forth between Demon and the patch in my hand, in shock. I hadn't expected this.

When I looked over at Cole he shrugged and held up his hands. "Don't look at me, Brother. I didn't want it. I like fucking people up."

My gaze scanned the faces around the room. Some of my brothers were standing against the wall, all big, burly, hard-core killers, and not one of their expressions revealed that they weren't on board with this. I cut my eyes back to Demon. It hadn't been something that I'd been actively seeking, but I couldn't deny the sense of pride and accomplishment that I felt over my new responsibilities.

"Wasn't expecting to come back to something like this."

"Why the fuck not?" Demon growled behind his grin. "You've been with Desert Rebels a long time, Sax. Been a good brother to all of us. You paid your dues as a prospect and soldier. As far as I'm concerned, getting an officer's patch has been long overdue."

Brothers backed up his commendations with enthusiastic words of agreement. I felt uncharacteristically humbled because I'd been gone almost a year and hadn't done anything during that time to deserve this honor. The fact that the club wanted me as VP and had waited for my return spoke volumes to me.

LD had left for Vegas months ago. I wondered who'd been serving as acting VP since then. I hadn't concerned myself with the club's goings on while I'd been on the road, and Demon hadn't kept me informed. That detached attitude ended now that I was back. I lived, breathed, and would die for the club. Nothing and no one was going to distract me from that.

"Thank you for the honor, Brothers. I won't let you down."

"So you accept?" Demon asked, as if I had any choice.

I snorted. "You doubted it?"

"Get that patch on your cut, Brother!" Cole gave me a hard slap on the back.

"Here." Demon tossed me a small tube. "Until you can get to the seamstress and get it sewed on."

I snatched the tube of glue in the air with a grin. I slipped off my cut. Cole helped me position the patch.

"Think of all the prime pussy that patch is gonna get you, VP." The comment came from Loco and was followed up with several snorts. "Thanks to you, we got us some new pussy in the clubhouse. She's a fucking wildcat in bed."

"Figured you'd be the first one to break her in," Oz laughed.

Loco's brows shot up. "Well most of you dumb fucks have old ladies, someone had to do it." He looked over at me. "You tried her out yet?"

I shook my head and instantly regretted it. My brothers knew that I'd been on the road with Goldie, and I knew that they would find it strange that I hadn't already fucked her. Not that I gave a fuck what any of them thought, but I knew that, in their eyes, if I'd fucked Goldie it would have solidified that I was over Holly and had moved on.

I released a heavy breath. "Plan to as soon as I leave church," I said, knowing that I was lying through my fucking teeth. "Got some celebrating to do."

A chorus of "hell yeah"s broke out, but quickly died down when it was noticed that Demon was sitting silently at the table. "We can do more celebrating after church," he said once the room was quiet again. "Right now we need to discuss the Knights."

"Been a while since I've heard that name," Dancer grumbled.

It had been at least a few years, not since we'd exchanged their president's brother for a peace treaty, right after they'd come across Demon riding solo one night and had attacked him. The kid, Freak, had been out to make a name for himself, but we'd captured him and used him for leverage.

"Stretch still their president?" Snake asked.

Demon nodded. "Got three of his brothers sitting at the table with him, too."

"I heard they want to make a move," Cole muttered. "To Vegas, of all places."

"Fuck. As if Vegas don't have enough clubs riding the streets."

Most weren't outlaw MCs, though. I gave Chewy a smirk. "Vegas is a big fucking place, Brother. We're not just talking the strip."

He shrugged. "Long as they don't cross over into our territory."

"That's not how we work there, and you know it," Demon snapped. "Too many fucking MCs to define borders. Sure, we have recognized zones, but there's an unspoken agreement that when one MC is crossing through another it's fast, peaceful, and respectful. Otherwise Vegas would turn into a war zone, and half of us would be dead or in prison."

"Too bad the Insane Boys hadn't adhered to that."

Snorts erupted in response to Reid's comment.

"Yeah, well, they're not around anymore, are they?" Demon snarled.

Neither are a lot of our brothers and old ladies, I thought to myself. Cole had filled me in on what had gone down at Grinders the night of Annabelle's birthday. A fucking massacre. LD and brothers from both clubs had gone after the IBMC fast and hard, finally killing their president, Dogface, after he'd attacked Jolene and LD at her place.

They'd been able to take care of that traitorous slut, Tamara, too.

"So, what trouble are they stirring up, Prez?"

Demon looked to our enforcer, Cole. A silent communication passed between them before Cole explained. "Bull caught wind that some of the Knights have been seen hanging around our businesses, like they're scoping them out. They're a small club. If they plan to relocate to Vegas, they're gonna need capitol."

"Fuck, you think they have the balls to rob us?" Loco snarled. He was always ready to fuck or fight.

Cole shrugged. "Not sure yet what, if anything, they're up to."

"Why doesn't LD take care of their asses then?" Dancer asked unwisely.

I glared at him for his stupid remark. The brother got his name because he was thin and fast and could dance his way out of a fight, but we'd brought him into the club because of his connections and expertise in working with explosives. Don't get me wrong, the man could fight when he needed to, I'd seen that with my own eyes, but it wasn't something that he went looking for.

"The fuck?" Demon shot him a scowl. "We're the same fucking MC, asshole. And last I heard I'm still the president of Desert Rebels. Not saying LD can't handle anything that comes his way, but we do it as a fucking club. As his enforcer, Bull did right by contacting Cole. We wait and watch, we don't go assuming shit until it actually happens. That's how wars start, and we don't want the other clubs thinking that we're overreacting, paranoid pussies."

"They watching any of the other MCs?" Oz wanted to know.

Cole shook his head. "Bull reached out to some of the clubs we're friendly with, and they haven't noticed anything."

"We're watching the Knights because of their suspicious activity. LD reached out to Stretch and warned him they were on our radar."

"Bet that went over good," I smirked.

"Why now?" Colton asked, leaning back in his chair. "After all this time of being quiet?"

"Who the hell knows?" Cole grumbled, running his hand over his head.

"We've beefed up our presence at Grinders and the tattoo shop. Nothing to worry about now, just wanted to give everyone a heads up."

"What about our brothels?"

Demon shook his head. "They're too far outside of Vegas, and too isolated. Be hard for anyone to scope them out without being seen." He looked over at me with a smirk. "That's it for now, Brothers. Let's go celebrate with our new VP!"

When he scooted back his chair, we all followed.

Chapter 7

H olly
When you had a baby, you had to be prepared for things to not go according to plan. I'd intended to leave right after seeing the men heading off to church, but Ava had chosen that time to have a messy bowel movement and I'd had to take her back upstairs to give her a bath. Annabelle had offered to do it, but she'd had Ava all night and I hadn't wanted to take advantage. She was already going to be taking Ava in the evenings when I worked, so she'd have plenty of time with my daughter.

Smelling fresh and clean, Ava and I headed back downstairs. It was obvious from the noise from below that the men were out of church, and I nearly stumbled when I glanced over at the bar and saw Sax with his arm around Goldie. The woman looked too comfortable against him, and I saw from her appearance that she'd already embraced the club slut persona as if she'd been born into it.

My heart lurched painfully at the sight. How was I supposed to deal with this? Especially after what had happened between us the night before? I was still slightly sore from his pounding. I hadn't been intimate with anyone since the attack that had caused this whole mess between me and Sax. Well, it wasn't exactly true that the attack had been responsible for the mess we were in—I was the reason we were no longer together.

When I'd found out that I was pregnant I hadn't been able to bear the thought that the baby might not be Sax's. Was it possible that Ava was his daughter? Yes. And it made me sick every time I thought about my deceit. Even if she were his, once he found out what I'd done he would never trust me again. Losing Sax had been the price I'd had to pay for having a child.

A girlish giggle drew my gaze to the bitch that was plastered against Sax. Goldie was a pretty girl, and she was rocking the low-riding short shorts and crop top that exposed her midriff and the fact that she wasn't wearing a bra.

42

Her hair was pulled up, exposing her neck. Sax's eyes met mine just as he turned slightly to run his nose along her flesh.

I looked away quickly, fighting back tears, and made my way back to where most of the old ladies were sitting. Somehow I found a smile in me as everyone welcomed me back to the table. There was something about their expressions and the atmosphere in the room that made me feel as if something big was going on.

"Let me have that baby!"

I automatically handed Ava off to a smiling Bobbie. "Next time she does a mess like that you can change her. I had to give her a bath."

"I don't care," Bobbie said, nuzzling Ava beneath her chin and making her squeal. "She smells so good!"

"That's because she's new." JoJo and everyone else laughed at her comment.

"You missed the excitement." I looked at Annie for her to continue. "Sax is the club's new VP."

I'd already made it clear to the girls that we weren't going to walk around on eggshells when it came to talking about Sax. Somehow I'd convinced them that I was over him and starting a new life with Ava. That was a big, fat lie, but a necessary one. I tried but couldn't bring myself to look back toward the bar, where it was obvious now that a celebration was going on. God, I knew that I would need to congratulate him. It was the right thing to do.

"Let me go congratulate him before I leave." I turned before anyone responded.

I took several calming breaths as I made my way over to him. He was surrounded by his brothers and all of the club girls, the center of their congratulations. Jealousy slammed through me, but I was determined to get through this. I could fake it when I needed to. Reid and Loco saw me approaching and moved aside to make room for me up against the bar. Goldie seemed to cling closer to Sax when she noticed me, a possessive look in her eyes that I didn't miss.

"Hey, honey, come over to congratulate our new VP?"

I barely acknowledged Dancer's comment.

Finally, Sax turned toward me, but he didn't speak. He stared down at me with hard eyes and a tightness to his mouth that revealed his displeasure with my appearance. "I just heard the good news and, um, wanted to congratulate you." My voice grew huskier with every word. It killed me to see his arm around Goldie, his hand against the bareness of her waist. Somehow I kept the smile on my face, even through the slight quivering of my bottom lip.

His gaze moved over me, taking in the short, clingy sundress that I wore, his eyes lingering on my breasts. Everything fit me a little tighter these days, so that when my nipples tightened against the material it was noticeable. I hated him at that moment, because his slight smirk revealed that he knew I was reacting to him. I always had.

Was he not going to talk to me? After a minute of waiting for a response, I swung around and rushed off to the restroom. I didn't want anyone to see how crushed I was over his cold indifference. I told myself that I deserved it, but still it hurt, especially to have to bear it in front of the club's watchful eyes. Before I left the room I'd seen some of the looks on his brother's faces, expressions that revealed that they knew what I was feeling. The fact that they couldn't look me in the eye told me a lot.

I made it to the bathroom, closed the door, and leaned against it for a minute to pull myself together. God, this was going to be harder than I'd thought. I had to get out of there. I went to the sink and splashed some cold water over my face, using a paper towel to pat it dry. A churning in my belly warned me that I could easily toss up my breakfast. My complexion was so pale that I pinched my cheeks to get some color into them.

The door opened and I looked in the mirror to see Sax walk in. My pulse jumped as I took in his expression, and I wondered what was going on. "I think you have the wrong restroom." I heard the nervousness in my voice.

"Don't need to take a piss." His tone was emotionless, but it still did something to me.

"Then what do you need, Sax?" I turned to face him, leaning against the counter. "It can't be sex. You seem to have that covered, with the way you and Goldie were all over each other." I prayed that he didn't hear the jealousy in my words.

He grinned, and I knew that he had. "Jealous, Baby?"

I squared my shoulders. "Why would I be jealous? We're both free to fuck whoever we want." I flinched at the callousness of my comment. It wasn't like me, and the way that Sax's face darkened revealed that he didn't like it. "What I mean is—"

"I know what you mean, Holly." He stepped further into the room. "I've spent the good part of a year getting over you so I could move on. Today I plan to move on with Goldie, and any of the other club whores who want my dick."

I swallowed hard, fighting back the tears that threatened to come. The thought of Sax with any woman was killing me. "You hate me."

He nodded slowly. "Yeah, you could say that."

"Then what are you doing here? Are you here to punish me?"

His eyes moved lazily up and down my body, causing my core to clench with arousal and my panties to become wet.

"Maybe before I move on with someone else I want more of what I had last night."

Oh, God, so did I but not like this. He hated me, but I couldn't help but hope that they were just words said because I'd hurt him, that he didn't really mean them. I still loved Sax, so much, and I knew that there would never be anyone else for me.

My heart jumped as I remembered how he'd fucked me the night before. It had been different. More raw and primal than what I was used to with him. We'd always had an active, intense sexual relationship, but in the past he'd been more considerate of me. Last night he'd taken what he'd wanted, setting me on fire with his desperate kind of invasion of my body.

He stepped closer to me, but I had nowhere to go. Would I stop him? Was I strong enough to deny him? I found myself breathing hard in anticipation, both fearful and excited. "What if I don't want it?"

My question didn't stop Sax, and before I knew it he had me trapped against the counter with his arms on either side of me. We were so close that I could feel the heat rolling off his body, could breathe in the warm whiskey on his breath. When I couldn't stand it any longer I raised my eyes to his. My lips parted, and a tiny sound escaped me. His dark gaze dropped to my mouth, and I dragged my bottom lip between my teeth. His nostrils flared in response, and his expression flushed with hunger.

I waited for him to grab me and ravish me like he had the night before, but something seemed to be holding him back. I knew he was aroused. The air was thick with it. I watched emotion flicker in his eyes and saw the indecision there. He was fighting against what he wanted to do and what he needed to do.

"Can't make up my mind if I want to fuck you or strangle you."

Tears filled my eyes. "I'm sorry." I was sorry that I'd ruined us with my selfishness and deceit.

He moved the few inches separating us and unexpectedly rested his forehead against mine and closed his eyes. "Me, too, Babe." The words were whispered against my lips. "Sorry I wasn't enough for you. Sorry I didn't give you the baby you wanted." There was so much anguish in his voice that it tore me up inside. The tears were flowing now, my mouth trembling as I fought to hold back sobs. When he spoke again I could barely hear him. "Have a good life, Babe. I'll try to leave you alone."

With that he turned and left, and I crumbled. I was such a fool. How was I going to live without him? If I could have gone back to undo the damage that I'd done, I would have. Maybe Sax would have forgiven me in time. I hadn't really given him a chance. I'd just taken the coward's way out, left him a note, and taken off.

As my sobs echoed off the bathroom tiles, I was sure that they could be heard outside at the bar. Hopefully the celebration was enough to drown them out. I had to pull myself together and get back out there to Ava. We needed to go home. But really, was I in any condition to drive?

The second time the door opened Raven walked in. Our eyes instantly met, and it didn't take her long to see the devastation on my face. She rushed to me and took me into her arms.

"Oh, honey," she said into my hair with understanding. "I saw Sax follow you, and when he came back out I thought I should check up on you."

I couldn't hold back my sobs as a fresh onset of tears exploded from me.

"I knew you weren't over that man."

"I'll never be over him, Raven," I confessed, pulling back and angrily brushing my cheeks. "I love him! I hate myself for what I've done to us."

"Then why did you break up with him? We've all been asking ourselves that for months. At first we believed it was because of what happened when the three of us were kidnapped, but it's about Ava, isn't it?"

I just stared at the concern in her eyes. Everyone knew Sax's thoughts about having a baby. It was on the tip of my tongue to just tell Raven everything, to confess my sins, but once the words were out there was no going back, and I wasn't sure that I was ready for that. Maybe I shouldn't have come back after all.

"Honey, it's not too late to undo it," Raven continued when the silence between us grew. "People break up all the time and then get back together. Sometimes a break is good for a relationship."

I half-laughed, half-sobbed. "I did something unforgivable," I whispered. Our eyes held, and I could see that Raven was considering my words, unsure about what she should say. Maybe she was afraid of what I'd say. "No. I made my bed, and I'll lie in it." God, that made me sound like such a martyr.

"Do you want to talk about it?" There was caring and sincerity in her soft tone, and I loved her for it. I knew that I could trust any one of the girls to be there for me if I needed them.

I shook my head. "Someday, but not today, and not here." I forced a smile to set Raven at ease. "And before someone claims that I've abandoned Ava, I'd better get out there." I glanced back in the mirror to see how bad my face looked. I looked a wreck.

Like a woman who'd had her heart broken.

Chapter 8

S^{ax} I sat back, relaxed against my headboard, legs crossed at the ankles, I played a jazz favorite of mine by Kenny G on my sax. "Alone" seemed appropriate to the way I was feeling these days, in spite of the fact that I was once again surrounded by my brothers. In many ways I felt more alone now than I had the whole time that I'd been on the road.

I was fucking pathetic.

I wished that I'd never seen Holly again, because it was messing with my fucking head. I'd kept to the declaration I'd made to my brothers on the day I'd received my VP patch. I was handling club business fine, but the rest of the time I was fixated on my ex-old lady and what had gone wrong with us. I missed everything about her. Hell, I missed everything about *us*. We'd been good together.

I was faking it, and my brothers weren't stupid, they knew it. Sure, I hung on to the club girls while I was out in the bar, gave attention to some of the hang arounds on Friday and Saturday nights, but I never took one back to my room. When the girls didn't get an invite to my bed, they tried fucking hard to get me to fuck them anywhere else. It wasn't lost on me that my VP patch drew them in like flies on shit, but I knew that all they wanted was bragging rights. Under different circumstances, I'd have been all over that.

The trouble was that I had two organs, my heart and my dick, that were refusing to let Holly go.

Truth was, I'd loved Holly since the moment I'd walked into the diner she'd been working at and saw her cute ass waiting tables. When she'd glanced up and our eyes had met that first time, it had been like a fucking ray of sunshine shining down on me. Her genuine smile and the glow shining in her friendly eyes had captured me and refused to let go. I'd gone back again and again just to watch her, never approaching her because I hadn't wanted to drag her into the danger and chaos of my world.

SAX

When my brothers and I had been asked by Moody, a nomad friend of the club, to rescue a woman out of the brothel she was being held at, and I'd walked in and found out that woman was Holly, our fates had been sealed. I'd had to have her, and I'd taken her to our clubhouse for safe keeping until the situation with Moody and his old lady was over. It hadn't taken me long to claim her ass.

She'd given me her fucking V-card.

I was finishing up the last notes of "Alone" when there was a movement at my open doorway. Goldie stood there, looking sexy in a short leather skirt and skimpy halter top that revealed more of her tits than it covered. The stiletto boots on her feet were decked out with silver spikes. Her face was already made up for the night, her blond hair braided and hanging over one tit. She was every man's fucking wet dream, but I felt nothing when I looked at her.

She had that coy, seductive look in her eyes, the kind that invited a man to put his dick in her, and I knew that if I let her get close she would try her damndest to get me to comply. A few years ago, before I'd met Holly, I would not have thought twice about dragging her into my room and fucking her six ways to Sunday. That's what club girls were there for. They were good at distracting us from the shit we didn't want to remember.

I lowered my sax, bringing my knee up.

"I love hearing you play," Goldie quipped softly with a smile.

She'd heard me before, when we'd been on the road. I'd got in the habit of ending most of my nights playing beneath the stars.

"What was the name of that song?"

"Alone."

Her laugh was low and husky as she took the few steps into my room to my bed. As she sat down, the scent of her strong perfume reached me. Her hand moved to where my pants hung over my boots, and her fingers began to walk up my leg.

"You don't have to be alone, Sax. I'll be glad to keep you company." Her fingers crested my bent knee and began to walk down my thigh. "I'd do whatever you want."

I smirked. "Sweetheart, save your moves for the guys downstairs, they're wasted on me."

She pouted, halting her fingers near my dick. "Why? You know I want you. I'm here for you."

"You're here for my brothers. I made that clear. If you came here thinking we'd be starting something up, you're going to be disappointed. It's not going to happen." I narrowed my eyes on her, hoping that I hadn't made a mistake in bringing her here. "If that was your reason for coming, maybe you should leave."

She released a sigh and removed her hand. "No, you were up front with me from the start. I just thought—" She shrugged. "You're stuck on someone else, aren't you?"

I held myself still, not responding. I knew that she must have heard talk about me and Holly.

She smiled. "There's nothing to say we can't be friends, right?"

Friends. I held back a snort. Men like me weren't friends with women unless they were *our* women. Goldie had a lot to learn about what it meant to be a club girl. Since I'd been the one to bring her to the club I'd been watching her on and off the last few nights, making sure that she was doing what she'd been brought here to do. She was friendly by nature, and seemed to have embraced the attention of my brothers, although the fact that she'd set her sights on me could become a problem.

I decided a little wakeup call would nip any thought of that in the bud. "How many of my brothers have you fucked since you've been here?" I could see it in her eyes, the subtle realization that her answer would matter.

She almost looked embarrassed. "Three."

That was a low number but I nodded, satisfied with her answer. I'd seen her going off with Loco more than once, and I was fairly sure she'd been with Snake as well. "Sweetheart, I don't mean to be cruel, but the cold, hard fact is that you belong to all of us. My brothers won't hesitate to fuck you, but that's where it ends. It's rare for a brother to get seriously involved with a woman who's already fucked around with his brothers."

She was quiet for a moment, reflecting on what I'd said. "I don't want to marry you, Sax. I just want to fuck you." There was a teasing light in her pretty eyes, a curve on her lips. I felt the slight flutter of her fingers next to my dick. "That's my job, right?"

I grinned, leaning forward. "I appreciate the thought, sweetheart, but not right now. I'll come to you if I'm looking to get laid." I sank back against the pillows.

Her laughter seemed a little forced as she slowly rose to her feet. "I guess I'll get downstairs where all the action is."

I smirked at her jab.

"Are you coming down?"

"Later." I watched the sway of her hips as she left my room, beating myself up for not tapping her fine ass. The truth was, I didn't want anyone but the woman who owned my fucking heart, and I would have felt like I was being unfaithful to Holly if I messed around with another woman right now.

Holly was back in Vegas. When we'd been together, we'd moved there to run the construction office and had shared an apartment for a while. After she'd taken off, I'd given it up for other members of the club to use until the lease was up. Annabelle had taken it over once she'd start running the office, and I'd found out that Holly had moved into a tiny home outside of Vegas. I didn't know much more than that, hadn't wanted to ask. The less I knew about her new life, the sooner I'd move on.

Yeah, I couldn't see that happening anytime soon.

I got up to go down to the party, which, from the sounds of it, was already going strong. When I got to the top of the stairs and glanced down I could see why. Some of the Vegas Watchdogs had shown up. Our two MCs had gotten close over the last couple of years. Some of their brothers worked on the construction sites with us, and they'd helped us take care of the Insane Boys. It didn't surprise me to see Demon and Cole sitting with their president, Trip, and his VP, Murphy. They were at the bar, their heads bent close together, and I could tell that they were having a serious conversation.

I stepped up between Demon and Trip. "What are you ladies gossiping about?"

"Hey, Brother." Trip leaned in, and we did the man-hug thing. "I hear congratulations are in order."

"Thanks, Brother," I grinned, and then I shot Murphy a look, following it up with a chin lift. "What brings you brothers here?"

"Just needed a change of scenery," Murphy answered, picking up his beer. Murphy was a bigger version of grizzly Adams, big as a fucking mountain and twice as hairy. In the dark, the man looked like a fucking Sasquatch. He was intimidating as hell, and I'd seen grown-ass men piss themselves when confronted by him.

"Like what you see so far?" I smirked, noticing that he had eyes on Lulu.

"Yeah, like it a fucking lot."

Demon snorted. "Be gentle with Lulu, yeah? She's sweet, and a favorite of my brothers."

Murphy pinned his eyes on Demon, a slight quirk on his lips. "I'm known as a gentle giant in the bedroom, Brother."

Cole turned on his stool and raised his arm to catch Lulu's attention. She scooted over to us immediately, a welcoming smile on her pretty face. She went up to Cole, but knew better than to touch him. That was one thing I liked about Lulu—she didn't mess around with the brothers who had old ladies.

"Yeah, honey?" She smiled up at Cole before letting her eyes wander around our little circle.

"Vegas Watchdogs are in the house. Think you can give Murphy here some of your time?"

Her smile grew bigger, making it clear that she wasn't afraid of Murphy's menacing size. She sidled up to him. "You want a little company, honey?" Her hand looked fucking tiny against the massive chest she was petting.

His growl could be heard over the music. "I want a fuck lot of your time, baby." He left his stool and took her hand. "Take me someplace private where your screams won't be heard."

The four of us laughed as we watched them walk away.

"My VP likes them small."

"Maybe it makes his dick feel bigger," Loco joked, joining us at the bar.

"So, you were saying?" Demon's edgy tone indicated that he wanted to get back to whatever they'd been discussing before I'd shown up.

It couldn't have been too important if Trip's VP hadn't stuck around.

Trip shrugged his wide shoulders. "Just giving you a heads up on some shit I've heard concerning the Knights. Seems their goal is to become the biggest and baddest in Nevada. They've been targeting smaller, weaker MCs and forcing them to move on or to patch over."

A heavy frown formed between Demon's eyes. "I'd caught wind of that, but thought it was bullshit. Stretch isn't that strong of a leader."

I agreed with him. I'd always thought of them as boy scouts playing at being bad asses. Their MC hadn't done anything noteworthy that would warrant changing their status to a serious MC.

Trip shrugged. "Don't have to be a strong leader if you got the fucking numbers backing you up. Bullets kill no matter who's holding the gun."

"You thinking he's amassing an army?" I inquired.

"Sure sounds like it to me," Colt added. "And what about the fact that they've been nosing around some of our businesses?"

Yeah, there was that. Demon had sent them a warning that we were on to them and it appeared that they'd stepped back, at least for the time being.

Demon released a heavy breath, running his hand over the scruff on his lower jaw. "Why the fuck now? The Knights have been practically dormant the last few years."

Snake and Reid came up and joined us at the bar.

"He's a sneaky bastard," Trip snorted. "Two of his brothers were doing time the last couple of years. Just got released. Word is, he was waiting for them to get out and quietly recruiting in the meantime."

We all knew that Hank and Screw had been in the slammer for selling drugs and stolen car parts.

"What are the other MCs in Vegas saying?"

"Jacked Up and the Guardians aren't worried," Trip smirked.

"Why would they? Their clubs have been around a damned long time and are going strong," Loco quipped.

"So have we," Demon snapped. "But you'd be a fool not to take it seriously. We need to get someone on the inside."

Trip sat back on his stool and crossed his arms. "I think I know someone who can help with that." He wasn't as big as some of us, wasn't muscled up, but his unfriendly expression, the heavy brows and narrowed eyes, and the scars lining one cheek were intimidating enough. He wore his long brown hair braided, his beard cut close to his jaw. Gauges decorated his ears, and he had piercings in one of his eyebrows and on his lip. "You know him, too."

"We know a lot of people," I muttered.

"Who?" Cole asked.

"Brody Savage."

Demon grunted. "Good man. Not connected to any club though. Not even a nomad."

"No, but he's a free agent," Trip said. "Takes on jobs for a price. Not afraid of a little danger."

"And he's damned good at what he does." I knew Savage, and his reputation put him in a position to pick and choose his jobs.

"He did a small job for me back when I needed someone to keep eyes on Raven." All eyes turned to Cole. "Before she became my old lady."

I laughed. "That time she ran from the club to Boulder City?"

Cole nodded, grinning. "Yeah. Had Savage stalk her for a week until I went and got her ass and brought her back."

A sound of disbelief escaped Trip. "That seems kind of tame for him."

"Yeah, well, he's getting older, just like the rest of us," Demon said with mild humor. "Christ, the man doesn't even need to work." He picked up his beer and drained it before asking, "What makes you think he'll want to get involved?"

"Nothing, but it won't hurt to ask. If he can become friendly with some of the Knights, he might be able to find out some information that would help us stay a step ahead of them."

Demon snorted. "When you say 'we' that mean our clubs are in this together?"

I knew what Demon was asking. If Savage took the job, we weren't going to foot the bill alone. He wanted to make sure that Trip understood that he would have to pay his share if they would both reap the rewards. Savage didn't work cheap, and this particular job could mean his life if the Knights found out what he was doing.

A slow smile spread across Trip's mouth. "Got no problem going in with you, Brother."

My president turned to me. "Get in touch with Savage, set up a meeting."

I responded with a chin lift. That wouldn't be an easy task.

Chapter 9

H olly
I walked in the back door of Grinders at precisely two minutes
before the start of my shift. I hated being late, and the last thing I wanted to
do was take advantage of Demon, who'd given me the temporary job. I was
just thankful that I'd be bringing money in to cover my bills and wouldn't
have to touch the little nest egg that I'd put aside for a rainy day.

My eyes met Candy's when I walked into the main room of the bar. She
was already filling drink orders. "Sorry," was the first thing out of my mouth.

"What for?" She always had a smile on her face. It was the nature of her
friendly personality. She had a tray in front of her and was preparing an order.

I liked Candy. Previously she'd worked as a dancer at the club, but had
gone to Bartending School so that she would have more opportunity. I
doubted that the tips were better than her previous position, but she didn't
complain. She'd worked at Grinders for several years, and had grown tired of
taking off her clothes and being pawed at by horny, unruly drunks.

"For almost being late," I laughed, watching her put the last glass onto
the tray. "Want me to take that?" Honey and Elsa seemed to be busy in their
sections.

She nodded. "Thanks, honey." She slid the tray in my direction. "Just
happens to be one of your tables. The one in the far back against the wall."

I glanced in that direction and saw a lone man sitting at the table. He
was watching Trina doing her thing on the pole, and she was working it as
if he were the only man in the room. I couldn't blame him for focusing on
her—Trina was beautiful, and she had a perfect body. The men loved her
bottled bright red hair and her large, augmented breasts. She made the most
tips of all the girls, and often disappeared into a back room with customers
several times a night.

"All these drinks for one man?" I smiled.

"He has friends coming."

I picked up the tray and turned towards the customer's table. The closer I got, the more I could see just how handsome the man was, in spite of his intense, closed-off expression. He wasn't wearing a cut like eighty percent of the other clientele were, yet he had the same dangerous vibe going on. The bomber-style leather jacket he was wearing revealed that he had a powerful, solid body. His black hair framed dark brown eyes in a strong face covered in scruff.

He noticed my approach and smiled as I drew closer. I noticed his eyes move over me with interest, but I didn't feel insulted by his gaze. I returned his smile and set the tray down.

"At first I thought you were just thirsty, until Candy told me you have friends coming," I teased. "How do you want these?"

"The tequila is mine, sweetheart. Just leave the tray, my friends can grab what's theirs."

I set the tequila down in front of him, careful not to lean over too far. I didn't mind showing a little cleavage for bigger tips, but I wasn't as obvious about the ploy as some of the other girls were. Some of them seemed to thrive on the attention, but I would never be one of those women who would disappear somewhere for a quick fuck with a patron. I'd made up my mind a long time ago that there would never be anyone but Sax for me. I knew that I wasn't being realistic, that someone would come along one day, someone I would settle for.

"Would you like anything to snack on?" I asked as I straightened up.

"Are you on the menu?"

I laughed. The teasing light in his eyes put me at ease, assuring me that his comment was meant as a joke. "Sorry. You'd probably have better luck with Trina." I glanced toward the striper pole that she was grinding on. Trina hadn't torn her gaze from the man, making it very clear what she wanted.

He shook his head. "I never go for average when I've got perfect standing in front of me."

This man was too much, but I recognized that it was all harmless flirting. I found myself giggling like a stupid school girl at the man's compliment, paying no mind when I felt movement behind me, assuming that someone was passing by to get to another booth or table.

"This one's off limits."

SAX

I tensed at the sound of the familiar voice behind me, my smile instantly evaporating. I didn't move as Sax, Cole, and Loco moved around me and slid into the booth. My eyes connected with the steely grit in Sax's. I felt my breath catch at the anger reflected there. Would he always look at me with such dislike? I steeled myself from revealing the hurt that I felt, exchanging a glance with Cole and Loco and forcing the smile back on my face.

"Hi, honey," Cole greeted, reaching for the beer.

"Got anything good to snack on back there?" Loco gave me a wink.

"We were just talking about tasty snacks, weren't we?" The stranger grinned in my direction.

It was obvious that he hadn't picked up on the hands-off vibe Sax had sent out when he'd first sat down, or he just didn't care. He wasn't intimidated by the bikers in the least, and I wondered how they knew each other.

"We didn't come here to fucking party," Sax snarled, drinking down his whiskey in one swallow. He slammed the glass back onto the tray. "Bring me the whole bottle," he demanded. It was clear that he wasn't happy to see me.

I raised my brow, not liking his demanding tone. "Well, since you asked so nicely, why don't you get it yourself?" As soon as the words left my mouth I regretted them. Sax's face flushed darkly, and I spun around and left before he could retaliate. Grinders belonged to the Desert Rebels, and he was the VP. He could fire me on the spot if he wanted to. *Shit!*

I didn't get far before I felt a rough hand wrap around my arm and then drag me past the bar to the back. Candy's eyes widened at me, but she knew better than to intervene. I made an effort to pull away. Sax grunted and tightened his hand around me, forcing me down the hall around a corner and then against the wall.

"Since when do you fucking work here?"

I rubbed my arm, facing his anger with my own. "Since Demon gave me a job," I said smartly.

"What else are you serving up besides drinks?" he growled, his eyes raking up and down my body.

I didn't like what he was implying. The accusation in his tone put me on the defensive. "None of your business!" I hissed in his face. "And your suspicions just confirm that you don't know me at all, Sax. I'm a server and sometimes bartender, and it's only temporary." Why was I explaining myself to him?

"I saw you flirting with Savage."

Was he jealous? I laughed. "It goes with the job, and he was flirting with me. It was harmless."

"What do you mean, 'it's temporary?'" he scowled. "Planning on running again?" There was something in his tone besides anger—accusation.

"I have a hostess job once Crickets opens up on the strip." I crossed my arms as if to keep a distance between us. I was weak where Sax was concerned, and my mind returned to the night when I'd awoken to find him unexpectedly in my bed.

"Good. The less I see of you, the fucking better." He turned and started to walk away.

"Sax—"

He halted but didn't turn back around.

"I'm sorry. I never meant to hurt you."

His shoulders tensed in response to my words. I wanted to tell him that I loved him, that I would always love him, but realized that would contradict the reason I'd given him for breaking up with him. "I wish things were different—"

He spun around and stepped back to me so fast that I caught my breath and sank back against the wall as if it offered some protection.

"Different?" he snarled the word down at me. "Different how, Holly? I thought we were good. That we would work out our differences like two people in a committed relationship would. It nearly gutted me when you were taken and raped. But I was willing to wait a fucking lifetime for you to come back to me, for you to heal and be my woman again. You're the one who threw it all away, Baby. You're the one who ran instead of fighting for us."

I shook my head, but couldn't find my words. Tears ran down my cheeks hearing the broken emotion reflected in his tone. The truth was right there, waiting to spill from my lips, but I was too afraid to utter the words that would destroy what little we had left between us.

Because the truth *would* destroy us.

"I came back here hoping that you were still gone. I prayed for it." His impassioned words hurt me deeply. "But here you are, and with a kid."

I was growing tired of his refusal to call Ava by her name. *"Ava, Sax. Her name is Ava,"* I said between my teeth. "And you don't want kids, so breaking it off with you was a no brainer. I wasn't going to have an abortion. I wasn't going to give her up. It doesn't matter who her father is, I loved her the second I saw the positive pregnancy test." I didn't realize what I'd just admitted to until I saw the dawning of realization fill his eyes.

Shit! Realizing my mistake, I started to leave, but he boxed me in with his arms.

"So you lied."

I blinked up at him, tightening my mouth.

"You knew you were pregnant before you left."

A shadow of doubt moved across his face, I could see that he was trying to put the pieces together, and the longer the silence continued between us, the more nervous I grew. My heart sped up and I closed my eyes against the growing suspicion in his. I forced myself to breathe slowly and deeply, hoping to calm the jittery energy causing my pulse to race. All I wanted to do was get away from Sax and back out onto the floor.

"Look at me."

I did as he asked and raised my chin a little in a defiant gesture that I was sure he'd recognize. When we'd been together he'd found my defiance cute, but now his expression remained frighteningly impassive. I swallowed hard. He had to know that he was making me very uncomfortable.

"Sax, I need to get back to work."

"Could Ava be mine?"

My stomach fell. I'd been expecting that question from him, but it didn't stop me from feeling sick. I wasn't ready to admit the truth of what I'd done. But I could answer him honestly. "I don't know who her father is."

"Not what I asked you."

Panic caused me to pull away from him. "I have to work, Sax!" I cried out when he grasped me by the hair and yanked me back. He forced me against the wall, crowding me in with his body and leaning his face in close. I'd never seen him like this before, and I had to admit that I was a little turned on by it.

"I want a DNA test," he gritted between his teeth, rage glittering in his eyes.

My eyes grew round. "Why? You don't even want kids." My mind raced as I tried to figure out how I was going to get out of this. I was ashamed by what I'd done, and if Ava turned out to be his he would instantly realize what I'd done. Tears filled my eyes as I stared up at him. If I thought Sax hated me now, it was nothing compared to what he would feel for me then.

"Maybe not, but if I ever found out I had one I'd do right by them."

I wanted more than anything for Ava to be his.

"Make the appointment and I'll be there to give a fucking sample."

"Sax—"

"Do it." With that, Sax released me and stomped off.

I stood there for a minute to pull myself together, and then hit the restroom to splash some water on my face and run my fingers through my hair. For the first time, I began to regret coming back. I was caught in a situation of my own making, and it was escalating faster than I could keep up with. The feeling that I'd turned a mole hill into a mountain wasn't lost on me. If I'd just been honest from the beginning, all of this could have been avoided, but the rape had messed with my thought processing and my ability to make common sense decisions back then.

My biggest regret was that I'd broken it off with Sax for the wrong reason.

I pulled my phone out of my back pocket and hit Jolene's number. During the months that I'd worked at the Desert Rebels construction office and she'd run Illuminations next door, we'd become fast friends. Of all the old ladies, we were the closest. She picked up on the first ring.

"Hi, honey," she breathed into the phone. "To what do I owe this pleasure?"

I could hear the smile in her voice, and for some reason her light-hearted tone brought tears back to my eyes. "I need you. I need my girl friends..."

There was immediate concern in her tone. "What's wrong? Are you alright?"

I took a deep breath as I struggled to regain my composure. "I just need to talk, but I can't now. I'm at work."

"Say no more, honey. I'll call the girls and we'll make a plan. I'll get back to you."

"Thank you," I said in a teary tone, hating myself for not being strong enough to keep it together.

I knew that I could count on my friends. They might not have been able to solve the problem caused by my own stupidity, but their support and unconditional love would buffer the fallout that was sure to come.

Chapter 10

S^{ax} "Why the fuck did no one tell me Holly was working at Grinders?"

"Didn't call church to discuss Holly," Demon said. "She's not your old lady anymore, Brother."

I didn't appreciate the brush off. I ground my back teeth until a sharp pain shot up the side of my head. Demon was right, but I still felt that withholding the information from me was a betrayal of sorts. "Thank fuck she isn't dancing and taking off her clothes, because if she were there would be heads rolling right now."

I heard some snickers, but as soon as I whipped my head around they stopped. Too many smirks to count were spread across my brothers' faces. I wanted to smash my fist into them, including Demon's. I crossed my arms and leaned back in my chair, prepared to hit the first brother who said the wrong fucking thing.

"Your meeting with Savage didn't exactly pan out."

I glanced over at Demon. I'd had a feeling that Savage wasn't going to take the job after our discussion at Grinders the other night. He was busy now, but asked us to give him a couple of days to see if he could work shit out. "He called then?"

Demon nodded. "This morning."

"Why'd he turn us down?" Oz asked.

"Got a commitment elsewhere." Demon leaned forward, elbows bent on the table as he steepled his fingers. "But he gave us a name of someone who might be available."

"Why doesn't one of us go in?"

"Don't want to take a chance the brother we send in will be recognized," Cole was quick to point out to Chewy.

Demon continued as if he hadn't been interrupted. "Ever hear of a nomad called Judge?"

More than one head nodded and "yeah" filtered through the room.

"Hell, yes." Colton spoke up.

"Jesus, don't tell us he used to run with your crew," Reid burst out.

Colton, along with a few others, had been patched over from Devil's Soldiers a few years ago. Their MC no longer existed.

Colton snorted. "Fuck, no. He's always been a nomad. Mean as hell motherfucker. Loyal to no one, unless you're payin' him for a job, and he'll expect half up front. Last I heard the fucker has two kids he's puttin' through college."

"We didn't ask for his resume, asshole."

He responded to Loco's sarcasm by giving him the finger.

"If he's not loyal then he can't be trusted." I snarled. Murmurs of agreement sounded throughout the room. I knew who Judge was, too, and if a man couldn't be loyal to anyone, he could flip sides on a dime. "I wouldn't want him at my back."

"Loyal, not stupid," Colton explained. "If you're payin' him he'll finish the job. He's not cheap, either."

"I've heard that about him," Oz quipped.

"That he'll finish the job, or that he's not cheap?" Dancer grinned.

"Both."

"The way you praise Judge, it almost sounds as if you have a personal gain in this."

The room grew quiet as everyone considered Cole's words and their implication and waited for Colton's reaction. He scratched his ear and shook his head. "Never met the man. Just know about him, and from what I've heard about his background, he'd probably get picked up by the Knights faster than Savage would have."

"That's fucking good enough for me," Demon announced, drawing everyone's attention his way. "I've already run it by Trip, and he's on board. Any ayes for hiring Judge to infiltrate the Knights?"

I scanned the room as arms shot up in the air. It looked as if everyone was on board.

"Any nays?"

Not one.

Demon swung his eyes to me. "You know what to do."

I gave him a chin lift before looking over at Oz. "Let's meet after church." Oz was our computer guru. It had taken him less than an hour to locate Savage. I expected it would take longer for him to find Judge, though. Nomads were good at not being found if they didn't want to be.

"We got trouble!"

I snapped my head in Cole's direction. He was sitting next to me, his head bent as he frowned down at something on his phone. His expression looked grim. "Just got a message from Bull." He got to his feet before he finished reading. "Their clubhouse was hit!"

"Fucks" exploded throughout the room as my brothers and I jumped to our feet to head out.

"How bad?" We were running shoulder to shoulder toward our bikes.

"Didn't say, just that the place was fucking shot up."

Brothers reached for their helmets and jumped on their bikes, their swift actions revealing their eagerness to take off. They revved up the powerful machines between their legs, forced to wait for Demon to take the lead. It sounded like thunder and the ground shook as we got in line and followed behind him through the gate. I was directly behind him, followed by Cole, and then the others. As we raced away from the clubhouse, I wondered what we were going to find at LD's.

I hadn't been there yet, hadn't had a chance. We went full throttle where we could. Once we reached the outskirts of Boulder City we jumped on the interstate to go the rest of the way. Now wasn't the time to take the scenic route. It didn't take long before we reached the exit and got off, and then we rode through parts of busy Vegas before winding up on a quiet road that took us the rest of the way to the clubhouse.

The first thing I noticed as we pulled through the gate and rode past the prospect who was manning it was that the clubhouse was in a good location. It was dark, so it was difficult to make out how much damage had been done to the building, but the broken windows were evident. There were a couple of wounded bikes in the front, if the way their riders were swearing and looking them over was any indication. I frowned, wondering where the rest of them were. I shut my bike down and shot a look toward Cole. "Did Bull say they went after the shooters?"

He shook his head as I brought my leg over my seat to get off. "They park behind the building for this very reason."

"Doesn't make for a fast getaway." Loco had obviously overheard.

"No, but it saves a fuck-ton of money on replacing bikes and bike parts," Oz quipped as we headed toward the door in a fast pace. "Think of how many bikes could have been crippled."

"Always a fucking pain in the ass," I agreed.

Demon burst through the door and the rest of us followed. I immediately scanned the large bar, taking in the slight chaos that still filled the room.

"Where the fuck is LD?"

The room quieted. Demon's shout drew everyone's attention to where he'd come to a stop.

Bull came out from somewhere in the back. "Gone, Prez. After the shooting died down he took some brothers after them."

"Did you see who the fuck did this?" I snarled.

"It was too dark to see, Brother."

"A fucking drive-by." The man who'd come to stand next to Bull had a patch that revealed that he was the secretary. "They hit fast and didn't hang around for introductions."

"What's the damage?" Demon asked.

Bull motioned to a brother who was sitting at one of the tables with two women fussing over him. It was obvious from the way they were dressed that they were club girls. Taking in the location of the blood on the wounded man, it looked as if he'd taken a hit to the arm and the leg.

"The prospect at the gate took a couple rounds. He heard them coming but didn't realize they meant trouble till shots were fired."

I nodded. "Good thing it was dark, or their aim would have been better."

"And we'd be planning a funeral," Bull said with a twist of disgust on his lips. "Had enough of that shit the last year."

No one said anything in response to that.

"Is Doc on the way?" I questioned, looking around.

"Yeah, I called him as soon as I heard gunfire." The secretary held out his hand. "I'm Blade, Brother." I grasped his hand. "Don't think I've met you before."

"Sax." We shook hands briefly. "I was away until recently." Normally I wouldn't have explained myself to anyone, but I felt it was necessary, considering that he was a brother and a patched officer to LD.

"Anyone else hurt?" Demon's gaze moved about the room, as if looking for the answer for himself.

"No, thank fuck," answered another brother whose name I didn't know. "Fuck!"

"Oh, stop being a baby," a feminine voice scolded. I glanced to where the girls were trying to staunch the flow of blood running out of the prospect.

"What's your name, kid?"

He glanced up, his eyes wild and glossy from pain. "Morgan."

"Could you make out anything?"

He shook his head, his lips turned down at the corners. "Everything happened too fucking fast. Once they started shooting, I started shooting back and took off for cover. I can't even tell you how many there were, but I do know this—they were fucking bikers. I couldn't see their colors, but I recognized that at least."

I cut my eyes to Demon. "You think some of us should go after LD and the others for backup?"

"Yeah. This could have been a plan to get some of our brothers away from the clubhouse to ambush them."

I headed back toward the door. "Loco, Reid, Colton—you brothers are with me."

I knew that whoever had hit the clubhouse wasn't heading back to Vegas because we would have met them on the road. We took off in the opposite direction, racing blindly in the night down a road that didn't have street lights, just the occasional reflector.

It wasn't long before we came upon LD and the rest of the brothers, heading back in our direction. We simultaneously slowed down and came to a slow crawl when we met up on the road. The savage look on LD's face revealed his anger and frustration, the brothers riding with him wearing the same tight-jawed expressions. They looked ready and geared up for war.

"Lost the fuckers!" LD shouted over the rumble of our bikes. "Too much of a head start!"

SAX

I gave him a chin lift and turned my bike around to head back to his clubhouse. It took us no more than five minutes to get back. "You think it was the Knights?" I asked as we headed inside.

"They're the only ones causing shit right now," LD snarled in a tone that said he thought so.

He nearly tore the door off the hinges when he snatched it open hard enough for it to slam back against the wall. I knew what he was looking for when his head snapped to the side, but Morgan wasn't there. Just some bloody rags.

"The girls are taking care of him in one of the rooms 'til Doc gets here."

I had a call coming in, and when I pulled my phone out, I saw Morty's name flash across the screen. He ran the tattoo shop for us. My first thought was that he must be working late tonight. "Yeah?" The first thing I heard in response was his rapid breathing, and a feeling in my gut told me that I wasn't going to like what he had to say.

"He's dead! He's dead! B-Bikers just sh-shot up the p-place!" He was tripping over his words in an effort to get them out. It was obvious he was scared shitless.

"Fuck! Calm down," I ordered. "Who's dead?" The sudden silence in the room revealed that everyone had stopped what they were doing to listen to my conversation.

"A cu-customer! I'd just finished him." He was breathing as if he'd just run a marathon. "We were at the register when the shooting started. It happened so fast! I heard the bikes but thought they were you guys!"

"Did you see who it was?"

"The Knights!"

"Shit! You sure?"

"Yeah, I saw the back of their cuts. What do I do?"

A civilian had been killed. There was only one thing he could do. "Okay, listen up. Call 911. Don't tell them or the cops that the shooters were bikers, just tell them it was a drive-by and you didn't see anything. Got it?"

I could hear Morty take a deep breath. "Yeah, okay."

"A couple brothers will be there in a few. Stay put."

I was about to put my phone away when another call came in. "The fuck?" I muttered to myself when I saw that it was Samson. He was the night manager at Grinders. I had a gut feeling we were in for more trouble. "What?"

As I listened to him relay what was going on, I noticed Demon and LD quietly step away from the brothers surrounding them and pulling out their phones, too.

Something was definitely going down.

Jesus Christ, the same fucking thing that had occurred here and at the tattoo shop had happened at Grinders! Bikers had driven by, shooting off their guns into the building. The whole time I listened to Samson explaining what had occurred, my only thought had been on Holly and whether or not she'd been working tonight. No one had been killed, but three people leaving the bar had been wounded in the parking lot. Samson had already called it in.

"Son-of-a-bitch!" LD snarled, when his call was over. "They hit the construction site we've been working."

"That was Trip," Demon began, pocketing his phone. "A couple of their businesses got hit, too." His sharp look encompassed everyone in the room, and I could tell that his mind was spinning.

Everyone looked to him for the answers. He had to be thinking about the brothels we owned and wondering when we'd get word that they'd been hit too. There was also the fact that we'd left our own clubhouse with low coverage.

"Fuck infiltrating the Knights," I snarled. "We need to do something about this shit now. They want war, we give it to them!"

More than one brother made his agreement known.

Demon and I locked eyes. I couldn't tell if he agreed with me or not, but as his VP I knew he'd weigh my words carefully. Maybe I'd overstepped my bounds, but after everything that had gone down tonight, we needed to retaliate sooner rather than later. Show those fuckers we weren't pussies.

"We need to go after those fuckers now!" Cappy, LD's VP, spoke up in a heated tone. He was an older brother, still in good shape, but right now his face was red, and I imagined that his blood pressure had risen, too.

"Agree!" LD said in a guttural tone, his jaw grinding and his eyes glittering with rage.

Demon took in the gazes of all the brothers in the room. He understood what we wanted. None of us wanted to wait to show the Knights that they were fucking with the wrong club. We were ready and eager now as we all stood looking at our president, waiting for his response.

"Looks like we're going to war, Brothers!"

Chapter 11

Holly

I'd wanted a baby so badly that I'd done a terrible thing. I'd stopped taking my birth control the month before Raven, Bobbie, and I had been kidnapped from the salon. I loved Sax more than life itself, but I couldn't give up my dream of having a child. I'd always dreamed of being a mother, and when JoJo and Ellie had their babies I'd allowed the longing to consume me. I'd sacrificed Sax, sacrificed all that we'd had together, for my selfish need to get what I'd wanted. And the worst part of all? I'd convinced myself that in the end he would come around, and if he didn't, I was prepared to leave the man I loved.

So stupid.

So selfish.

I'd hurt us both with my decision. I was ashamed.

The stark silence in the room was telling. I'd shocked the women of the MC so much that they were speechless, staring at me in stunned disbelief. The only one who wasn't there was Annabelle. Apparently, she and Jolene's younger brother, Danny, were in a serious relationship and spent all of their free time together. I felt mortified, tears swimming in my eyes after the awful truth I'd just spewed to them. Did they hate me now? I didn't see hate in their eyes, I didn't see condemnation. Maybe disappointment and regret because I'd done the wrong thing, which I had. As each one processed what I'd just confessed, I wiped my cheeks and held back the sobs by clenching my jaw.

I deserved whatever they threw at me.

"I'm a terrible person," I finally said to break the awful silence. I firmly believed that.

"No, no, no!" Jolene admonished sharply, rushing over to sit next to me on the sofa. She put her arm around me. "We've all made mistakes," she said firmly.

"Yeah, honey." Raven joined us on the couch and sat on the other side of me. "We've all done things we're not proud of."

"You can't undo it, but you can move on from it." Bobbie also came over to sit with us. "And you don't get to sit here and make yourself out to be a bad person, honey."

JoJo spoke up, sitting next to Bobbie. "We won't let you."

"So it's possible that Ava could be Sax's?" Annie asked.

I met her eyes where she sat across from me and nodded. "I'm afraid to find out."

"You can't let him think Ava is the result of, um, what those men did to you," Raven said in a firm tone. "Especially if it turns out that he's the father. That's not fair to either of you."

"Is this why you broke it off with Sax?" Bobbie asked with a frown.

I nodded without meeting her eyes. "As soon as I found out I was pregnant I told him we were over." I buried my face in my hands and broke down. "Don't you see? I stopped taking my pills so I would have Sax's baby. If it turns out that Ava is the result of the attack, then it's my fault. He'll never forgive me for that." I paused for a second. "I didn't have the guts to tell Sax when I found out I was pregnant."

"You were scared," JoJo said knowingly.

Among other things, I thought. "The guilt I felt..." I wiped my face and pushed my hair back behind my ears. "I still feel..."

"Honey, you have to come clean and tell Sax. And you have to get Ava tested to see if he's her daddy, and then go from there. Once that is done, you'll feel better."

I'd never feel better. I stared at Bobbie as if she were crazy. "I'll lose him forever!" I whisper yelled. "Either way, he'll never forgive me!" I firmly believed that. Trust was a big thing.

"Honey—" She took my hand. "Will it be any different than now? At least Sax will know the truth about why you broke it off with him. He'll know that it wasn't because you stopped loving him. Will he be angry? Most definitely. You know our men. But maybe once he processes it he'll surprise you."

I snorted. "You don't believe that any more than I do," I told her. "I do know our men. Trustworthiness is important to them. He'll never forgive me for this, especially if Ava isn't his. If I hadn't stopped taking my pills..."

"Oh, God, honey, you're being too hard on yourself." Raven grasped my other hand, drawing my eyes to her. "You didn't stop taking your pills to trap Sax."

No, but I did stop taking them to get pregnant, knowing that he didn't want children. That was worse.

Annie laughed softly. "You already have the man."

Had *the man,* I tought to myself, but I didn't correct her.

"Can I ask you something, honey?"

I nodded at JoJo's question, and waited.

"Did you ever find out why Sax feels so strongly about not having children?"

I shook my head sadly. "No. He won't talk about it, except to say he doesn't want to raise a child in the MC."

"Could it be that simple?" Raven murmured.

No one had a response to that, but I got the feeling that they didn't believe his reasons any more than I did. Our men were hard-core in a lot of ways, and they may have fought tooth and nail to convince their brothers that they didn't need a good woman by their sides, but when it happened they were all in. That included the babies that followed. Maybe that's what I'd been looking for with Sax.

"Thank you all for not hating me." I felt another bout of tears coming on, but managed to hold them off. I loved these ladies.

"We're here as your friends, not to judge you or your actions. We may not agree with what you did, but speaking for myself, I can certainly understand it. I know what it's like to want something so badly that you'd do just about anything to get it."

I was glad to hear something from Ellie. Up until that point she'd been silent. "I have to admit I feel better now that I've told all of you."

"Talking about shit does help," Jolene smiled.

"Sax has demanded a DNA test..."

"Well then he must already have suspicions that Ava could be his."

Bobbie and Annie nodded in agreement with Raven's comment.

"No matter what happens after you tell Sax, no matter how the DNA results turn out, we're here for you. We'll help you get through it. Nothing will change the fact that you have a beautiful baby girl. Sometimes sacrifices have to be made to find our own happiness."

I wondered if Ellie was speaking from experience. I gave her an appreciative smile. Her words meant a lot to me. "I don't know what I'd do without you guys." I meant it. "Your friendship and support means a lot to me." I wiped the remaining wetness from my eyes and took a deep breath.

"Oh, oh! I think I hear the thunder of motorcycles coming." The softness that came across Jolene's face and the look of happiness in her eyes revealed her excitement at the prospect of seeing LD.

I could hear it, too, and with every second that passed the rumbling grew louder. It was clear that there was more than one bike headed our way, and since we were at Jolene and LD's house it was a given that LD would be part of it. Anxiousness churned in my belly at the possibility that Sax was with them. I wasn't ready to face him after what I'd just divulged to the girls. I still felt guilt and shame over my actions, and I wondered if he'd see it on my face. He knew me, probably better than anyone else did.

My anxiety dropped several notches when none of the three men who entered the house was Sax.

Jolene rose to her feet upon seeing the state that LD was in. "Baby, what happened?"

Cole and Reid seemed to have the same hard looks on their faces, as they were also joined by their old ladies, Raven and Ellie. I sensed something bad was going on as I watched how the couples interacted with each other. It was clear that the girls knew instinctively that something was very wrong.

"Trouble." LD's one-word comment was brash and hard.

"Where's Izzy?" Reid wanted to know, his face shadowed with deep concern.

Ellie's expression quickly fell into a look of fear for the well-being of their daughter. "At the clubhouse. All the children are. Lulu is watching them." Reid's look relaxed slightly.

"Going on lockdown, Babe," Cole mumbled down at Raven.

"Both clubhouses?" Bobbie's brow furrowed as she rose to her feet.

LD nodded. "Yup. We need to get our families there."

"What's going on?"

LD stared silently down at Jolene, tightening his mouth.

"I know—club business." She reached up to give his chin a kiss.

"I need to get Ava." I knew that she was safe at the clubhouse, but I wanted to see her and hold her.

"You're going on lockdown, too, honey."

I looked at Cole. "But she's at Demon's clubhouse." There was no way that I was leaving my daughter there while I went to LD's clubhouse, and I was pretty sure that no one in the room expected that I would, either. I was in LD's territory when it came to lockdown.

"Doesn't matter what clubhouse you go to," Cole explained.

"We need to get a move on," LD snapped impatiently.

The man was scary when he was in full-on alpha mode. His size alone was enough to give someone nightmares if they didn't know him. He had his arm wrapped around Jolene and was holding her protectively against his body. They were a good fit—Jolene was tall and built like an Amazon goddess. She was beautiful, inside and out.

Cole and Reid were holding their women just as tightly. I missed the connection of having a man who looked out for me, one who would give up his life for me if it came down to it. I'd had that once with Sax.

I got to my feet, as did Bobbie, Annie, and JoJo.

"What about Annabelle and Danny?" Jolene questioned in her soft, Southern accent. "They went to some park today."

"Already got a handle on it, Babe. They'll be waiting for you at the clubhouse." LD's answer seemed to satisfy her. "Let's head out."

I knew one thing—I didn't have a room at either clubhouse, which also meant that I didn't have any clothes or toiletries. Not to mention that I had nothing for Ava. The other women would be able to go straight to the clubhouse, but I needed to get supplies. There was no telling how long we would be locked up. "I need to make a run to my house to pick up some things for me and Ava first."

"Figured that," Cole grinned. "Spider, the prospect outside will go with you, but make it quick, okay?"

I nodded, thankful that I had my own car. Lulu had come by earlier and picked up Ava so that I wouldn't have to make the trip to Demon's clubhouse twice. The others had come together in one of the club's large SUVs, having left their vehicles at the clubhouse. I exchanged looks with the girls, their concern evident on their faces.

"Do you want me to come with you?" Jolene asked.

LD answered before I could. "No, Babe."

Her smile disappeared as she glanced up at her tall man. "You're going straight to the clubhouse with me."

I smiled to put her at ease. "I'll be okay, Spider will be with me."

"We need to go." Cole looked down at Raven. "You girls go back in the SUV, Reid and I will be right behind you."

Raven nodded.

"We come up on any trouble, you don't stop. You haul ass 'till you're through the gates and safe, got me?"

"But—"

Cole glared down at Raven, a silent message passing between them. "Got you." She lifted on her toes so they could share a heated kiss. Cole's hand lightly caressed over her tiny baby bump, which brought an instantaneous smile to my lips.

As we piled outside I wanted to ask about Sax, but held my tongue. I would be seeing him soon anyway. I wasn't too happy that I would be staying at his clubhouse and would have to see him with club whores, but I had no choice. Ava was already there, so it only made sense. I didn't want to put her in danger by picking her up just to bring her to a different clubhouse.

I met Spider's look with a smile. "I guess you're with me."

In the past, I'd felt sorry for the prospects. They were essentially nothing but gofers. They did all the work, were treated like crap, and got none of the perks of belonging to the club. They were also treated like punching bags to any member who was aggressive or was high on adrenaline and needed to fight it out. Some of them put up with it for two years or longer just for the chance to be patched in. Once Sax had explained the process to me, telling me that they'd all gone through it, I understood that it was a trial period to prove themselves worthy of becoming full-fledged members.

"I got ya, sweetheart," Spider said with a flirty grin.

I climbed into my car and waved back at the girls as they plowed into the SUV in front of me. I'd see them again soon. Cole and Reid climbed onto their bikes, while LD broke away from Jolene and walked to Spider.

"Take Holly straight to her house, and then to the clubhouse. You see anything..." LD didn't finish his sentence, but it was clear that Spider didn't need him to. "You radio in. Don't engage unless they make the first move."

Spider nodded at LD's directions and then looked back at me. "You ready?"

Jolene and I gave each other a finger wave. She, at least, would have Danny and Annabelle with her. I wasn't familiar with the members and their old ladies at LD's clubhouse, which had been created while I'd been away. I was kind of glad to be going to Demon's.

I still had a hard time believing that Jolene and LD were together. I'd never thought that LD would find a woman that would put up with his dark moods. Jolene had broken down the barriers around his stone heart and won him over. I was happy for them both.

I started my car and took off down the drive. I noticed in my rearview mirror that LD and Spider continued to converse for a minute, but as I neared the road they parted and Spider was soon behind me.

I headed home, anxious to get to Demon's clubhouse and have Ava in my arms again.

Chapter 12

H olly
I was tossing clothes into the small suitcase laid out on my bed when I heard the familiar sound of a motorcycle rumbling outside my house. I didn't think anything of it. Spider was waiting for me, and I assumed that one of his brothers from the club had joined him. I couldn't say that I was exactly happy to be going on lockdown, but I knew the drill by now, and I'd have been a fool to deny Ava the protection of the club. I would do whatever it took to keep her safe.

Even if it meant being around Sax.

Glancing down at the contents in the suitcase, I had to chuckle. Ava's things took up more than half of the room. I shoved some of her clothes aside to make room for my meager things. I knew there were a washer and dryer at the clubhouse, so that made packing easier.

As I went to the bathroom to gather a few toiletries, I heard the sound of a motorcycle revving up and taking off. A moment later I heard my front door opening, and then the noise of boots stomping through my tiny house. "Almost done, Spider," I called out, leaving the bathroom with an arm load of toiletries. I set them on the bed, deciding I should put them into a plastic bag before packing them. The bags were in the kitchen. I turned to head out of my bedroom and came to a startled stop. My breath caught at the sight of Sax standing in the threshold, watching me.

"Spider is gone," he said bluntly.

God, he looked hot. His hair was a little longer than he usually wore it, and the five o'clock shadow on his jaw defined the strong, square cut of it. Eyes that had always reminded me of rich mahogany gleamed with an intimate knowledge that made my underwear wet. The way they moved over me caused me to shiver with awareness. I wet my lips. "What are you doing here?"

"Spider had something to take care of."

Why did I get the feeling that he was lying? "So I'm important enough for the VP of Desert Rebels to drop whatever he was doing to pick me up?"

He shrugged. "I happened to be in the neighborhood."

Yeah, okay.

"Did you make that appointment yet?"

I knew exactly what he was talking about, and I released a huff. "Sax, it's only been two days." I wasn't in any hurry to find out if Ava was his or not, and I'd been busy—busy with work, busy with taking care of an active baby, busy putting off the inevitable and stressing over the whole thing. Talking to the girls and telling them my awful secret had actually made me feel better, but the thought of hurting Sax even more made me sick inside.

Or maybe I was more afraid of what his reaction would be to the results.

To hell with a plastic bag. I turned away from him, crammed my toiletries into my suitcase, and slammed it closed. "I will," I said with little conviction, avoiding his eyes. Before I looked up again, Sax had moved further into my bedroom. The speed in which he moved and the look of purpose in his eyes caused me to gasp and take a step back. Another sharp gasp escaped me when I found my back pressed against the wall and Sax practically on top of me.

"What are you so afraid of?" he growled down at me. "What the fuck you hiding from me?"

He saw too much.

I couldn't even bring myself to shake my head in denial. We locked eyes, the tension growing between us. I dragged my bottom lip between my teeth in a nervous effort to hold myself together. The heat between us was palpable and sexual in nature. It always had been. All the scents that I associated with him were there, turning me on. Old leather, smoke, and the light scent of the aftershave he liked. His own personal musk. The longer the silence went on, the harder it was to keep from throwing myself at him. I wanted to kiss him. I wanted to touch him. I watched his jaw clench and his nostrils flare with arousal. Sax may have wanted me too, but I could see the truth in his eyes—he wanted to lash out and hurt me just as badly.

I swallowed hard, blinking back the emotion that threatened to expose my weakness for him. His hooded gaze dropped to my lips, and he closed his eyes as if he were fighting against himself. Slowly he shook his head, breathing in deeply. I could tell that he was struggling for control. Every

78

instinct I had warned me that I should get away from him, but I knew that the minute I moved he'd be on me. I wasn't sure I could handle Sax's hands on me again.

"Why are you really here, Sax?" My words were soft, barely above a whisper. "Are you here to hurt me?"

His eyes snapped open, anger changing the brown until they were almost obsidian. "Maybe," he said gruffly, shocking me. "Hurt you or fuck you."

What was I supposed to say to that? I felt my pulse jump, and caught my breath as more wetness pooled between my legs. I slowly shook my head, but I wasn't sure if I was denying my arousal, or if it was my way of telling Sax that he couldn't do either. I tried not to recall the night that he'd shown up in my room at the clubhouse, but a sharp tingle traveled down my spine as I remembered his rough hands and hard mouth on me, giving me pleasure.

While he took it.

I opened my mouth to say again that I was sorry, but clamped it shut. Once he found out the truth of what I'd done, he would hurt me, and I would deserve it. I knew that I should just tell him now and get it over with, but I was so afraid. The girls thought that in time he might forgive me, but if Ava turned out not to be his, I knew in my heart that I'd lose him forever.

"I fucking hate you," he growled low, surprising me.

"I know," I whispered in a tortured voice. "I hate me, too."

Without warning, Sax's mouth slammed down onto mine and his hand moved to the back of my head as he crushed me into the wall at my back. I couldn't halt the moan of desire that rushed up my throat, and I opened my mouth to his probing tongue. I'd take him even in hate. As his tongue filled my mouth and thrust against mine, I thrust back, moaning at the sharp charge of heat that coursed through my blood.

My nipples become tight buds in reaction to his hard body grinding against mine. When his hand moved there and pinched hard, I whimpered against his mouth, accepting the pain because I knew it would turn to pleasure. I began to move my hips in accordance with his grinding movements, relishing the knowledge that I was turning him on as much as he was making me hot. I swallowed his growls of arousal. Knowing that Sax was lost in the moment flooded my senses with a heightened level of lust.

No other man before him had ever made me feel the things he did. I curled my hands into the defined muscles of his biceps, hoping the bite of my nails would reveal the extent of my hunger for him. It did more than that. He grunted, and without breaking the kiss, reached between us and hooked his hand in the top of my blouse, tearing it open down the front. Before I could fully grasp what he'd done, he pushed the cups of my bra up out of the way and covered my nipples with his mouth.

"Oh!" I cried out, arching into the wet heat of his caress. I looked down to watch him suck and bite at my aching flesh. Both hands shaped and squeezed my breasts, while his mouth left no inch of them untouched. I lost my hands in his hair, holding him to me, and leaned my head back against the wall and closed my eyes. "Yes!" I whispered sharply. "Yes!" His hard cock was nestled right over my pubic bone and I rode it shamelessly, chasing the orgasm that was building between my legs. "Oh, Jesus!" I was so close!

I scraped my nails over his scalp, hearing his hiss. He retaliated by nipping my nipple, causing another flood in my panties, and then his hand was there, violently undoing my pants and reaching inside. As soon as his finger slid between my folds and touched my clit, I cried out. My knees buckled, but Sax easily held me in place.

"I might hate you, but I'll never get enough of your pussy, Baby," he grated against my lips as his finger moved over my clit in the way he knew I liked. "Long as you're here, it's mine."

What?! What was he saying? My heart raced, every nerve in my body attuned to his administrations, and in the moment I was too far gone to fully comprehend his words or question them. In the past I would have felt thrilled that he wanted me that fiercely, but our circumstances were different now. We weren't together. So did he only want me for sex? The rest of my thoughts went right out my head when he sank two fingers inside me and curled them against my G-spot.

Sax knew exactly where my sweet spot was and wasted no time stimulating it. I opened my legs wider, the pleasure his touch was providing too intense for me to ignore. My lower body trembled, my hips moved into his thrusting fingers. We were both breathing heavily, the sound interrupted only by the occasional whimper or groan.

SAX

"Oh, God, Sax!" I felt the telltale rush of my impending orgasm, the electric connection from my core to my pulsing clit.

Sax knew my body. He knew how to read the signs that I was about to come. Suddenly he yanked my pants and panties down with rapid force. I barely had the wherewithal to lift my feet so he could remove them completely. He sank to his knees, and I looked down at his handsome face between my legs, his nose buried in my pussy. I nearly came right then when I heard him inhale several deep breaths, and then his tongue split my folds and he licked me from the back up to my clit.

I cried out with pleasure, the heat and pressure of his mouth on my clit overwhelming. He sucked hard, and I had to brace my hands against his shoulders to remain on my feet. I moved my hips instinctively, chasing the relief I knew was around the corner. As Sax's mouth worked the bundle of nerves between my legs, he thrust his fingers in and out of my body.

"Sax!"

"Come for me, Baby." He replaced his fingers with his tongue, fucking me deep. "I'm hungry for your cream."

My eyes rolled back as I let my body fly. I came hard and moaned loudly as wave after wave of spine-tingling pleasure surged through me in one, violent explosion that eventually trickled down to aftershocks. During the peak of my orgasm, Sax continued to fuck me with his tongue, slurping up my juices. His hands clenched tightly into my ass as he held me in place against his mouth.

When he was done he pulled away and rose to his feet, slamming his mouth down on mine so that I could taste myself. When he'd finished ravishing my mouth and renewing my arousal with blinding speed, he made quick work at removing his boots and pants. Excitement thrummed through me in anticipation of what was coming. I started to lower myself to my knees. It was only fair that I return the pleasure he'd given me.

"No!" His sharp command and the tight grasp of my arm kept me in place. My questioning eyes traveled up to his. There was an intensity shining in his that I'd not seen before. "I need to be in you this time."

His jaw was set and I knew arguing would get me nowhere, and anyway, I didn't want to argue with him. He kissed me again roughly, pushing me closer to my bed until my knees were against it.

"Get on the bed," he ordered harshly.

We were inches apart, and the tip of his cock brushed against my thigh, leaving a wet trail. Before, he would have lowered us down together and we would have made love. A flashback of that night at Demon's clubhouse reminded me that we hadn't made love that night, either. Sax had fucked me as if I were one of the club whores. I had to admit that his lack of control had been exciting.

"On your fucking knees with your ass in the air."

I did as he demanded with anticipation. "Is this how it's going to be from here on out?" I felt compelled to ask.

"What?" he grated, climbing onto the bed behind me. I could feel his hot cock bobbing between my thighs.

"Fucking me like a club whore?"

He lined up his cock and slammed his hips forward, penetrating me with one, rough plunge. I gasped, and would have shot forward if not for the powerful hand grasping my hip. His long, drawn out groan revealed his pleasure at the feel of sinking inside me, and he did fill me.

"Yes." He began to fuck me hard and deep. He grabbed me by the hair and pulled my head back. "I like fucking whores. I don't have to hold back with them."

His hurtful words brought tears to my eyes. So he was fucking the whores again? Well, what did I expect? I knew that sooner or later he'd have urges that would send him into their arms. The thought of him with another woman crushed me. I buried my face against the pillow to cushion my sobs and wipe my tears away, letting Sax rut behind me like an angry beast. I could feel the rage in the way his hands gripped my hips, in the way he pulled me sharply back on his cock as he plowed into me until his balls slapped against me.

I couldn't help but feel turned on as well. How sick was that, to allow Sax to take me the way that he was, without feeling? His breathing turned harsh, and a hand found its way to my clit. He rubbed and pinched it.

"Come... again... Baby!" he said between thrusts.

The sound of his voice told me that he was getting ready to come. I clenched down hard on his cock, satisfied to hear his grunt. He tilted my hips until his cock hit all the right places. The friction became too much, and my orgasm shrouded me in a mind-blowing, earth-shattering mess that left me twitching and gasping for air.

"Oh, shhhit!" I heard Sax swear, and then he held himself still as he flooded my insides with his warm cum. Every release from his cock dragged a groan from him.

I squeezed as hard as I could around his girth, enjoying the feel of his cock as it swelled against my walls and continued to spill. But the bliss didn't last long as it slowly dawned on me that he hadn't used a condom. When we'd been together we'd used both condoms and the pill, and now that he was fucking whores...

"Oh, no," I muttered beneath my breath, angry at myself for being so careless. I collapsed onto the bed. "I'm going to have to get checked after this."

Chapter 13

S^{ax}

"What the fuck?"

I pulled out and rolled off Holly. Fucking her had been the last thing on my mind when I'd come here. No, that wasn't really true—fucking her was always on my mind.

I didn't want to admit it, but I still loved the woman.

I pulled the pillow behind me so that I could half-recline and turned my eyes on her. She was covered in sweat and her hair was a mess. Some of the wayward strands were clinging to her damp skin. I reached forward and tugged one that was sticking to the side of her neck, blowing gently on her skin. She slowly turned to look in my direction. The sadness in her eyes caught me by surprise, and I could tell that she'd been crying.

Fuck.

"You didn't wear a condom," she explained.

I narrowed my eyes, thinking the worst. "Are you saying you're not on birth control?" I nearly yelled at her. Her eyes rounded, and the panic on her face was very real. "Fuck, Holly!"

"Don't you dare blame me for this!" She sat up, her whole body flushed, as she reached for the second pillow on her bed and brought it up in front of her. "And I said that I need to get checked because you're fucking whores now. No telling what kind of disease—"

I stared at her, not about to confess that I'd led her to believe that I'd moved on simply to hurt her. I was angry as fuck that she wasn't on birth control. "You're the only woman I've ever fucked bare." I could tell that this wasn't the response she'd been hoping for. "And you've always been on birth control."

"That was then, this is now," was her maddening response.

There was more, I knew there was. I knew Holly, and she hadn't shifted her eyes away from me fast enough to disguise the guilt in them. Interesting.

SAX

What did she have to feel guilty about? I was in trouble, because the fact that she wasn't on birth control didn't stop me from wanting her again, and right fucking now. Afraid that I'd do just that, I left the bed and went to get my pants. I jerked them on and didn't turn back to her until I was doing them up.

"Get dressed. We need to get out of here." I grabbed for my boots and sat on the end of the bed.

"I was ready," she said quietly behind me. I felt the bed bounce slightly with her movements.

"And get back on birth control."

"You can't tell me what to do, Sax."

I stood and watched her as she walked around naked, snatching up clothes. Fuck, I liked what having a kid had done to her curves. Her full tits bounced with her brisk movements and turned my dick hard again. A smirk curled my mouth when she picked up her ruined blouse. She held it up for inspection, and then tossed it aside with a sigh and walked to her closet. My dick punched against my zipper at the sight of her shapely ass as she picked through her hanging clothes.

Holly was comfortable being naked in front of me, and for a minute I forgot that we weren't together anymore. I fought the urge to go up to her, lower my zipper, and take out my dick and bend her over for a quick, hard fuck. Jesus, I'd just gotten off, but the thought of losing myself in her again made me reach down to adjust my boner.

"You know what I find interesting, Baby?" She turned from the closet with a shirt in her hands. "That you broke shit off between us, yet you still let me fuck you."

She huffed. "I have needs, too."

"Are you saying you're letting me use you to scratch an itch?" She slipped the shirt over her head, hiding her fantastic tits from me. It was the kind that hung low, exposing one, sexy shoulder.

Holly stared at me for a minute, her eyes filled with hurt. "The sex has always been good between us, Sax."

An inadequate answer if I'd ever heard one. "Even hate sex?" I smirked. "Because I have to tell you, Baby, unless the word 'no' comes out of your mouth, I'm going to continue fucking you."

"So you really do hate me?" She cast her eyes downward, as if she were afraid of what she'd see in mine.

I barely made out the words, she spoke so low. I steeled myself from the regret I detected in her voice. She was the one who'd ruined us, and I would never understand it.

"I told you how I felt the other day." I didn't want to repeat the lie that I'd grated down into her face. I would never hate her.

After a few seconds of silence, I barked, "What? Nothing to say to that?"

She moved away to where her pants were. "There's nothing I can say," she admitted, slipping into a pair of panties. "Except that I ruined a good thing."

Ruined a good thing? "Understatement."

She pulled her pants on. They were old jeans, and tight as sin after the few pounds she'd put on. My mouth watered at the way they outlined the perfect curves of her ass.

"Is this suitcase ready to go?" I had to get away from her for a minute.

"Yes." She sat down on the bed to slip into her sneakers.

I grabbed it and headed out to put it into her car. Christ, a year ago, after the sexual assault, she'd told me that she'd needed time and that I should just move on, but now she was still letting me in her pants. That was a serious contradiction in my book. I'd wanted to help her deal with what she'd gone through. She was my woman, and I'd felt a measure of blame for what she'd suffered because I hadn't protected her. So I'd kept my distance physically, knowing that she would probably need time before she'd want me to touch her again, and had supported her emotionally. Fuck, the whole club had been there for her. But it hadn't been enough.

We needed to get to the clubhouse where Holly would be safe. We, including the Vegas Watchdogs, were going to war, and we were going to hit the Knights fast and hard. Both MCs wanted those little fuckers gone, and not just out of Nevada. They'd hit six of our businesses in one night, which had resulted in the deaths of innocent bystanders and two of Trip's brothers. Demon had called an emergency meeting, and the two clubs had hatched out the details of going to war.

But before we did, we had to lockdown our families.

Holly stepped outside, turned, and locked her door. I'd been leaning against her trunk and now I straightened, letting her come to me. Our gazes clung in the few feet separating us. I couldn't stop my eyes from drifting down her body in a lazy sweep, appreciating the way her nipples beaded against the soft material of her shirt. The enticing space between her legs was nice, too. I didn't try to disguise my body's reaction to her. It wasn't anything she wasn't used to seeing anyway.

It was going to be hell having her at the clubhouse again, the distraction something I didn't need right now. I wanted to stay away from her, but she was my weakness, my drug of choice, and we had too much fucking history. I'd known the very first second that our eyes had met that she was *the* one for me. Years later, I still felt that way.

"Let's go," I snapped, showing my frustration. Holly just glared back at me, but climbed inside her car. She could push my buttons so easily, but she seemed to be holding back. I walked to the driver's side window and looked down at her. "Not expecting any trouble, but if we run into any you get your ass to the clubhouse as fast as you can."

"I will."

I could tell that she wanted to ask what was going on, but she no longer had that right. We didn't talk about club business with anyone, but when a brother had an old lady, some information was bound to be shared between them. I knew that Demon and Cole shared shit with their old ladies because once in a while they'd let it slip.

I started to walk away when she called me back. "Sax?"

I halted and looked over my shoulder and waited.

"Be careful."

I acknowledged her with a chin lift and continued to where my bike was parked in front of her car. Climbing on, I slipped my helmet over my head, and flipped on the Bluetooth. "Cole?"

"Here, Brother."

"Leaving Holly's now. Be at the club in a few."

"What's taking you so long?"

I could hear the smirk in his voice. "None of your fucking business," I grinned. His laughter came over, and then there was silence.

I started my bike and waited to hear for Holly to start the car, and then we both pulled out onto the road and made a u-turn to head in the other direction. I didn't like the location of Holly's house. It was too far outside the city limits, and if she had any trouble it would take emergency personnel a while to reach her. The road she lived on was too quiet, houses too far apart and hidden by the native Nevada vegetation that grew wild throughout the state.

She was vulnerable and an easy target.

I was going to have to do something about that.

I remained alert for signs of trouble, kept my speed down so Holly could keep up. There were too many places that would have been ideal for an ambush, and the Knights had made it clear that they wanted to run us out of Nevada. There was bad blood between our clubs that had begun a few years ago. We'd killed some of Stretch's brothers and taken his blood brother, Freak, hostage after they'd tried to take Demon out. Stretch had been forced to meet our demands in order to get Freak back alive. That kind of shit always brought the possibility of retribution, even after years had passed.

Had to wonder, too, if the Knights had targeted Vegas Watchdogs simply because they were associated with us.

Shit. We were coming up on a wide corner, and I could make out a white van coming our way, the kind of utility van used in commercial business. No windows, except for the driver and passenger sides, and they were tinted darkly. There were no logos on it to indicate that it belonged to any business, and it looked fairly new. I instinctively reached for my revolver at my back and slipped if free, keeping it down at my side and out of sight.

A white or light-colored van had been seen leaving Trip's garage the night that it had been set on fire, and I wasn't taking any chances, not with Holly. I checked my rearview mirror. She was about sixty-feet behind me. I sped up, wanting to put more distance between us in case the people in the van made a move. As the vehicle reached us, I kept my eyes on it until it was well past, and then I followed its progress in my mirror to make sure that it kept going.

Satisfied, I tucked my gun away. No sooner had I let down my guard when a voice came over my Bluetooth.

"Brother, where are you?"

It was Cole, and something was wrong. I could hear it in his voice. "'Bout five miles from the clubhouse. What's up?"

"We're heading out as soon as you get here. Just got word Stretch has a meet set up somewhere at Copeland."

Copeland was an industrial park that had been built in the seventies or eighties and was far enough away from residential areas that nosey civilians wouldn't cause any problems. There were a lot of empty warehouses on the property, big, empty concrete buildings ideal for the kind of illegal activity MCs were into.

"What kind of meet?"

"With Toledo."

Fuck. That said it all. Toledo was a gun runner from Mexico, an evil bastard, loyal to no one, and he often worked both sides. The only reason he was still alive was that no one wanted to eliminate a good resource for weapons. He managed to get his fucking hands on anything you needed—guns, explosives, flame throwers, mortars, you name it, and he could get it. Desert Rebels had done business with him a long time ago, before we'd decided to go legit. If Stretch had made a deal with him, that could mean big trouble for every MC in Nevada.

I doubted the Knights could afford the big-ticket items that Toledo dealt in, but a few assault rifles and grenades would give them deadlier leverage. The meet was a new development, and the warehouse was a prime location for a fight that would probably lead to a shootout.

I exhaled loudly.

Looked like war was going to come earlier than planned.

Chapter 14

H olly
    I couldn't wait to get Ava in my arms again. As soon as we pulled
through the gates of the clubhouse grounds, I parked my car and rushed
toward the door with every intention of snatching her from Lulu's arms, but
Sax had other ideas. I'd barely noticed him getting off his bike, and was taken
aback when he reached out and grasped my arm, halting my progress.

Our eyes clashed and I waited, sensing that he had something to say.
"Some serious shit is going down right now, Babe. You and Ava stay here until
it's safe to leave."

I knew that. I'd been around the club long enough to know that
lockdown wasn't done without a good reason. Why did Sax feel that he had
to warn me now? Was this his way of showing me that he still cared about
me? And he'd called me "babe", had that been a slip up?

"I will," I said. He unclasped his hand, and I went inside the clubhouse.
My eyes instantly locked on where Ava was playing on a blanket on the floor
in front of the TV. Lulu was sitting with her, watching over Ava and several
other children as they watched a Disney movie.

Ava looked up, and a big smile lit up her face when she saw me. I rushed
over to her and scooped her up into my arms. "Oh, baby, mommy missed
you!" I gushed, raining kisses all over her squealing face. Her tiny hands lost
themselves in my hair as she hugged me to her. I looked down at Lulu. "Was
she good?"

She nodded enthusiastically. "Very good. She's an angel." She got to her
feet.

"You must be tired."

"Not at all. She took a good, long nap."

I laughed, looking toward the door when it opened. Sax walked inside,
his eyes zeroing in on me and Ava. His sharp gaze moved over her as if he
were searching for something. A resemblance, maybe? Everyone knew that

he didn't want kids, but he'd never said that he didn't like them. Sadness sent a pang to my heart, and I wondered if anything would change if she turned out to be his.

Then I remembered my horrible betrayal and how I'd come to have her in the first place.

Still, even if I could have, I wouldn't undo what I'd done now that I had Ava. She brought so much happiness to my life, and since I planned on having more children, Sax and I could never be together.

He continued to walk through the room as if we weren't there. "Do you know what's going on?" I asked Lulu. Sometimes the club girls heard things when they were mingling with the men.

She nodded and looked around before speaking to make sure that she wouldn't be overheard. "Some of the businesses were hit the other night, all at the same time."

God, I prayed that no one had been hurt. I wondered if Grinders had been one of the properties hit, but I hadn't heard from Samson. It didn't matter now, because we were all on lockdown and I wasn't going anywhere.

"Now the men are all hyped-up for war. You can practically smell the bloodlust in the air."

Well, that was certainly descriptive. I smiled. "Bloodlust?"

She shrugged with a giggle. "You know these men. They like a good fight. Apparently one of the MCs they had trouble with in the past has shown back up."

I didn't need to ask Lulu how she knew so much. The men loved her, and more than that they trusted her. She was easy to talk to and good at listening, I'd heard Bull say once. She was more than just a club girl to them, she'd become a friend, too. I often wondered what had pushed her to become an outlet for the men to appease their sexual drives, but she seemed to like sex, too.

Suddenly, several men stormed into the room from the room in which church was held, led by Demon and Sax. Loco, Snake, Chewy, Cole, Colton, and Reid looked like men with a purpose as they made a beeline for the door. Lulu and I exchanged knowing looks, while the kids watching TV remained riveted to the screen. There were other mothers in the room, too, and they looked on with concern.

Movement at the top of the stairs drew my gaze there, and I saw Bobbie leading the way down with Raven, Ellie, and Annie right behind her. Ellie had her daughter, Izzy, in her arms. JoJo trailed leisurely behind, carrying her and Oz's son, Samuel. They were practically running, and I realized that they wanted to catch up to the men. They continued through the room and straight out the door. I couldn't miss the fear and worry in their eyes. JoJo was the only one who stopped when she came to where Lulu and I were standing with the kids.

"Demon just text Bobbie and told her the guys are leaving."

"This is bad, isn't it?" I couldn't help murmur, meeting JoJo's eyes. She nodded, setting Samuel down on the blanket where the toys were. Ava, who was contentedly running her hands through my hair, saw him and indicated that she wanted down, probably because she'd claimed those toys as her own. "Where's Oz?"

She released a breath of relief for the safety of her man, but there was still worry in her eyes. "In the computer room. Demon has him looking for something."

The loud rumble of bikes starting up reverberated throughout the building. A minute later the girls came back inside, some with tears swimming in their eyes. God, this was not good sign. I knew in my heart that they knew what was going on, and glanced out the window as the men rode past.

Raven caught my eye and forced a smile, wiping at her eyes. "I'm just hormonal," she tried to explain away.

She was hormonal, yes, but those tears were caused by worry about Cole, and not by the baby she was carrying. She couldn't disguise the fear reflected in her eyes.

I went to her and wrapped my arms around her. "Honey..."

"I'm okay, really."

I pulled back and met her eyes. "None of us are okay with this," I murmured softly. I pushed thoughts of Sax and any possibility that something bad could happen to him aside.

"They'll be okay," Bobbie insisted, but she didn't sound very convinced of that. "Our men are tough."

Tough, but not invincible, I thought to myself. There was no reason to voice what they all already knew. None of us had been blind to the way the men in the club lived their lives when we'd entered into relationships with them, or that danger always seemed to be present. The Desert Rebels had spent years turning their MC around for the better, but they still walked the fine line between legal and illegal activity. The one percent patch that they all wore was a challenge to other MCs, and sometimes the Desert Rebels were forced to protect their reputation by showing their strength.

Ellie set Izzy down on the floor with Ava and Samuel. Apparently, Samuel felt threatened being sandwiched between two girls and got up and began to wander off. He didn't go far, just to where some of the other mothers were sitting. I guessed that they were the wives of the soldiers, because I didn't recognize them.

"I'm glad the Vegas Watchdogs are in this with them."

Annie's comment piqued my interest. That was news to me, but hearing it made me feel better. I also realized that if the two clubs had joined together, the trouble they were facing must be huge. I tried to push aside the worry over something that I had no control of, but that had never worked in the past, and it wasn't working now. I loved everyone in the club—they were family to me—and I couldn't stop myself from worrying over their safety.

"Did anyone check to make sure Annabelle is okay?" JoJo inquired, keeping an eye on her son.

Raven spoke up. "I did. She and Danny are at LD's clubhouse."

"Those two lovebirds are joined at the hip," Ellie laughed.

"Well, he does treat her like she walks on water," Annie added.

"Any talk of a wedding?" I asked. It was nice that we'd moved on to talk that was safe and would keep our minds off what might be happening to our men.

"Yeah, but not lately. Demon told them to slow down and for Danny to keep his dick in his pants. That Annabelle better not turn up pregnant." Bobbie made a face and rolled her eyes. "Typical big brother."

We all laughed at that. Annabelle had been through a lot, and I was pleased to see that she was happy and had found someone. Years ago she'd been attacked and left for dead. It had taken months of healing, and more months of therapy, before she'd gradually returned to her old self again. I knew that there were still triggers for her, and nightmares that kept her from forgetting entirely, but she wasn't letting it cripple her or keep her from living.

Danny was a good fit for her. He wasn't a member of the club, but he did jobs for them and he helped his sister, Jolene, run Illuminations, a lighting fixtures business next to the MC's construction office. He'd once been a pool hustler, but he'd gotten himself into big trouble owing the wrong people money, and after the debts had been paid, LD had nipped that behavior in the bud. Jolene had told me all about it. She also credited Danny's change for the better to Annabelle's influence.

I felt a little hand against my lower leg and glanced down to see Ava clinging to my pants. Smiling, I held my hands down to her. "Take mommy's hands, honey." I pulled her to her feet, laughing as her little legs wobbled back and forth. She squealed with joy, staring up at me with drool dribbling down her chin. I let her take a few steps before picking her up. She wouldn't be walking for a while.

I wondered if she was hungry.

"She might be hungry," Lulu said, as if reading my mind.

I laughed. "I was just thinking the same thing." I glanced around, and it suddenly occurred to me that I had no place to go to feed Ava in private, because I was unsure of where I would be staying during this lockdown. Bobbie and Demon would be using their apartment upstairs, and Sax would be staying in his room. I supposed that I would probably be staying with the other wives and children in the back room where the cots would be set up. Maybe I could find a private spot in the kitchen to feed her.

"You're staying in Sax's room," Bobbie said, guessing my dilemma.

That came as a surprise to me. "But..."

She shrugged. "It's what he wants, honey. A prospect has already set up a crib in there for you."

I still hesitated. Where would Sax be staying? With Goldie? I didn't see her or any of the other club girls, except for Lulu. Demon would have told them to stay scarce while the old ladies and their children were around. Good. I didn't want to see any triumphant looks in their eyes that would lead me to conclude that they were fucking Sax. The club sluts could be devious and mean bitches. Tamara, who was gone now, thank God, had been the worst.

"Why don't we all go up to my apartment until it's time to start dinner? We'll have more privacy to talk, and Holly can feed Ava and put her down if she needs to."

"I think Izzy's ready for a nap, too."

"Do you have wine?" Annie joked, getting a raised brow and a smirk from Bobbie in response that clearly said that she thought Annie was crazy for asking because Bobbie *always* had wine. Annie laughed. "Doesn't hurt to ask. Some of us are going to need something stronger than baby's milk while we're waiting."

"Ew!" JoJo said with disgust, while everyone else laughed at Annie's comment.

We turned toward the stairs and followed Bobbie to her and Demon's room. I sank down into a chair and prepared to feed Ava. She settled against me easily and latched on to a nipple instinctively to drink, her little hand curled against my breast. As I gazed down at her, love made my heart swell to overflowing. I ran my hand over her hair, smiling, and thinking that it was time to wean her off of breast milk.

"She looks so content."

I smiled up at Raven. "Aren't most babies when they're eating? Are you planning on breast feeding?"

"Definitely."

"Okay, which ones of you bitches wants wine? Or should I say, can drink wine?" Bobbie was in her miniscule kitchen, pulling out glasses. Two bottles of wine already sat on the counter.

"None for me," Raven sighed.

"Or me." Not while I was still breast feeding.

"Okay, I've got orange juice for you two."

Annie was helping Bobbie in the kitchen. She'd pulled out a block of cheese and was slicing some off for us to snack on. Ellie was sitting on one side of the bed where she'd laid Izzy down, rubbing her tummy as the toddler fought sleep. JoJo was on the other side with Samuel, keeping him occupied with some toys. Raven sat with her legs curled beneath her on the sofa opposite me. She was positively glowing, as most expectant mothers did.

I looked back down at Ava. She was still sucking away, but her eyes were closed. Sometimes I wondered how I'd got so lucky to have a perfect little girl. The only thing that would have made it more perfect was if Sax were her father. Sometimes I thought I saw little glimpses of him in her, but I knew that it was just wishful thinking.

I needed to make that appointment.

Once Ava was done I scooted to the floor and lay her in the chair to finish her nap, and then I took out my phone, did some research, and ordered a home DNA test kit.

It seemed almost too easy.

Four cheek swabs for each participant.

Results within a week.

Chapter 15

S^{ax}

    Thanks to Oz, it hadn't taken us long to zone in on the warehouse that was being used for the meeting between the Knights and Toledo. He'd discovered that the Knights had purchased one of the buildings under a bogus company name a month ago. The sale and purchase agreement had been signed by someone named Agnes Prachett, who was supposedly using the warehouse as a supply house for wholesale cosmetics and shit. A little digging had revealed that Agnes Prachett was Stretch's aunt. Dumb fuck. Stretch had probably thought that since they had different last names, no connection would be made.

There was only one road into the industrial park, and it ran the full length of the park and divided it into two sections. Two of the buildings near the entrance were occupied, if the maintained landscaping was any indication. There were also several vehicles in the parking lot, probably the after-hours cleaning crew. Railroad tracks ran along the length of one side at the back where the buildings had been used as warehouses back in the day. Most were empty now, except for one that was being used for heavy duty truck repairs. The huge bay doors were closed, but I guessed that inside they were housing semis, dump trucks, and possibly some heavy duty farm equipment, anything too big for a regular garage to handle.

The meeting was set up for nine, but we got there early. We didn't want to alert any of the Knights that we were in the area. The warehouse right next door to Sketch's was the perfect place to hide our bikes. We jimmied a door to get inside and arranged them in front of the bay door, ready for when we'd need to take off. Spider was staying behind to guard the bikes and to make sure that the bay door was up when we were ready to make our escape.

Confrontations between MCs were usually quick and brutal. When shit got messy you could count on chaos and death and neither side wanted to get caught by the cops.

Unsure of what to expect when we got to Stretch's warehouse, we'd sent Cole, Bull, and Trip's enforcer, Bigfoot (BF), over to scan the area, while the rest of us waited, double checking our weapons. Most of us had more than one gun on us, as well as a knife or two. I knew that LD would be carrying his favorite weapon of choice, at least when it came to one-on-one fighting. He was quick and efficient with a well-aimed slash of his knife.

We didn't know how many Knights we would be facing, but the goal was to take Stretch out and hopefully some of his top officers. The reality was that most meetings only included a few members on each side. If that was the case for today's meeting, getting our hands on Stretch or any of his blood brothers would work out in our favor in the long-run. We needed to show the Knights what happened to assholes that fucked with us.

The back door opened, and the three enforcers stomped in, their expressions serious. Bigfoot had gotten his name due to his freakishly big feet. The man wore a size sixteen boot. He was as tall as LD, six-foot-seven, and built like Bull, big all over. Bigfoot was an old friend, and he and Murphy were blood brothers, same mother but different fathers.

LD was the first to speak when they reached us. "Any trouble getting in?"

Cole shook his head, but it was Bull who answered. "Found a way in through the fucking roof," he smirked. "Left the side door ajar."

"What's it look like over there?" Trip asked.

Cole snorted. "Like a fucking warehouse filled with beauty products and shit."

"They went all out to make it look legit," BF added with a smirk that you could barely see through his bushy blonde beard. "Opened up a few boxes to see what was inside."

"And?" his president asked.

BF shrugged. "The ones I checked had product in them. Don't mean they all did."

Demon was standing with his legs parted and his arms crossed over his massive chest. He nodded, listening. "That all? Just a bunch of boxes?"

"Fuck, no," Bull responded. "They got an office set up over there—desk, computer, phone. Even tossed a few invoices and shit over the top to make it look like someone sits there working."

"Anything else?" LD growled, his stance similar to Demon's and Trip's. The three presidents stood like imposing sentries, their expressions set in severe lines that revealed that they were taking shit seriously and were out for blood. Fuck, we all were. There we were, fourteen brothers all standing by, waiting to go to war, eager to fight for our MCs and what was ours.

Cole ran his hands through his hair and released a long breath. "There's fucking cameras everywhere."

"The fuck?" Demon snarled. Even with a patch over one eye, he managed to make a frown work.

BF nodded. "They went all out to try and make the place look legit. Chances are they're duds."

"We don't know that for sure," Trip said, shaking his head.

"They are," LD said with gruff conviction. "No way would either side want a deal like this to go down while it's being recorded."

I had to agree. Most likely the cameras were set up as another ruse to give the impression that there was genuine business taking place there. Chances were that most of those fucking boxes were empty, too.

"Unless they're fucking stupid."

No one responded to Snake's comment.

"So we're going to take a chance?" Trip's brows rose high with disbelief.

It grew quiet. Was he looking for a way out, or was he just paranoid about the cameras? He didn't strike me as a coward.

"No worries." Loco stepped forward. His Mohawk was the color of the rainbow, which sometimes gave people the wrong idea about his sexual identity. Even as scary as he looked, he'd been hit on a couple of times by men. It was funny as shit to watch. "We'll kill them once the shooting begins."

"Problem solved," I smirked.

"There's plenty of places to hide," Bull spoke up. "Plenty of stacked boxes—"

I didn't let him finish. "Boxes won't stop fucking bullets."

Several brothers muttered under their breath in agreement. Bull's look told me that he'd already considered that. We didn't want any casualties, unless those casualties were the Knights.

"There's also salon furniture, those big ass chairs they use for pedicures, and other furniture scattered around," Bull continued.

I snorted at his use of the word "pedicure."

"They got two vans parked by the bay doors." Cole smirked. "White, could be the ones that were used during the drive-bys the other night, but they have logos on them now—*Prachett's Cosmetic and Beauty Supplies.*"

"Someone must be funding them," Chewy muttered as if to himself.

"That's a discussion for another day."

Demon was getting antsy, and I couldn't blame him. It was getting close to the time for us to move on to the other warehouse and get into position. I wanted this shit to be over with, too, but at the same time I could feel the anticipation running through my blood. It had been a while since I'd been involved in any club drama, since I'd tasted the high of a good fight.

"Okay, listen up!" Demon began, then waited for the men to gather in close. "It's time. Don't know how many Knights we'll be facing. Doesn't matter. Stretch and any of his brothers are our targets. We take out as many as we can. Need to show these assholes what happens when they mess with us. Send them a message."

"What about Toledo?" Colton asked.

"Don't worry about that weasel. His men will get him out of there once the shooting starts," LD snarled.

"When we get over there, find a place to hole up until the time is right. Want to hear what's going down before we make our move. Once the shooting starts, we need to finish up quickly and then get the fuck out of here."

Demon didn't need to remind us about the few vehicles we'd seen when we'd driven into Copeland. With civilians around, one call to the cops was all it would take for things to blow up, and we sure as shit didn't need any witnesses.

"Lucky, Singer, and Randy will stay outside," Trip began, drawing everyone's attention. "With the exception of Toledo and his men, no one escapes."

His three brothers nodded their understanding.

"It's fucking dark out there, Brothers," one of Trip's men half-joked. "Make sure you shoot the right fuckers."

Sniggers followed in response to his quip.

Demon growled. "Let's go!"

We fell in step behind Demon, LD, and Trip and ran to the other warehouse. The bay doors faced the railroad tracks, and the side door that had been left ajar was at the back of the building on the other side. We moved with stealth and purpose once inside the warehouse, seeking out places to lay in wait like an army of fucking ants. I spied a wide steel beam, grabbed a stack of boxes, and moved them in front of it for cover.

I heard the door click when someone closed it behind the last brother. There were no windows in the warehouse. When the lights were flicked off, it was pitch black. The sudden silence was eerie. I pulled out my phone and checked the time. It was ten minutes till nine. Almost immediately the sound of bikes could be heard approaching the building. I made sure my phone was on silent and waited.

It was hard to judge how many Knights there were from the sound of their bikes alone. There had to be at least one vehicle that Toledo and his men would have come in. I could hear talking through the bay doors, but couldn't make out the words. The side door we'd come in through was opened, and someone flipped on the lights. I peeked around the box in front of me and saw someone wearing a Knights' cut push a button that raised one of the bay doors, and then a black van drove into the warehouse. I ducked back out of sight before I was seen.

Directly across from me were LD and Loco. I pulled my weapon, and they did the same. We heard the sound of the vehicle being turned off, and then doors were opened. The bay door rolled down again.

"Let's make this exchange fast," I heard Stretch say. He sounded nervous. "I have somewhere else to be."

Yeah, he was probably planning on hitting another one of our businesses. I had one eye on what was going on as I watched from behind my box.

"Nice setup you have here."

Toledo was as round as he was tall, dressed in an expensive suit that seemed inappropriate for an arms dealer. There was nothing that appeared to be tough or threatening about him, from his leather loafers to his shiny bald head, but he knew his weapons. I heard the light tapping of his shoes on the concrete floor as he walked around, puffing on a fat Cuban cigar. I tensed, ready to act if he discovered one of us, but he didn't venture any further than the center of the room. Two armed men guarded him closely.

Stretch's brother, Hank, was there, but I didn't see any of their other brothers. "Did you bring everything we ordered?"

"Everything, and some surprises," Toledo joked. "You have the thirty grand?"

Fuck! That was no drop in the bucket. Looked like we were going to be leaving with plenty of loot. Where the fuck did the Knights get that kind of money?

Toledo stepped forward to open the sliding doors.

"We don't like fucking surprises," Stretch snarled. His hand reached behind him and rested on the handle of the gun tucked into his pants, ready to pull it if he needed to.

"You'll like this," Toledo laughed. "Since you're in the business of selling flesh."

That was news to me. I didn't like where this was going, and from the looks that were exchanged between my brothers, I could see that they didn't either. LD and Loco were watching things unfold as closely as I was.

Toledo nodded at one of his men, which prompted him to move toward the open van door. Next thing I knew, he was pulling a woman out. A girl, really, she couldn't have been older than thirteen, and she was wearing jeans and a t-shirt. A second woman, who was nearly naked, was pulled out roughly behind the girl, and both were made to stand against the van.

They were terrified, visibly shaking, their faces streaked with tears, but there was also glaring anger in the older woman's eyes. Duct tape covered their mouths, and their hands were tied in front of them. They looked like they'd been roughed up, the older woman more so. She had bruises and a black eye. Both had brown hair and brown eyes, their features similar. Fuck, were they mother and daughter?

Shit. I wondered how this was going to play out now that there were civilians present.

"Nice surprise," one of Stretch's boys grated in a vulgar tone. He grabbed the front of his pants. "I'll take the young one."

He was ignored. I would make sure to shoot his fucking dick off if I got the chance. The way he was eye-balling the kid turned my stomach.

"Thought you could get rid of them for me," Toledo grinned. "No charge, and you keep what you get for them."

"Who the fuck are they?"

"My sister-in-law and her kid." Stretch's gaze whipped back in Toledo's direction in surprise. "She's been causing trouble for me since her sister—my wife—disappeared."

That explained a lot, such as why the older woman wasn't putting up more of a fight. They must have threatened to hurt her kid, and I was willing to bet that Toledo had helped his wife 'disappear'.

"We'll take them off your hands," Hank offered, his tone cold.

I shot a glance at LD, wondering when the fuck Demon was going to make his move.

"Ransom," Stretch barked, shooting a glance at one of his boys as he grabbed each woman by the arm and hauled them away from the van. "Lock these bitches up somewhere." He handed the women off to the other man and turned back to the van. "Now what about the fucking guns?"

I breathed a sigh of relief that the girls were out of harm's way and kept my eyes on them as Ransom led them as far as the office and then forced them to sit on the floor. I was sure that I wasn't the only one. We would make sure that they made it back home again.

"Show us what you got." Hank stepped up next to Toledo and looked inside the van. A big smile spread across his face and he looked back at Stretch, nodding his head with satisfaction.

Demon and Trip stepped out from behind their hiding places. "How about we show you what *we* got?"

I knew that was our cue. We came out shooting, and I watched as Toledo's men pushed him into the van, jumped in behind him, and slammed the doors closed. In the next instant the squealing sound of tires on concrete could be heard as the driver backed up, forgetting that the bay doors were closed, and rammed into them.

I smirked and fired my weapon, hitting my first intended target right between his mother-fucking legs.

Chapter 16

Holly

It was early when I made my way downstairs, the time of morning when darkness gradually gives way to light, and things are still quiet. Someone else was also up, because I could smell the enticing aroma of coffee before I even made it to the kitchen. My lips curled up in a smile as I took in the sight of Loco sleeping against the bar, his mouth hanging half-open and drool running out of the side and onto his arm where he laid his head. Chewy was prone on the sofa with Cherry, one of the club girls, splayed out on top of him.

Well, that answered my question about whether or not the men had returned. I wondered what time they'd made it back, and if everyone was okay. No news was good news, I guessed. They'd obviously kept quiet because I hadn't heard a thing once my head had hit the pillow the night before.

When Sax and I had been together, he had always returned, as most of the men did, wound up with adrenaline pumping through his veins in response to whatever danger the club had faced. Fucking their women or fighting a brother was their go-to outlet for relieving that stress.

I wondered where Sax had spent the night, then immediately pushed the thought aside. I had no claim over him anymore, even though I knew it would kill me to see him with another woman. Just because we'd fucked a few times since I'd come home didn't mean anything to men like him. These bikers liked sex and plenty of it, and I'd hardly said no to him. I didn't have it in me to deny Sax.

I stepped into the kitchen and halted abruptly, my heart dropping at the sight of Sax leaning against the counter, minus a shirt, his jeans half-opened as if he'd put them on in a hurry and hadn't bothered to do them up. The denim outlined his thick, powerful thighs. His hair looked wild, as if someone had been running their fingers through it, and he was barefoot. And plastered right up against him was Goldie in all her near naked glory.

My first thought was that when the club was on lockdown, the club sluts were told to stay clothed, which she clearly wasn't. The little boy shorts she had on were lacey and tucked up her butt crack. The tiny string tied at her back suggested that she had on some kind of top, but it had to be miniscule, because I couldn't see any signs of it from my viewpoint.

"I know you need relief, baby. The girls told me how it is when you guys return from a fight. I'm here for you."

As she attempted to entice Sax, she rubbed her breasts over his naked chest, her hands roaming over his torso as she leaned in to kiss the side of his neck.

"I'll let you fuck me in the ass if you want."

Sax just stood there, his arms at his sides.

I was frozen in place, fighting the tears and hating myself, because this was all my fault. I deserved to be punished for pushing him away. This was karma getting even with me. I watched as Goldie's hand roamed down his side to the front where his jeans were open. I held my breath, not sure how I would react if she wiggled inside to touch his cock. I couldn't see if Sax was hard or not. I didn't want to know.

"You have a big cock, baby." She was saying all the right things to turn him on. "Let me suck it." She dropped to her knees, and that's when Sax noticed me standing there.

There was a flicker of something dark in his eyes before the look on his face turned savage. It was a look that I was familiar with, one that I'd seen before when he'd come home from dealing with trouble in the club, the same look that always warned that he was going to take me hard and fast up against the nearest surface. His hand fell down to Goldie's hair, pulling her head away from him. Her gasp echoed through the kitchen as she stared up at him with open-mouthed confusion.

"Don't let me interrupt. I'm just here for coffee." I don't know where I found the words, but I knew that I couldn't continue to stand there and do nothing.

Goldie reacted with a gasp as she looked my way, and then covered her initial reaction with a knowing smirk. She was learning fast from the other girls. She already had her slutty bitch expression down pat.

"You're not interrupting anything," Sax grated.

TORY RICHARDS

"Yet," Goldie smiled. Her hand began to roam up his leg on the outside of his jeans.

Why wasn't he pushing her away? I wanted to scream for her to take her hands off my man, but everyone knew that we were no longer together.

"Let's go back to my bed, baby."

Oh, God...he'd spent the night with her?

"Shut it," Sax growled.

I felt sick inside. I couldn't take the sight of them together any longer and made my way to the coffee maker. Cups had already been laid out, so I filled one and fixed it the way I liked it. As I was taking my first sip, I glanced up at the clock over the sink to see that it was only six o'clock. I should probably start making breakfast.

I purposely kept my back to Sax and Goldie, praying that they left.

"Get up and go put some clothes on," I heard Sax demand. "I'm sure you were told the fucking rules when we're on lockdown."

I heard Goldie make a disappointed sound and could just imagine the pout on her face. Wordlessly she left the kitchen, leaving behind a trail of stale perfume. I wondered how many times Sax had been with her, if he was fucking the other club girls, too.

Suddenly I felt his presence behind me, and then his warm breath against my neck as he leaned in. "*You* sent me into her bed," he whispered into my ear. "It's your fault I'm putting my dick in other bitches."

I closed my eyes tightly, as if it would keep out his hurtful words. I felt my heart race and wondered if it was the caffeine. What he was saying didn't make sense to me. "Then why are you still fucking me?" I found the strength to ask, keeping my back to him.

"You should be asking yourself that question, Baby," he grated in a cold voice. "You make it so fucking easy."

I sucked in my breath because, God, he was right. I'd made it all too easy for him, and my only excuse was that I'd never stopped loving Sax, had never stopped wanting him. Down deep I knew that once he discovered the level of my deceit, he wouldn't want anything to do with me, and then it would truly be over.

I should have never come back.

"Look who I've got!" Annie breezed into the kitchen with a bright-eyed Ava in her arms. "I heard this little munchkin when I was passing your room."

My heart warmed at the sight of my daughter. "She was still sleeping when I came down for coffee." I had planned to bring it up to my room to drink.

Sax stepped away from me, and I immediately felt the cold air replace the warmth of his body. "Hi, baby." I leaned forward to kiss Ava on her forehead. "Thank you for bringing her down." I set my cup down and reached for her.

"I changed her for you." We exchanged smiles before Annie turned her attention toward Sax. "Good morning."

"Morning." He turned and poured himself a cup of coffee.

"I bet she's hungry." Annie ran a finger gently over Ava's chubby cheek.

"She's always hungry, aren't you, baby?"

"I can't wait to have one of my own." Annie's gaze moved back and forth between Sax and me. There was a question in her eyes that she wisely didn't ask.

"Are you and Colton trying?"

Annie nodded. "Yeah, it's time. We've been married eight years."

My eyes widened with surprise. "I didn't know that." I arranged Ava against my cocked hip, knowing that she would let me know when she was ready to eat. Her curious focused behind me as she watched Sax at the coffee maker.

A sigh escaped Annie. "Yeah, we got married when we were still teenagers, and he was in another MC. With everyone starting to have babies around here...." She let her sentence trail off with a shrug.

"You won't regret it," I said, forgetting about Sax for a moment. "Having a little mini you or Colton running around, knowing that he or she is part of you both, it just makes your life feel complete. I can't imagine life without Ava. She brought me back from a dark time." It was true. Finding out that I was pregnant after the sexual assault had helped me to heal and move on.

"Baby." Colton walked into the room and went straight to Annie, giving her a kiss on the cheek.

Colton was a handsome man, but at the moment he looked like death warmed over. His hair was sticking up everywhere, and his eyes were bloodshot. He was slightly pale, too, and I noticed that there was a bloody bandage wrapped around his ribs beneath his cut. I refrained from asking what had happened, knowing that it wouldn't do any good. "Club business" would be the standard reply, though I was certain that Annie knew the details.

I could see that Colton was okay, so I asked instead, "Did anyone else get hurt?"

"No one who matters," Sax muttered.

He and Sax exchanged silent looks that spoke volumes before Colton said, "No worries, honey."

Annie made a sound of annoyance. "If you say so. Doc's been in with Snake since you returned."

"He'll be okay, Babe, swear." He crossed his heart and reached out to run his finger down Ava's nose. "Good morning, little darlin'."

Ava giggled and reached out for his finger.

"You sure got yourself a cutie here."

My heart swelled with pride. "Thank you."

"She looks just like her mama."

If there was a compliment in there somewhere, I didn't hear it in Sax's cold tone. I met his eyes in surprise that he'd looked at Ava long enough to come to that conclusion. It was true, though, Ava looked just like me. If she had any of her father in her I couldn't see it, which pleased me immensely. If her daddy turned out to be one of my rapists, I wouldn't be reminded of him every day when I looked into my daughter's face.

Ava pulled Colton's finger toward her mouth, but Annie quickly snatched it away. "You don't want that nasty old finger in your mouth, sweetheart."

He gave Annie a look of hurt. "I washed my hands after I took my morning piss."

"Good to know," I laughed along with them. "But you might want to be careful of the teeth Ava has coming in."

"That must hurt," Annie smiled knowingly.

A soft laugh escaped me as I rubbed noses with Ava. "That's why starting today I'm weaning her off breast feeding."

Loco walked into the kitchen at the tail end of my statement, a smile spreading across his face. "Always wondered what breast milk tasted like."

Annie and I exchanged amused glances before I decided to call his bluff. "Would you like a taste?"

His eyes flicked down to my breasts, and then over to Sax. Sax was glaring angrily at Loco. "No thanks. I like my dick right where it is," he joked, moving on to the coffee maker.

"Well if you change your mind, I have a bottle already pumped in the fridge."

"Where's the fun in that?"

Annie slapped Colton behind the head. "What?" The teasing gleam in his eyes revealed that he already knew what. He gave Annie a wink.

Oz poked his head into the room. "Church in five. Bring me coffee!" With that he was gone.

"I'll fix him one." Annie moved next to Loco, shooting Colton a look over her shoulder. "I'll fix you one, too, Baby."

That left Sax and me staring at each other. "You going to attend church without a shirt and boots?" I ran my gaze over his torso, trying not to be obvious about it. The sight of him took my breath away and got my libido running. Sax had always been lean and muscular, but he'd added some bulk since I'd been gone. There was a prominent bulge in his pants, but I knew from experience that it wasn't a hard-on.

"My shirt and boots are out in the bar."

His smirk told me that he'd caught me ogling him. He looked tired. I hadn't noticed it before. I didn't want to think about the possibility that his tiredness was a result of a night spent in someone else's room and someone else's bed.

"You can have your room back, Sax. Ava and I can sleep somewhere else."

He ran his hand over the whiskers on his lower jaw, his eyes not leaving mine. "No, use it. Plenty of other places for me to lay my head."

No doubt. Ava was beginning to whine, a clear sign that she was hungry. Sax's eyes moved to her, and my heart jumped at the tiniest sign of softening in his hard gaze. It happened quickly and was gone, but I knew what I'd seen.

"How old is Ava?"

His question caught me off-guard. "Six months."

Ava was gnawing on her little fist, and I knew that if I didn't feed her soon, she was going to let out a wail that would wake everyone in the clubhouse.

"From the looks of it, you'd better feed her."

With that, he left me standing there.

Chapter 17

Sax

By the time we'd finished with the Knights, we didn't get back to the clubhouse until two. Snake and Colton weren't the only ones who came away with wounds from the confrontation. LD's VP, Cappy, got hit in the shoulder, and Trip lost one of his soldiers. During the ten-minute long shootout we took out Stretch and his brother, Hank, and the few of their men. The fact that none of Stretch's other blood brothers had been there meant that there was more trouble to come.

I glanced around the table. Not all of us had gone to fight, and it was clear which of us had. We hadn't gotten much sleep, and it was apparent in the bloodshot eyes and haggard expressions. Some of us had come back and gone straight to the bar to drink away the angst and the adrenaline required to take another man's life, while others had fucked the images out of their heads.

I'd done neither.

I'd spent the night in Goldie's bed after ignoring her invitation for more and sending her away.

"We're not waiting for the fucking Knights to come to us," Demon growled from where he sat at the head of the table.

He looked disheveled and rough, and if I'd had to guess I would have said that he'd done a whole lot of fucking his woman and drinking before coming down. It didn't look as if he'd gotten any sleep.

"Once the Dunlap brothers find out about Stretch and Hank, they'll come gunning for us," Chewy said, speaking aloud what we all already knew in our guts.

Stretch's blood brothers included Screw, Hank, Radar, and Freak. Freak was the youngest at about eighteen, and seemed to be MIA. He hadn't been seen since we'd used him as a bargaining chip to strike a deal with the Knights that required them to stay out of our territory and stop causing trouble. They'd been quiet until recently.

"That's what we want," Cole said, leaning back in his chair with a semi-smirk on his tired face. "Pissed off assholes make mistakes."

"Makes them dangerous, too," I added.

Demon and several others nodded their agreement.

"We're not going to give those fucking bastards time to catch their breath. We're going to hit them hard and fast and without mercy, especially now we know they're dealing in flesh, too."

The mother and daughter that Toledo had tried to get rid of had gone to Trip's clubhouse with him and his brothers. They couldn't very well return home, knowing how badly Toledo wanted to get rid of them. They weren't safe. Trip was going to help them sort shit out.

Demon cut his eyes to Dancer, one of the brothers who hadn't come with us to the warehouse. Dancer had been an Explosive Ordinance Disposal Specialist in the army, or EOD Specialist. The brother was on the small side, thin and darkly tanned at about five-feet-four, with blonde hair and sharp blue eyes. He liked being outdoors and working with his hands. I knew that he was twenty-eight, but he didn't look a day over twenty. Poor asshole still got carded when we went to places that didn't know him.

"What do you have?"

I didn't see any of Dancer's usual cockiness show through in response to Demon's inquiry, which was good, considering the seriousness of it. He took a minute to think before leaning forward and folding his hands on the table.

"Got some C-4. I can rig up some remote detonators."

"We'll need Molotov cocktails, too," I suggested. "For the drive-bys."

Demon showed his agreement by giving me a nod. "Gonna start out by hitting their porn studio, give them a taste of their own medicine. When they come running to see what the fuck is going on we'll pick them off."

"What about the cops?" Reid questioned.

"What *about* the cops?" Cole returned with a grin. "Won't be any cops showing up at their studio. At least not until later."

Reid wasn't convinced. "How do you know?"

"The studio is a fucking trailer in the desert, Brother, twenty miles from anywhere. Hell, they use fucking generators for power," Oz laughed.

"So why the fuck we wasting time on a dump?" Loco's question was valid.

"To send a fucking message, asshole, and the porn business is lucrative. Any place they're making money is a target."

Loco held his middle finger up at Chewy. "And how do we get to this place that's out in bumfuck nowhere without being seen?"

Demon crossed his arms and looked at Oz. "Tell em what you found out, Brother."

"While some of you were out having fun last night, I was here on the computer. Found out the Knights have tapped into an evil business venture that sick fucks in the world thrive on. They're making a shit-ton of money with very little coming out of their own pockets."

"What is it?" I growled, losing patience.

Oz continued, unfazed. "Mondays and Thursdays they get a delivery of fresh, young girls, two or three at a time, tops. That's why Toledo thought Stretch could get rid of his sister-in-law and her kid for him. He knew about it. The Knights video those girls while they're being raped and beaten. Then the girls are sold and never seen again."

The thought of that happening to the thirteen-year-old girl from last night sickened me.

"They're taken across the border?" Colton scowled.

"No, Brother. They're purchased by one of the sick fucks watching them on live stream while they're being assaulted."

"Fuck!" I snarled, feeling my blood pressure rising.

"Are any of those girls there willingly?"

Oz shot Loco a twisted scowl for even asking. "Yeah, because being raped and beaten is a dream all women have, dumb ass." He shook his head with disgust. "I checked out some of their porn, and the girls are switched out almost weekly."

"Son-of-a-bitch!" Cole snapped, slamming his fist down on the table. "I take it we don't know where the girls are being held before they're taken to the trailer?"

Oz shook his head. "Haven't been able to find that out, but there's probably more than one location."

"You say they have a delivery on Thursday nights?"

Oz nodded.

"I bet they're using a white van to transport them."

I bet that Colton was right, considering that a white van had been seen at some of the places the Knights had hit. Cole and I made eye contact, and I sensed that we were both thinking the same thing. We'd taken one of the Knights' vans when we'd left their warehouse the night before. Snake had been too hurt to ride, so we'd put his and Chewy's bikes in the back of the van, and Chewy had driven him back to the club. It was in the garage out back.

"Need to get the van we brought back painted so we can use it tomorrow night." I glanced over at Oz. "Where is this trailer?"

"Somewhere off Route 66."

"Shit, that's the road LD and Jolene live on. Better warn them." Cole was texting as he spoke.

As the rest of us planned, Demon just sat back and listened silently, but if I knew him he was using the time to figure shit out and put a plan in place. His eyes touched on all of the brothers at the table, but he didn't speak until Cole looked up from his phone. Then he turned his attention to Dancer.

"Can you have shit ready for tomorrow night?"

Dancer nodded with the confidence of someone who knew his skill well.

"Okay then. All in favor of hitting the porn house tomorrow night, hands up."

Everyone raised their hand. Demon cut his gaze to Cole. "Thoughts about how this will go down?"

Cole set his eyes on Oz. "How far off Route 66 are they located?"

"About a mile. The road isn't marked, but I'll map out the coordinates for you."

"Is there a set time that they deliver the girls?"

"Anytime after dark."

Nodding with satisfaction, he turned to Reid. "Get those logos on the van painted over today so it will be dry by tomorrow night. Then I want you to dent and scratch the hell out of it, break one of the taillights, maybe one of the side view mirrors."

"The fuck?" Reid stared at Cole as if he'd lost his mind.

"Don't want the Knights to recognize it." His next comments were addressed to the room. "Since we don't know what direction they'll be coming from we'll park the van at their turnoff, make it look like it's broken down. Raise the hood. In the meantime, we'll be hiding inside. When they stop to take a look we'll get the jump on them. Move any girls they have with them over to the wrecked van and drive in like we're making a regular delivery."

A grunt of doubt escaped Loco. "What if they don't stop?" Leave it to him to play devil's advocate.

"Trust me, Brother, they will," I said with self-assurance. I knew that if we came across an abandoned vehicle anywhere near one of our properties, we would stop to check it out, especially out in the middle of nowhere where we might be doing something illegal. "It'll be too fucking close to their studio for them to just ignore and drive on by."

"Sax is right." Demon leaned forward. "Go on."

"Loco, Chewy, Sax, and Reid will go with me."

"I'm going, too, Brother." There was a grin on Demon's lips. "Not going to miss out on all the fucking fun."

"So will Dancer and his explosives. Once we get inside he can blow the fucking place up. At the same time Spider, Oz, and Colton can hit their titty bar near the strip with cocktails." Cole exchanged a look with Colton. "If you're up to it, Brother."

"What the fuck you mean, 'if I'm up to it?'" Colton growled. "This is just a fucking scratch." He indicated the bandage wrapped around his ribs.

"Then what the fuck did you mean when I heard you tell Annie to kiss it and make it better when I walked by your room this morning?"

Even though he was grinning, Colton gave Cole the finger. "I was talking about my dick, *Brother*."

"Whatever women we find there tomorrow night, we get them home to their families," I said once the laughter had died down.

"Unless they need to go to the hospital," Demon added.

Loco snorted. "If there are any there willingly, bring them here. We can use some fresh pussy." The brother was always thinking about his dick.

I shook my head and rubbed my eyes, wishing now that I'd brought a cup of coffee with me. I hadn't gotten much sleep in Goldie's bed. It was too fucking soft and smelled heavily of perfume.

"If we hit their bar during business hours there'll be civilians there." Chewy was leaning back in his chair, stretching his arms over his head.

Demon was quick to make clear that we weren't in the business of hurting civilians. "Don't want any fucking civilians killed. No guns. Toss a few cocktails and get out of there. More interested in burning the fucking place down than taking out any Knights."

The Knights had screwed up the night they'd gone around Vegas causing property damage for us and the Vegas Watchdogs. They'd not only left witnesses to their crimes, they'd killed innocent people. The cops were out looking for the members responsible, but they had their work cut out for them. Even if they found witnesses who were willing to talk it was going to be hard for anyone to identify the right bikers in a lineup. Plus, it had been dark when shit had gone down.

The cops knew better than to expect any collaboration from us or Vegas Watchdogs. Trouble between MCs was handled between clubs. MCs were already under scrutiny from their local cops and the Feds.

"Sounds good. Anyone in disagreement?"

If anyone had planned to speak up, they lost their chance when the door opened and Doc walked in. Heads turned in his direction. "Snake is good," he said before anyone had the chance to open their mouths. "I got the bullet out. How, I don't know, but he got lucky. It just missed his jugular. I stitched him up, gave him antibiotics and something for pain. Mitzi is with him now."

"That was fucking close," I muttered.

"Too fucking close," Demon mirrored.

"He needs to be still and get rest, and I've got him on a drip for the next twenty-four hours. I'll be back later tonight to check on him, but he should sleep until then."

"Thanks, Doc."

"Thanks" didn't seem adequate for saving a brother's life.

Chapter 18

Holly

I put my phone to my ear and waited for Samson to pick up. I was scheduled for a shift that night, and though I knew about the recent trouble at Grinders, I doubted that they would be closed. The people who worked there weren't all club members, including Samson. When the Desert Rebels had purchased the bar years ago, they'd kept Samson on because he'd worked there since the beginning and knew what was what. He'd turned out to be a good asset for them.

I liked Samson. He was a tough old man who'd become like a surrogate father to some of the girls who worked at the bar. He looked out for and was protective of them, but he could also dish out tough love when it was needed. He expected to be treated as he treated others, with fairness and respect.

"Hello?"

The frog in his voice revealed that I'd probably woken him up. "It's almost noontime, Sam, and you're still in bed?" I teased with a smile.

He groaned and cleared his throat. "Holly? Jesus, this is early for me, sweetheart. Everything okay?"

"Yes. I'm just calling about my shift tonight. Am I still scheduled?"

I could hear him moving around on his end, and then he released a deep breath. "Yeah I still have you down, but figured you wouldn't be coming in while you're on lockdown at the clubhouse."

Damn. I knew that I wasn't supposed to leave, but I hated letting Samson down, and I needed the work. I only had one more week at Grinders before I started my new job at Crickets, and I didn't want to have to dig into my savings. Still, I doubted Demon was going to let me leave the clubhouse. Lockdown meant no one in, and no one out, unless it was one of the men. The last thing anyone wanted to do was to get on Demon's bad side by ignoring his orders.

Samson made a sound between a laugh and a grunt. "I can almost hear you thinking, sweetheart."

I laughed and confessed, "I may have been contemplating sneaking out for just a minute." Even though I had thought about it, being kidnapped twice in my lifetime was enough. I wasn't about to tempt fate. I supposed I was going to have to dig into my savings after all, because rent was coming up.

"I hope you're smarter than that," Samson grumbled. "We'll miss you, but we will get by."

I knew they would. "Don't worry, I'm not going to do anything stupid. I have Ava to think about now. This was my last week," I reminded him. "I guess you should go ahead and replace me."

He snorted. "Sweetheart, the club created that position just for you. I won't be replacing you."

That didn't surprise me. The Desert Rebels took care of their own, and they still considered me family. I had to wonder if it was because I'd been with Sax for so long and had also formed deep friendships with members in the club.

"Don't be a stranger," Samson said in his gruff voice.

"Oh, don't worry. I'm sure there will be girls' nights in my future," I laughed. We said our goodbyes and I let my mind drift to my new job at Crickets. God, I prayed that we were done with lockdown by the time I was supposed to start, because it was going to be a problem if we were. I knew that they couldn't keep me in the clubhouse if I really wanted to leave, but did I really want to cause bad feelings with the people who were my friends? The people who I loved? They were looking out for me and Ava.

I smiled down at Ava. I'd brought her outside for some fresh air and sun, laying her on a blanket with some toys. She'd played and looked around for a little while, mesmerized watching the other children running on the playground. Gradually she'd drifted off. The noise of their laughter and chatter hadn't bothered her in the least.

I reached for my iced tea. I was sitting next to Ava with my legs criss-crossed, or "criss-cross applesauce" as one of the older kids on the playground had laughed out earlier as he'd run past me. The mothers with children on the playground were obviously taking turns watching them, because I'd watched two arrive and then two take off more than once. Our little group was doing the same thing, and I'd volunteered to take the first shift. A playpen had been brought out, and both Izzy and Samuel were playing contentedly in it. One of the prospects had erected a large beach umbrella over our area to protect us from the hot desert sun.

The ground around the playpen was littered with the toys that Izzy and Samuel had tossed out. I'd picked them up a dozen times before I'd realized they were just going to keep doing it as long as I picked up after them, so I quit. A couple of the bigger kids had run over and picked the toys up once or twice, too, but they were smarter than I was, giving up much sooner.

I watched one of the mothers, Kathy, I believe her name was, fan herself. "There's room over here if you want to get out from under the sun," I called out.

She returned my smile and walked over. "Thanks. I'm not a sun worshiper as some are. I don't care for the heat either, but when you have kids you can't keep them cooped up inside."

I could tell by her pale complexion that she wasn't an outdoorsy type. She was pretty enough to be a model, and it was obvious that she took care of herself. Her short, blonde hair was shaved on the sides and long on top in a flipped over style, and her hourglass shape belied the fact that she'd had any kids, much less the three I'd seen her with today.

"Lockdown isn't easy for anyone," I agreed, making room for her on the blanket.

"Especially for my crew." She had three boys. "Holly, right?"

I nodded. "Kathy?"

She nodded in turn. "How old is your little one?"

"Ava is six months."

"She's a sweetheart. My boys are four, six, and eight." She looked out at the playground, as if searching for them. "I hope this last one is a girl."

My jaw dropped with surprise before I could stop it. "You're pregnant?"

Kathy laughed with a nod. "Just found out. I told Dale this is it. No more. I'm not going to provide him with a baseball team."

We both laughed at that. I didn't recognize her husband's name. "What does Dale do?"

"He's a writer when he's not playing warrior. Once in a while the club calls him in to help out with something. Of course, he doesn't share the details with me because it's considered—" She did air quotes, "'club business.'"

I detected a measure of bitterness in Kathy's tone. "You don't like him being part of the MC?"

She inhaled a deep breath and released it, pulling her gaze away from the playground. "I know when he's called in that whatever he's doing is dangerous. I don't like that part. But then there are the other things, like the charity runs, and helping out in the community, the club barbeques..." She shrugged. "I don't mean to complain."

I understood how she felt. Belonging to an MC wasn't for everyone, and when your man belonged that meant you did, too. "How long has Dale been a member?"

"Fifteen years," she said without hesitation. "How about your man?"

I didn't feel like getting into it with her about my situation with Sax, so I just said, "About the same."

Samuel and Izzy were both on their feet and watching us, and I wondered if they'd finally tossed all their toys out. I got up and went to them to make sure that they weren't getting overheated. They seemed fine, but I got them each a bottle anyway, and while they threw themselves down to drink, I went around and picked up all their toys. "Last time," I laughed, throwing a look over my shoulder at Kathy.

About that time I heard familiar giggling, and looked over to see JoJo and Ellie walking in my direction. My smile disappeared when I noticed that Goldie and Cherry were also walking a ways behind them. Great. What were they doing out here?

"How are they behaving?" JoJo walked directly to the playpen and glanced down at her son.

"We decided to give you an early break," Ellie smiled, doing the same thing as JoJo. "Hi, Kathy." She reached for Izzy, touching her skin, and I knew that she was doing the same exact thing that I'd done only moments before, checking to make sure she that her daughter wasn't hot.

"Ladies." Kathy's friendly tone included them both in her response.

"What time is it?" I asked.

Ellie glanced down at her watch. "Five till one."

I rolled my eyes and snorted. They were supposed to relieve me at one. "Thanks for the *early* break."

Ellie giggled but ignored me. "They look like they're getting ready for a nap." She looked at JoJo. "Should we leave them or take them inside?"

"I say we leave them. By the time we get them inside and set up they'll have got their second wind."

Someone began to cry on the playground, drawing our attention. Kathy immediately got to her feet. "That one is mine. See you ladies around." She rushed to the playground, where her youngest was crying. The other mother had already made her way there and was examining his knee.

"She has three boys," Ellie murmured in awe, stepping away from the playpen.

"Four. Don't forget her husband. Men are just big boys," JoJo joked, following Ellie over to where I was sitting. Her gaze flickered briefly toward the picnic tables. "I don't know who thought it would be a good idea to put the smokers next to the playground," she complained.

I took a quick look. Goldie and Cherry had both lit up a cigarette and were puffing away. They were close, and judging from their smirks, they'd heard what JoJo had said. "At least they have clothes on now," I murmured low, remembering the way Goldie had been dressed that morning.

"Yeah, we heard about that. Demon was pissed when he found out. He has strict rules about the club whores not running around half-naked when we're on lockdown."

I glared at JoJo. "A bikini top that barely covers your nipples and boy shorts up the crack of your ass is not half-naked. She may as well have been nude."

"I'm surprised he even allows them to be here when the wives and families are here."

"They're considered club property, honey," I reminded Ellie. "And the club protects their own." I knew that Ellie and JoJo understood what the deal was. Hell, they'd both been old ladies long before I'd come on the scene.

I heard the sound of snickering behind me, and I knew that I should stop before my mouth got me into trouble.

"That's right, bitch," I heard Goldie say behind me.

JoJo gasped, but I chose to ignore Goldie.

"I belong to the club more than you do now. You're not even an old lady anymore."

It hadn't taken her long to find out about me and Sax.

"Enough," JoJo warned, shooting Goldie a scowl. "Holly is family. You have a problem with anyone being here, you take it up with Demon." She gave an evil grin. "Or better yet, take it up with Sax, since he's VP."

I rolled my eyes and barely held back a groan. JoJo was a sweetheart for coming to my defense, but I wasn't sure that mentioning Sax was a good idea.

"When I'm with Sax we don't talk."

I winced, literally winced, at Goldie's response.

"We're too busy sucking and fucking."

"I seriously doubt that," Ellie countered assuredly. "Sax has been in love with Holly for years. I can't see him wasting his time on a skank like you."

Goldie threw her head back and laughed loudly. "Love and sex are two different things. And Sax is an animal in bed. He was in my bed last night."

My cheeks were burning as I kept my back to her. "Yes, you already made that clear this morning."

JoJo and Ellie reacted with the same stunned, open-mouth, round-eyed expressions. Goldie shrugged with a cunning gleam in her eyes.

"I'll have him in my bed again tonight, too..." She paused for effect. "Or maybe I'll let him fuck me on his bike. That was our favorite place when we were on the road on the way here."

Sax and I had fucked many times on his bike. The idea that he'd had another woman on the back of his bike, and the visual of them together turned my stomach. Finally, I'd had enough, and I turned to face the bitch. "You're a beautiful woman, Goldie. Your insecurities and bitchiness takes away from that. You should have more respect for yourself than to be with someone who only wants to fuck you. You haven't been at the clubhouse long, and yet you've already turned into a slutty whore who only wants to sink her claws into a biker and stir up trouble."

I heard JoJo and Ellie snort behind me.

"You're the jealous bitch making a fool out of yourself with a man who doesn't want you anymore." She took a puff of her cigarette and blew it out in one long stream.

"For your information, Holly is the one who broke it off with Sax."

I knew Ellie was just trying to help.

Goldie shrugged with indifference. "And she fucked up by having another man's brat."

Thank God for her sake that she hadn't said bastard. I resisted the urge to get up and slap Goldie's face. She was trying to provoke me into a reaction, and I wasn't going to give her the satisfaction. I glanced down at Ava and smiled. Looking at her made everything okay, made me feel good inside. Even Goldie's harsh, hateful words didn't hurt as much.

"I'm going back to check on Snake." They were the first words Cherry had spoken since she and Goldie had walked up. She'd been with the MC long enough to know to keep her mouth shut and mind her own business.

"Wait for me!" Goldie got up and quickly followed Cherry. "Maybe I'll find Sax and suck his big cock." Her laughter drifted away the further she walked.

I clenched my teeth.

"Honey—" JoJo reached over and touched my arm. "You know these bitches talk trash half the time. They're the jealous ones, because they know they're not good enough to be old ladies."

I smiled at her attempt to make me feel better. "I'm good," I lied. "I just didn't realize that staying part of the club after I broke up with Sax was going to mean so much drama."

Ava began to stir. It was time for me to take her inside to change and feed her.

"Why don't you leave her?" Ellie suggested as I got up and reached for Ava's diaper bag.

"She's going to want some food in a few minutes. I've got some applesauce and cereal in the kitchen. Maybe you can take her for a little while tonight while I get my shower?"

"Sure, honey. We're going to watch some Disney movies tonight with the rest of the kids, see how long they can occupy our little monsters."

"If they're the cartoons they might hold Ava's interest for a little while." I scooped my daughter up and gave her a kiss. "See you guys later."

As I walked toward the front of the building, my attention was drawn to a buzzing noise coming from the direction of the warehouse. Reid was spray painting the side of a van. Noticing me looking his way, he gave a wave, but continued working. As I continued walking, I thought to myself that he must have been doing work for someone outside of the club, because I'd never seen anyone in the club driving a white van.

Chapter 19

S ax

Fuck. The three hours of sleep that I'd managed to grab after church weren't nearly enough, but it would have to do if I wanted to sleep tonight. I'd made it by on less with a little help from a hot shower and some booze. With a solid plan in place for tomorrow night, I couldn't wait for the shit with the Knights to be done. Taking out one of their main avenues of revenue, along with more of their brothers, was getting us closer to wiping the fuckers off the map.

We're going to put a halt to their sick twisted business of selling flesh.

I stepped out of the shower and wrapped a towel around my waist before grabbing another to rub over my head. My hair was getting too fucking long. Holly had always kept it trimmed for me, but I hadn't bothered with it since our split. As I brushed my teeth and trimmed up my beard, preferring to keep a little stubble, I thought about the woman who I loved and hated at the same time.

I thought about little Ava, too, and the possibility that she could be mine.

Did I want her to be mine? Fuck yeah, for several reasons. I didn't want Holly to have to live with the constant reminder of the men who'd assaulted her. She hadn't deserved that, no woman did. She didn't deserve to live with that kind of pain. She was strong and kind and I knew that she loved Ava no matter what, but if Ava turned out to be one of her rapists' then she would never be able to completely let go of what had happened to her.

I'd always insisted that I didn't want kids, using the lie that I didn't want to raise one in the club. But fear was the real reason that I'd refused to give Holly the baby she'd wanted so badly. I'd never told her about my family, choosing instead to keep it simple by telling her that they were all dead. Less lies that way.

Less shame.

Jesus Christ. I threw the razor in the sink and gripped the porcelain, staring at my reflection. I wanted so badly to turn back the clock for a fucking do over. The problem was I didn't know how far back I would even go. I snorted as if it were even a possibility. If it had been an option, Holly and I would probably have never met, because knowing what I knew now, I would have chosen not to be born.

A noise coming from my bedroom drew me out of the bathroom to check it out. I paused in the doorway, seeing Holly halfway into the room with Ava asleep in her arms. Our eyes met, and she halted. It was obvious that she hadn't expected to see me. She'd been heading toward the crib.

"Stay."

She hesitated only briefly before continuing to the crib and laying Ava down carefully. She settled the baby on her back and drew a light blanket over her before straightening and turning my way.

"She sleeps a lot."

Her smile was instant and genuine. "She's a baby, Sax. They sleep a lot in the beginning."

Her eyes moved over me, causing me to smirk and my dick to stir. She'd always had that effect on me. The sex between us had always been intense and satisfying, like it was the first time every time, and Holly had always been down with whatever I'd thrown at her. She liked it rough, she liked different, and she demanded as much as she gave. Thinking about her soft curves and tight pussy made me hard as fuck within seconds, but I resisted the pull.

I could tell that she had questions. Hell, I had questions, too. The problem with Holly and me was that we both had secrets. My gaze dropped with lazy interest down her body, taking in the shape of her full, rounded tits in her tank, and the tightness of her shorts between her luscious thighs. Her legs were tanned and strong, and I tried not to remember how they felt wrapped around my body when I was plowing into her. What turned me on the most was the graceful column of her neck and shoulders, exposed because she'd pulled her hair up in a messy bun.

I liked sucking on that silky flesh and taking in her scent, liked sinking my teeth into her in the primitive act of an animal claiming its mate. Fuck, these kinds of thoughts were getting me nowhere, because I didn't intend to fuck Holly again. If I kept going down that road I would never move on, so I was going to ignore what my body wanted if it killed me.

"Um, she won't sleep long, and then we'll be out of your hair." She seemed nervous, which was funny, considering our history. "I, ah, ordered a home DNA kit. When it comes in I'll let you know."

Good. I wanted that shit over with. "Sit," I said, gesturing towards the bed.

She looked toward the bed, then back at me. "Why?"

"We need to talk." She had that fight or flight look in her eyes. "We'll keep it low so we won't wake Ava."

She took a deep breath and moved to sit on the end of the bed. "Okay."

I decided to stay where I was, and leaned against the doorjamb, crossing my arms. "I want some answers."

"Are we going to play twenty questions?" She crossed her legs and leaned back, resting her hands behind her on the bed.

The position made those tits jut out. I could see her nipples were hard through the thin material of her top, see those large, dark areolas. I sucked in my breath as fire raced through my veins. "No, I'm the only one asking the questions," I clarified.

She laughed softly, and when she realized where my eyes were focused she straightened up. "I have questions, too, Sax."

I ignored that. "I want to know the real fucking reason you ended us."

"I found out I was pregnant." I thought that was all she was going to say until she added, "I knew that I was going to keep the baby and that you didn't want kids, so it seemed like the only solution."

"There's something you're not telling me. I feel it in my gut." Holly's eyes shifted away, and I knew that my instincts were right. She looked guilty as fuck. "I've had some time to think, and you know what I find interesting?" She just stared at me, but I could see the worry in her eyes. "We were together a long time and you never got pregnant, so why did it happen then? How does that fucking happen?"

Again she avoided my eyes, as if she were afraid that I would see the truth in hers. She focused her gaze on Ava as if she could draw strength from her.

"Do you remember you were so adamant about us not having a baby that you used a condom even while I was on birth control? Those...men..."

"Fuck, don't say it!" I grated, loud enough that Ava jerked but then quickly settled down again. Christ, I couldn't handle hearing about anything those fuckers had done to her when I was supposed to be protecting her. The image of them holding Holly down while they took turns raping her, beating her, sent me into a blind rage that made me want to destroy something or kill someone.

I wanted to kill those bastards a second time, and I hoped they were burning in hell.

And then I remembered something. I hadn't used a condom every time. There'd been times that I'd lost control and taken her bare. Fuck. I hadn't even bothered to suit up at all since we'd been back, and Holly had all but admitted that she wasn't on birth control. Why that didn't bother me, I didn't know.

She opened her mouth to say something, and then quickly shut it again. What had she been about to say? Her eyes were downcast, as if she were searching for the right words.

"I didn't wear a condom every time, but you were still on birth control—" I halted abruptly, not because Holly interrupted me, but because I heard her soft, tearful whisper. I frowned. "What?"

She didn't look at me. "I have to tell you something." Her words were so low it was hard to make them out. "Something that will make you hate me even more than you already do."

I didn't waste my breath trying to deny it, she was probably right. When she finally turned her face to me, I recognized the stark devastation on it. My stomach lurched with the depth of her misery. Tears flowed freely down her cheeks, her mouth was trembling. This was costing her.

"I wanted a baby so badly that I did a horrible thing," she confessed, wiping her cheeks, but the tears kept coming. "So badly, Sax, that I convinced myself that if it happened you would accept and welcome a child." She sobbed. "I was banking on the belief that you loved me enough to forgive me anything. But then the assault happened, and I realized how much I'd messed up."

I stepped away from the doorway, my hands fisted at my sides. What had she done? Judging from her tearful outpouring it was big, at least in her eyes. The only thing I could imagine was that she'd betrayed me in some way. "What the fuck did you do?"

At first I didn't think Holly was going to answer me. She looked away, sucking in air, her entire body trembling. She wiped her cheeks one last time and uttered brokenly, "I-I sto-stopped taking m-my birth con-control."

I went numb and stood frozen in place, shaking my head with disbelief. It took a solid minute before I could digest her words and the meaning behind them. She'd stopped taking her pills? How could she? Apparently what I'd wanted hadn't mattered, and she'd been counting on me to forgive her? For being dishonest with me? What the fuck?!

"When?" I snapped.

"Does it matter?"

"When?!" I was so fucking angry that I was shaking.

"Right before the assault."

Right before the assault. *Shit!* How long before the assault? Had we had sex? Did it matter? *Christ!* I reached up and pulled at my hair, turning around and walking away from her. I didn't trust myself not to hurt her, I was so angry. She'd made up her mind that she was going to have a baby no matter what, and she'd been willing to trick me to accomplish that! I was fucking livid. I paced back and forth like a wild animal, clenching and unclenching my fists.

"I made a mistake!" she whisper shouted. "I'm sorry!"

I stopped and snapped my head in her direction. "You're *sorry?*" I snorted. "Sorry hardly erases your deceit, Holly. The woman I knew and loved would have never resorted to lying and deception to get what she wanted. That's all on you." I was so fucking angry that I felt my control slipping. "Once there's no trust between two people, there's fucking nothing."

"I know that! God, Sax, I know that. But have you ever wanted something so badly that you would have done anything to get it? Even if the only way you could obtain it was to lie?"

I clenched my jaw because, yeah, I had.

"Was it so wrong with me wanting a baby with the man I love?"

It was not her wanting it that was wrong, but the way she'd gone about doing it. Maybe denying her needs had made me a selfish bastard. She hadn't known that I didn't want kids when she'd entered into a relationship with me. Her happiness had always been important to me, but making the choice to go off birth control without at least discussing it first... *Jesus, fuck!* It enraged me. I went to her and yanked her to her feet.

"You were off birth control when you were assaulted. You may very well have let one of them put a baby in your belly. Do you get that?!" I knew I was being cruel, but the whole situation was fucked up.

Holly gasped and slapped me hard, tears running down her face. "You don't think I live with that thought every day?" Her voice was hoarse with emotion, her lips trembling. "And I didn't *let* anything happen to me." She put her hands on my chest and tried to push me away. "I'm paying for my fucked-up mistake now, aren't I?" There was bitterness in her tone.

"Which fucked up mistake—having a baby, or losing me?"

She gasped. "Let me go, Sax."

"Gladly," I sneered, releasing her so roughly that she fell back onto the bed.

I. Was. Done.

I spun around and gathered up some clean clothes before disappearing into the bathroom again. Once I was dressed, I returned to the bedroom to get my boots. I ignored Holly, who was still sitting quietly on the bed. Every few seconds I heard her sniffle, but I refused to let it suck me in. I never could stand to see her hurt, but she'd done this to herself. I wasn't sure if I could ever forgive her for what she'd done. All I knew right now was that I couldn't stand to look at her.

Once I'd put on my boots I walked out.

I needed space.

I needed to be alone.

Chapter 20

Holly

Hearing the click of the door as it closed behind Sax allowed me to release the breath I'd been holding. I sank back on the bed and closed my eyes. The girls would be proud of me for finally telling him what I'd done. Now I just had to live with the fallout. The truth hadn't set me free, as the saying went. It had only damaged what little relationship we'd had left. I didn't blame Sax for hating me. I deserved it after what I'd done to him.

I knew how he and his brothers felt about loyalty, and how they dealt with disloyalty, especially disloyalty to the club. They had each other's backs, and if one brother got hurt, they all reacted to it. They took brotherhood to a whole other level when it came to their commitment to the club bylaws.

I let the tears flow down the side of my head and onto the bed. I was pretty sure that there was no future for Sax and me. No forgiveness. He might understand my desperation to have a baby, but he would never understand why I'd lied to him to achieve what I'd wanted. Looking back now, I'd been a fool to think that things would work out, for banking on love above all else. All I could hope for now was that one day we could be friends. I needed to have Sax in my life in some way.

Gradually, the tears stopped. I relaxed enough to doze off, until I heard Ava vocalizing that she was awake from her nap. Usually the first few minutes after she woke she'd lay there and entertain herself with baby chatter. I often wondered what went on inside her little head. What did babies think about?

I rolled off the bed and went to the bathroom to wash my face and run a brush through my hair, then pinned it back up. I couldn't say that the nap had refreshed me. The tears had left my face a blotchy mess, and my eyes were swollen and red, revealing the depth of the raw emotions that were tearing me up inside. *Suck it up,* I told myself. The hard part was over.

When I reached the crib, Ava was checking out her toes as if it were the first time that she was seeing them. Her little face was so serious until she noticed me smiling down at her, and then she threw her little legs out and wiggled happily.

"Did you have a good nap, honey?" I reached for her and cuddled her against me tightly, kissing her little chubby cheeks. "Mommy got a nap, too," I cooed, taking her over to the bed to change her. After a quick change, I headed out, scanning the room below as I went down the stairs. Dinnertime was coming up, and I wanted to help out in the kitchen.

The room was bustling with activity of all sorts. It looked more like a gathering at a community center than a biker's clubhouse. While the older children and teenagers were sitting around doing their own thing on their phones and tablets, the younger ones were once again on the floor in front of the TV, watching cartoons. Most of the women were gathered around in little clusters while their men were off doing their own thing. Several were playing pool, and the stools around the bar were full.

Cherry, Goldie, Mitzi, and Lulu were there, too, keeping their distance from the wives and their men. They were overdressed for club girls, but still looked a world apart from the other women. Lulu shot me a finger wave from where she sat on Razor's lap. She was such a sweetheart. I often wondered why she'd settled for being one of the club's sluts when she deserved so much more. She'd been the first one to welcome me and make me feel comfortable when Sax had brought me here. She'd taught me a lot about club life.

My smile must have seemed like an invite to her, because she jumped from Loco's lap and rushed toward me. There was a joyful gleam in her eyes as they shot back and forth from me to Ava.

"God, she's so cute!" As soon as she was close enough she reached for my daughter's little hand. Ava giggled, her expression revealing her trust of Lulu. "Can I have her?"

I laughed. "You can borrow her," I countered. "But she'll want to eat soon."

Ava went willingly to her. "I can feed her," Lulu insisted. "Is there a bottle in the fridge?"

I nodded. "She'll also get a little cereal with applesauce mixed into it."

"I think we can handle that. Can't we, baby?" She kissed Ava on the cheek and turned to head to the kitchen.

I watched for a minute, smiling, before I noticed the looks of disgust on some of the wives' faces who had witnessed the exchange. They obviously didn't know Lulu, but they knew what she was, and it was clear that they disagreed with my decision to let a club girl handle my daughter. Kathy was sitting with them, a look of regret on her face. Did she feel the same way? The smile she offered me said that she didn't. I walked over to the table, not knowing what I was going to say until I opened my mouth and the words poured out.

"I can see by some of your expressions that you think it's a bad idea to let Lulu take Ava, but let me tell you something—Lulu is the sweetest, most caring and loving person in this whole clubhouse. She'd do anything for any one of you, and she'd do it with a smile on her face. I trust her with my daughter." I purposely kept my tone calm and friendly. "She may be here for the *unmarried* men, but you should get to know her before passing judgment."

One of them, an older woman, scoffed. "We know why those sluts are here, and apparently it doesn't matter if the men are married or not." She nodded over my shoulder.

I followed the direction of her gaze and saw Goldie sitting on the lap of one of the brothers that I didn't know. Even from where I was I could see the gold band on his finger. I looked back at the woman. "That's not Lulu, and it takes two to tango."

Kathy burst out with laughter, getting a shocked look from the women. "What? She's right, Aggie. You should look at what's right in front of your eyes. And you know that Kramer is a no good cheat, and has been for years. Why you put up with it is anyone's guess, but that woman isn't forcing him to let her sit on his lap."

Aggie pressed her lips and remained silent, but her eyes told a different story. Inside she was fuming. There was something else there, too, and I recognized it for what it was—pain. When I glanced back at Goldie and Kramer, it became clear to me where that pain was coming from. Holy shit! Was Kramer Aggie's husband? I met Kathy's eyes, and she confirmed my silent question with a subtle nod. I instantly felt sorry for Aggie. Why would any woman put up with a cheating husband?

I was really beginning to dislike Goldie.

"Holly!"

The sound of my name drew my eyes to the bar. Bobbie and Raven were there with Cole and Demon, along with Sax. I hesitated only briefly before making my way there, a forced smile on my face. Sax had his back to me, and the minute I let my presence be known he twirled on his stool, got up, and left. Both women stared after him with slight surprise.

I tried to make light of it. "Must be something I said."

Demon snorted. "More like something you did, sweetheart."

My smile vanished. Sax hadn't wasted any time in telling his brothers what I'd done. It was difficult meeting the coldness in Demon's eyes. The same disapproval was in Cole's hard glare.

"I'm sorrier than you know, because my selfish mistake cost me the love of my life, but I'm not sorry that I have Ava. I'll understand if you want me to leave."

Demon made a sound between impatience and a growl. "Hell, don't want you to leave, Holly, you and Ava are family. Just fucking disappointed in you, that's all."

I nodded, accepting Demon's words.

"Glad you told him the truth about why you left," Cole added. "Now he can stop beating himself up thinking that it was something he did."

Sax had been blaming himself?

"Drink, Holly?"

"No thanks, Spider."

"Not everyone knows."

I looked at Demon, waiting for an explanation.

"Says this is between you and him, and he doesn't want his brothers treating you different. Not that they would. Fuck, we all make mistakes. But he's still protecting you, girl."

"Maybe if he finds out that Ava's his, shit will be different." Cole gave me a wink.

I doubted that, but forced a small smile for his benefit.

"Are you going to help out in the kitchen, honey?"

I breathed a sigh of relief when Raven changed the subject. "Yeah. That's my intention."

"Then let's go so we can feed these men and get these kids off to bed." Bobbie jumped off her stool and Raven followed, and the three of us walked to the kitchen.

As we stepped into the kitchen, Raven and Bobbie walked to the fridge and began pulling food out, but I came to an abrupt stop, my eyes transfixed on Lulu and Sax. They had their heads tilted together and seemed to be talking as Lulu fed Ava in her highchair. Sax watched Ava closely as she eagerly opened her little mouth every time Lulu got close with the spoon. My heart skipped a beat when he picked up the cloth on the highchair and wiped it gently across her cherub mouth. Then something Lulu said caused them both to laugh.

The sexy smile on his rugged features warmed my heart and made me realize how much I'd missed that smile, especially when it was directed at me. I wondered what Lulu had said to bring it out, but it didn't last long.

Lulu finished up with Ava, removing the food-stained bib and pulling the tray back to lift Ava from the seat. She and Sax both turned to leave, and that's when they realized that I was in the room.

"There's mommy," Lulu gushed when they got closer to me.

Sax's stony expression was closed off, but he couldn't hide from his hard eyes the painful truth that I'd hurt him. I wanted to ask what they'd been laughing about, but knew that it wasn't any of my business.

I reached for Ava's outstretched hand and brought it to my lips. "Do you want me to take her now?" I slathered kisses all over her palm until she began to squeal, which then caused me to giggle. I'd noticed she'd been drooling more lately, and suspected that she was going to be teething soon. "Mommy loves you, baby girl!" I pretended to nibble on her fingers.

"No!" Lulu shook her head vigorously. "I still want to give her a bottle." She held the one up in her hand that I hadn't noticed before. "We're good."

My eyes darted briefly to Sax, and then back to her. "I'm going to help get dinner ready then."

As they continued out of the room it struck me how much they looked just like a happy little family. I ignored the pang in my heart and joined Raven and Bobbie at the counter. There was a ton of vegetables in front of them. They both looked up when I joined them, a look in their eyes that said that they knew what I was feeling. "So it looks like we're having veggies for dinner?"

"We're making a humongous salad," Bobbie explained. "To go with the spaghetti."

I looked around and saw several crock pots on the opposite counter.

Raven saw where I was looking. "Annie and Lulu made the sauce earlier."

"Do you gals need any help in here?" All three of us turned to see Kathy come into the kitchen.

"If you want to get the garlic bread ready, that would be great."

"Anything to get off my ass," Kathy laughed as she headed toward the loaves of French bread that were laid out on the island in the middle of the kitchen. "Lockdown sucks."

We all mumbled our agreement.

"I'll start the pasta." I went to the stove area and pulled three huge pots out of the bottom cupboard. "What kind of sauce did they make?" I asked as I filled the pots with water.

"There's meatballs, sausage, and a vegetarian one." Raven made a yummy sound. "Lulu makes her own meatballs, and they're to die for."

"I think we all know that," Kathy laughed as she sliced the bread down the middle. "Everything Lulu makes is yummy."

Kathy and I exchanged a quick look.

Once the pots were on the stove, I had nothing left to do but wait for the water to boil. I leaned against the counter and turned back towards the other women. "How about I make macaroni for the kids?"

Bobbie turned and gave me a thumbs-up. "Good idea. It will be less messy for them than spaghetti."

"Is there anything for dessert?" Raven smiled, rubbing her baby bump. "I'm just asking for the little one in here."

"I'm sure there's something." I hoped there was, because I felt like having something sweet, too.

"Demon sent us in here to help."

We all turned to see Mitzi, Cherry, and Goldie standing just inside the door. Cherry and Mitzi both had smiles on their faces and looked ready to go. They were used to doing multiple jobs at the clubhouse, and when we weren't on lockdown they usually did most of the cooking. Goldie, on the other hand, looked uninterested, as if all of this was beneath her. I didn't let her see my smirk as I turned to check on the water, adding a little salt to it. I'd let Bobbie or one of the other women deal with Goldie's ass.

"Since we have the food under control, why don't you three deal with setting up the plates, napkins, and silverware?"

I liked the assertive way that Bobbie directed the three women, leaving no doubt that she was not giving them a choice in the matter. "Oh, and the drinks."

"How come Lulu doesn't have to help?"

I kept my back to the room, adding a little oil to the pot that I was going to cook the macaroni in so that it wouldn't stick. "Lulu already did her part."

"What, fuck your ex-boyfriend?"

There were gasps in response to Goldie's vindictive words.

"I saw them playing house out there with your little bas—"

"Don't fucking say it, bitch!" Bobbie snapped, spinning around to face her. She looked pissed. "Maybe the other girls didn't warn you about what happens when you disrespect one of us, but you'd better learn real fast."

They faced-off for a moment before Goldie wisely backed down. She'd have been a fool not to. She knew that Bobbie was Demon's old lady, and that her opinion carried a lot of weight in the club when it came to certain decisions. Goldie would have been stupid not to accept her warning. Once Bobbie was convinced that Goldie was cowed and was going to watch her mouth, she turned back to resume chopping the vegetables. Goldie shot me a glare before joining Mitzi and Cherry.

I added the pasta to the boiling water. Kathy slipped the garlic bread into the oven, and then went over to stir the three crock pots of spaghetti sauce. The kitchen smelled like an Italian restaurant, and I began to feel hungry. Bobbie brought the huge salad bowl with tongs over and set it down on the island near the bowls. I was stirring the pasta, and on her way past me she shot me a wink.

God, I loved these women.

We had our own little sisterhood.

Chapter 21

S^{ax}

The van was in place, the hood was up. All we had to do was stay out of sight and wait. Reid had done a good job banging it up. To the casual observer passing by, it would just look like an old vehicle broken down on the side of the road. Abandoned. Darkness would help. That was *if* anyone passed by.

Spider, Colton, and Oz were on their way to the Knights' titty bar. They wouldn't strike until they heard from us that we were on our way in. We wanted both hits to be made as close to the same time as possible.

The Knights wouldn't know what hit them.

"It's fucking hot in here," Chewy complained.

"Whining won't help," Demon snapped from the passenger seat next to me.

"Least you two fuckers have windows." The brother sounded like a five-year-old.

Cole snorted from his position by the side door, ready to slide it open when the time came. "Make sure you brothers have your silencers on."

"If we have to transfer any girls over I'll stay behind and protect them," Loco offered.

"Nice fucking try, Brother," I grinned.

Reid slapped the back of his head. "These women will be traumatized, stupid. They don't need your horny ass coming on to them."

About that time headlights appeared down the road in front of us. "Everyone down!" I shouted, just as the lights hit our windshield and illuminated the inside of the van. The windows were tinted, but I didn't want to take a chance that we'd be seen. I waited until the slight curve in the road caused the lights to shift away from us before popping my head up. "They're slowing down! Someone text Oz and tell them to move in."

SAX

The sound of gravel beneath tires indicated that they'd pulled off to the side of the road somewhere behind us, and then there was the tell-tale sound of someone opening a truck door. They'd left their vehicle running, which told me that someone was still inside the van with the girls. If it was the driver than we were fucked. He could take off at the first sign of trouble. I glanced over at Demon.

"Fuck," he said low. He looked out at his side mirror. "Someone is coming up on my side." He cast a glance back at Cole. "The driver's door is still closed."

"Shit!" Cole whisper yelled. "See anyone coming up your side, Sax?"

I checked my mirror. "No one."

"Let me know the second the fucker reaches your door, Prez. I'll sneak out and take care of the driver while you're taking care of him."

"Get ready," Demon said. "Now!"

Cole slid the door open and jumped from the van at a run, his gun in his hand. As I opened my door just as the others were jumping to the ground I heard the muted pop pop of Demon's gun, and then the same exact sound when Cole took out the driver. Then screaming erupted from the women inside the van. I slid the door open and saw two women huddled together, bruised and extremely terrified, their eyes swollen and faces streaked with tears.

I put my finger up to my mouth. "Sshh! Quiet. We're not here to hurt you. We're here to help," I said, praying that their screams hadn't carried all the way to the trailer. "We're going to transfer you to our van—"

"Why?" one of them asked, sobbing.

"Don't have time to explain right now." Reid showed up next to me and the two of us helped the women out of the van. "It's only for a little while."

"Come with me," Reid said in a calm tone.

"We need to move out!" Cole stated. He grabbed the dead driver and hauled him from the van, tossing him off the road and into the dirt so he wouldn't be noticed.

We plowed into the van and took off down the road. The trailer turned out to be a lot more than the old tin box that I'd been expecting. It was a newer manufactured home, the kind you saw in retirement communities.

Either Oz had been given incorrect info, or the Knights had done some upgrading. I wondered what other surprises we were going to find.

Cole pulled up to the side of the main building, out of sight of the entrance door. We didn't know how many Knights we'd be dealing with, or if there were guards. The plan was to storm the studio, but there was also another building on the property that we hadn't expected. A hunch told me that it was probably where they held the girls. It wasn't as nice as the main building, and looked as if it was used mainly for storage.

"Chewy, Loco, you check out the other building!" Cole commanded in a harsh whisper the minute we were all outside the van. "The rest come with me."

Demon stayed close to Cole's backside, and Reid and I followed as we rushed around the building toward the door. Movement in the shadows drew our attention, and several of us fired off a shot, content that the threat was gone when we heard a grunt. Cole kicked in the door and we rushed inside with our weapons ready. The first two men we came across went down before they could even reach for their guns.

"Spread out!" Demon growled.

We hadn't gotten far when three other fuckers came running into the room. I managed to nail the first one, while the other two shot in our direction, causing us to scramble for cover. I saw movement out of the corner of my eye as another Knight entered the room from a different direction. Our eyes met, but he didn't have time to line up his shot. Before I could get a shot off, he chopped the gun out of my hand, and we began fighting each other for control.

I pushed him down the tight hallway. I didn't trust his brothers not to shoot blindly, not caring of who they hit. We went at each other like two bulls, bouncing back and forth against the walls while our fists pounded against hard muscles and flesh. His fist glanced off my face, the ring he was wearing splitting my cheek open. With a snarl I brought my fist up and clipped him beneath the chin in a solid uppercut. Blood and spit went flying. His retaliation caught me square in the eye, and for a second I saw stars. My head flew back, hitting the wall before I gave it a shake and came back at him with several punches to his nose and mouth. Several punches to my torso took my breath away, but I knew that if I went down, I wouldn't get back up

As I dropped to my knees I slammed my fist directly into his balls. I knew it was a cheap shot, but we were fighting for life or death. He released a sound like an animal on the verge of dying as he reached for his balls and his body slowly started to crumble. Before he could recover I got to my feet and brought my knee up, hitting him in the throat. He went down. I looked around for my gun, picked it up, and fired one shot between his eyes.

I stood panting for breath. The shooting had stopped. Reid and Demon were heading down the hallway opposite where I was standing, so I decided to check the rooms at my end. I walked into the first bedroom, which appeared to be set up as a studio, cameras facing a round bed. There was a mirror on the ceiling that would reflect anything that might happen on the bed. The décor was strictly a porn setting. I squinted, swearing as I realized that mixed among the various stains on the bed was blood.

Fuck.

I left that room and checked two other similar rooms, finding them empty. Dancer was heading down the hallway as I was heading back. "How much time do you need?"

"Give me ten to set it up. I can detonate after we leave."

I nodded and continued to the main room. The door opened, and Chewy and Loco came inside. I raised a brow, silently asking what had gone down. From their expressions I knew that it wasn't good.

"Found two girls in that fucking hot box," Loco said, grinding his back teeth until a muscle jerked in his jaw. "One of them is just a kid, Brother. A fucking kid."

Jesus H. Christ. I thought about the blood that I'd seen on the bed. Had that been hers? Had those fucking bastards raped a kid?

"Took out two of them," Chewy said as Demon, Cole, and Reid returned.

"Where are the girls?" I frowned.

"Outside. Didn't know what we'd find in here."

"We'd better get gone." Cole tucked his gun away. He glanced up when Dancer came back into the room. "You done?"

"Yup. Set explosives up in that shed, too. Time the Knights get here, this place is going to look like a fucking crater," he grinned.

"Good." Demon was already at the door. "Let's go."

We'd barely made it outside when he paused and pulled out his phone. A smirk moved across his face. "Oz said it's done."

"The fucking Knights won't know which way to go," Loco remarked as he moved toward the two cowering girls.

Jesus fuck. The one looked to be about ten, maybe eleven-years-old at most. I went over to her. Her eyes were downcast, and I could feel her trembling when I put my finger beneath her small chin and gently pulled her head up to meet her eyes. God, hers were big and so full of innocence. "We're going to get you home, okay, sweetheart?"

She nodded slowly, her bottom lip quivering.

"Did any of those men touch you?"

Before she could respond, the woman next to her said, "They were saving her. They said they could get more money for a virgin."

Fucking hell. I ground my teeth until a sharp pain shot up the side of my jaw. Thank God she wouldn't have to deal with the aftermath of being raped. From the look of the woman in front of me, it seemed like she hadn't avoided anything. In spite of that, there was gratitude swimming in her eyes

"We got to go, Brother," Demon insisted.

Loco and Chewy carried the barefoot girls to the van. We plowed inside and took off down the road and back to the van we'd arrived in. I glanced back at the girls where they sat on the floor. The older one was holding the little girl close to her, trying to comfort her in her own way. "What are your names?"

"Shanna," the woman answered. "This is Tara.

"How long were you with those men?"

"Two days," Shanna answered, looking down at the floor. "Too long."

"We have a doctor at the clubhouse if you need one."

She shook her head, keeping her eyes down.

"There's two other girls. I promise we'll get you all home."

As we pulled up next to the other van, Demon growled, "Reid, you drive the other van back, Brother."

Reid got up without question.

"I gotta go too, Prez." Dancer followed behind Reid after he opened the door and jumped to the ground. "Detonator's over there."

"After we take off, you know what to do," Cole said.

"Got it." He closed the door behind him.

"Let's get the fuck out of here." I didn't want to face any more Knights tonight with the girls present.

"We're not going to watch the fireworks?" Chewy joked.

Oh, we'd be watching them. Well, I would, because I had a window. If I knew Dancer he'd set up enough explosives to light up the fucking sky for miles around, which was another reason that I wanted to put distance between us and this place. It was going to draw the cops.

As soon as Reid took off we pulled in right behind him. A minute later a huge explosion shook the ground and lit the sky, followed by several more. I looked out the window, watching as flaming debris fell to the ground. Both buildings had been obliterated, and what little was left of them was burning out of control. I released a breath of relief and relaxed back in my seat for the ride back to the clubhouse.

If the Knights hadn't thought we were at war before, they did now.

Chapter 22

H olly
    It was nearing the end of the week, and we were still on lockdown. The men rode out nearly every day, sometimes twice a day, to take care of "club business." They often returned looking as if they'd been in a fight, scraped and bloodied, but still worked up. They would come through the clubhouse door mean and moody, and anyone close by would scramble out of their way, the wives included. First they'd hit the bar, then they'd grab their women and disappear. These men needed an outlet when the day was done, and if they didn't have old ladies, they grabbed a club girl.

Those were the times when I secretly watched Sax, waiting for him to tear my heart out, but he had yet to take any of the club girls off somewhere. He'd just sit at the bar and drink, and once in a while I'd catch him watching me, but for the most part we stayed away from each other. Where he was sleeping at night, I had no clue. After that first day he hadn't returned to his room.

I busied myself with taking care of Ava and helping out where I could, but I knew I would need to make a decision soon about whether or not I would stay. The first day of my new job was almost here, and I couldn't afford to screw things up. They wouldn't understand or even care about lockdown. They had a restaurant to open. I decided it would probably be a good idea to touch base with them, just to make sure the restaurant was still opening on time.

Ava was good, entertaining herself on a blanket in front of the TV. JoJo and Ellie were there with their toddlers. I pulled out my phone and indicated to JoJo that I needed to make a call. She nodded, and I went to the kitchen where I wouldn't be interrupted. The room was empty. I checked my contacts for the Crickets' manager who'd hired me and hit his number.

As I waited for Mr. Mathis to answer his phone I jumped up onto the island to sit. Low-key noise from the bar carried to me, but not enough to be distracting. Finally, on the fourth ring he answered.

"Hello?"

"Mr. Mathis?"

"Yes."

"This is Holly—"

"Holly?" His tone suggested that he was surprised to be hearing from me, and his nervous laughter warned me that something was not right. "I hope you're not calling to get your job back. I've already hired a new hostess."

As his words quickly sank in, my smile disappeared and my stomach dropped. What was he talking about? "I don't understand what you mean. I thought the position was mine. That's why I'm calling, to see if the restaurant is still opening on Saturday."

"Um, well . . ." He cleared his throat. "This is certainly awkward." I could just imagine the furrow between his thick, white eyebrows. "I came in Monday and had a message on my desk saying that you'd changed your mind about the job."

"What? I didn't change my mind! Who left a message?" This was *not* happening to me. "Did you talk to your assistant? Because I did not change my mind," I reiterated. "I need that job, Mr. Mathis."

"To be totally honest, I was surprised that you'd changed your mind, so I did speak with Angie and she said that a man had called. He said that something else had come along and that you would have to pass on the position."

A man? I digested his words, more confused now than ever. Who would do something like this? My mind raced, but no one came to mind. Someone was messing with my life. "I don't suppose he left a name?" I sighed, not expecting much.

"As a matter of fact, he did. Unusual name, too, which is why I remember it—Sax."

Sax?! Why would he do this? He didn't want me at Grinders, he didn't want me around the clubhouse. Unless he knew that I'd want to leave the clubhouse so I could start the job at Crickets, and he didn't want me to leave while the club was on lockdown. But going behind my back and causing me to lose a new job was a bit extreme, and why would he even care? It was my life, and I couldn't put it on hold indefinitely.

"Is there anything available, Mr. Mathis?" If I could just get my foot in the door...

"I'm sorry, Holly. I really am. This close to opening, everything has been filled. But I'll keep your resume, and if something opens up you'll be the first one I call."

"Thank you. I appreciate that." I wanted to cry with disappointment.

As we ended the call I fought the urge to throw my phone across the room. Disappointment quickly turned to anger. Sax had no right to interfere in my life. I needed that job, and now I had no job and no money coming in. What the hell was he thinking? That he was protecting Ava and me by manipulating our situation? The more I stewed over it, the angrier I got. I jumped down off the island and stormed out to the bar.

I scanned the crowded room for Sax, my heart pounding. By the time I found him playing pool with Cole, Colton, and Oz I was fuming. And then I saw Goldie. Perfect. She was there too, eyeing Sax up and down, her intentions so obvious that it made me sick. I made my way over to them, too infuriated to care that I was about to make a fool out of myself.

Cole and Oz saw me coming, their happy-go-lucky expressions quickly changing when they realized that something was wrong and that I was on the warpath. They were holding their pool cues and waiting for their turn to make a shot. Colton and Sax had their backs to me. Sax was bent over the table, about to take his turn. Goldie noticed me approaching and moved to his side, getting as close as she could in an attempt to get between us.

I ignored the bitch.

I didn't wait for Sax to take his shot. I grabbed his arm to get his attention. "How could you, Sax?!"

The pool cue missed the ball and hit the table as I pulled him around to face me. He turned, angry and swearing. "The fuck?!"

"You had no right to call Crickets and tell them I no longer wanted that job! I needed that job, you asshole! How do you expect me to pay my bills, huh?"

"I have no fucking idea what you're talking about!" he growled back with a heavy frown.

SAX

"I just got off the phone with the manager, Sax! He said you called him, he knew your name. Why would you do that, you jerk?! You had no fucking right to interfere in my life!"

"Settle the fuck down—"

"*You* settle down! I know why you did it. You're all alike! It's all about control with you guys—"

"Holly," Sax warned in a guttural growl, a flash of anger in his eyes. "Don't say something you'll regret, woman."

I knew that I was going too far. The look in Cole's eyes said it, too, but I didn't care. I was hurt and angry. "Or what, Sax? What will you do to me for speaking the truth? You had no right to make a decision that concerned me!"

"Doesn't feel good, does it?" he snarled back.

The truth behind his harsh words hit me hard, because that's exactly what I'd done to him. It took me a minute to breathe, and I tried to calm my racing heart. "You knew I'd have to leave for that job, and you wanted to keep me here on lockdown!"

"Why the fuck would I do that when I want you gone?"

Goldie giggled. Colton looked down regretfully and slowly shook his head, for whom I wasn't sure.

I jerked back as if his hurtful words had physically hit me, and blinked as my eyes filled with tears. Cole and Oz just stood there quietly. The room had quieted behind me, telling me that we had an audience. I was too afraid to look and see what was on everyone's faces, knowing that I'd screwed up.

You didn't disrespect a member of the club, especially in front of his brothers, and Sax was the VP.

It was hard to tell what he was thinking, but his body language was easy to read. He was rigid with anger. If he wanted me gone it didn't make sense that he'd made that call, but the fact that Mr. Mathis had mentioned his name couldn't be ignored either. Someone was playing games.

"Are you done with your fucking tantrum?"

I gasped with disbelief.

"I don't know what the fuck is going on, but I do know this—I didn't call anyone about any job you had lined up. I want you out of Grinders. I want you out of this clubhouse. I want you out of my sight. Is that clear enough for you?"

His cruel words caused me to reach for a discarded pool cue. I didn't know what I was going to do with it until I raised it and slammed it down on the edge of the pool table."You're an asshole, Sax, and a liar!" I said between my teeth, convinced that he was lying.

"Jesus Christ, woman!"

"Just be glad that wasn't your head!"

I heard a few snorts behind me as I stood there, shocked by my own actions. There was amusement in Goldie's eyes, along with something else. She was enjoying this, and a little too much. I narrowed my eyes distrustfully at the other woman. I looked back at Sax. His expression was dark and frightening in its intensity.

We'd had our fights, but none like this. Maybe I was a little out of control. Maybe this was about more than just losing a job. It didn't help my mood seeing Goldie hanging around Sax all week like a bitch in heat.

Realizing that I had to get out of there, I tossed the pool cue onto the pool table and spun around to make my escape.

"You can go to hell!" I said pointedly over my shoulder. I met the amusement in JoJo and Raven's eyes as they sat playing with the kids. Annie's mouth was frozen open with surprise. Ellie's worried look revealed that I may have gone too far.

I thought I was going to make my escape until I heard, "Oh, no you don't, you little brat."

I didn't see Sax move because I was moving swiftly through the room toward the stairs. I avoided everyone's eyes, still panting with anger and a little embarrassed. I'd seen a lot of women go after their men in the clubhouse, and while it had created entertainment for all, I'd always thought myself above giving into my emotions and causing a scene.

Suddenly a hand on my shoulder flipped me around. Before I could question him, Sax bent, put his shoulder against my belly, and lifted me off my feet in a fireman's hold.

This couldn't be good. "Put me down!" I screeched.

"I will." He continued toward the stairs. "Just as soon as I have you over my knee and my hand on your ass!"

Laughter erupted around us. "No, Sax!" He'd never taken a hand to me before. Sure, we'd played around a little, but his tone implied that this was punishment and he was going to make it sting. "Put me down!"

Somehow Sax managed to walk up the stairs with me hanging over his shoulder, making the effort seem like a piece of cake. I'd never returned to my pre-baby weight, and yet he wasn't even huffing. I seethed the whole way and struggled to get down. A hard slap on my behind took my breath away. He'd held nothing back, and I wondered if that was a prelude to what was to come.

I wondered if maybe this was just an act to save face in front of his brothers, and that once we got to wherever it was he was taking me, he'd put me down and we would talk like two grown adults. On second thought, I didn't believe that for a minute, and the closer we got to his room, the more scared I grew.

"I hate you!" I cried out childishly.

"You're going to hate me more in a minute."

Chapter 23

S^{ax}

I tossed Holly onto the bed before slamming the door closed and facing her again. I couldn't remember the last time I'd been this angry at her. If we'd still been together, I would have laughed her tirade off, maybe grabbed her and kissed her breathlessly before slapping her on the ass and telling her to cool off. My brothers wouldn't have thought anything of it. But we weren't together, and she'd crossed the line throwing her little tantrum. Demon, especially, would expect me to rein her in and remind her where she was and how shit worked.

Holly disrespecting me disrespected the club, and my brothers would be waiting to hear her screams downstairs. I crossed my arms and glared down at her flushed face and fiery eyes. She was pissed, but there was also apprehension on her face. She had to be thinking that I'd never had to "handle" her before, had only ever put my hands on her to give her pleasure, but again, these were different times. There were no exceptions because of the history between two people.

"You went too far."

"I don't give a shit!"

I saw red at her flippant attitude. "You will." I reached for her ankle, but she scooted up to the head of the bed.

Growling with irritation, I reached again, this time snatching it. She let out a squeal and tried to kick me with her other foot until I grabbed that one, too.

"No! Don't you dare!"

I loved a challenge, and smirked. I easily yanked her to the foot of the bed and caught her up in my arms, grunting when she brushed against my dick as she struggled to get away. Fuck, that felt good. I'd been fucking horny all week, and not taking the opportunity to work it out with one of the club sluts was my own fault.

"No, Sax!"

I ignored her, sitting on the edge of the bed and forcing her over my knee. She tensed when she felt my hand at the back of her shorts, and I yanked them and her panties down to bare her sweet ass. I stared down at the two full moons for a minute, my mouth watering at the smooth, flawless flesh I'd exposed. It was going to be fucking hard to keep to my agenda, harder than I'd thought it would be. She sucked in her breath as I smoothed my palm over one cheek until she gradually relaxed, and then when she wasn't expecting it I brought my hand down in a slap that burned my palm and echoed through the room.

So did her scream. "God damn you, Sax!"

She stiffened. I brought my palm down again, this time on the opposite cheek.

"Ouch! This is childish." She tensed again. "And it fucking hurts!"

"Obviously not enough if you can still talk."

I slapped her again, and this time she remained silent except for a hiss. I grinned at the evil pleasure surging through me, and spanked her earnestly, mesmerized by the beautiful flesh turning red with my hand prints. Her gasps turned into sobs as she tried to wiggle off my lap, but an arm across her waist held her where I wanted her. Unfortunately, she was right over my straining dick, and every move she made dragged a groan from me. By the time I counted to fifteen she was sobbing uncontrollably and her bottom looked like a bright red apple.

An apple I wanted to bite in to.

I stopped and took a minute to pull myself together. I was breathing hard with unexpected arousal, my dick hard as stone as I stared down at a beautiful sight. Holly's bright ass was hot as fuck, and I had to fight the urge to run my hand over it to sooth the sting. This was about punishment, and showing her mercy now would defeat the purpose.

I grabbed her by the hair and pulled her head back enough so our eyes could meet. "You know better than to cause a scene like that in front of my brothers, Holly. Exceptions may be made for old ladies, but you gave up that privilege." I had to steel myself from the anguish on her face and the tears that I'd caused. It tore me up inside that I'd been the one to put them there.

She remained stubbornly silent. Sighing, I released her hair and she faced the floor again.

"You want to tell me again what the fuck happened?" My eyes kept returning to her delectable ass. The sight was keeping my dick hard. Hell, who was I kidding? I've been hard since I'd returned home and found that she'd come back. A year without her had only revealed how fucking much I wanted this woman in my life.

But after what she'd done...

She sniffled. "I told you, someone called Crickets and told them that I'd changed my mind about the job that I was supposed to start on Saturday night. The manager said they used your name. Now I have no job."

I didn't believe in coincidences, and two men going by the name of "Sax" and living in the same area was suspicious. Clearly someone had impersonated me. "You know that you can still work at Grinders."

"That's not the point, Sax. And besides, you don't want me there."

Yeah, but not for the reasons she thought. I ground my back teeth in frustration and started to pull her panties and shorts back up, but her hiss caused me to hesitate. Regret filled me as I realized that I might have overdone it. I gave in and smoothed my palm over her hot, swollen flesh. At first Holly twitched away from my hand, but then she relaxed with a sigh.

"You need the job, Holly." My tone booked no argument. What I wanted didn't matter. She had Ava to think about.

I could feel her bottom cooling down, watched as the red faded slightly. I could have rubbed her satiny flesh all fucking day. Her soft mewls kept my heart racing and my dick throbbing. As I stared down at my hand rubbing her skin, it struck me that Holly didn't seem to mind that I was touching her so intimately. If anything, her deep breathing indicated that she liked it.

I wasn't doing myself any favors by giving in to the temptation to touch Holly, but I couldn't seem to find the strength to ignore her. She'd been my drug of choice for so long, and the fucking truth was I craved her as much today as I had in the beginning. I felt her shiver, and I knew that what I was doing was turning her on.

"I'll see if I can find out who this *other* Sax is, but I promise you it wasn't me."

"Thank you," she responded in a whispery, slightly lazy tone.

I couldn't ignore the enticing crack separating her luscious cheeks anymore, and let my finger dip and explore. I started at the top and ran my finger down to the tiny star that marked her backdoor entrance and played with it a little. She caught her breath and tensed slightly, but we both knew that she liked anal play. I half-expected her to protest, and when she didn't, my finger continued to travel through her wet slit all the way up to her clit. Even though I couldn't see it, I could tell the little jewel was engorged and surrounded by slickness. Holly whimpered as I flicked over it.

"Jesus, you're soaked." I flicked my finger a second time, causing her to twitch and suck in her breath. "I can't seem to keep my hands off you." My voice was hoarse with arousal. I wanted to flip her around and fuck her raw, fuck the anger out of my system, and fuck in a new beginning, but I knew that wasn't the solution.

Her breathless response made me rethink that.

"Only for you, Sax." Her tone was thick with emotion.

I ground my back teeth. At this rate I wouldn't have any left by the time I left the room. My dick ached with the need to sink inside her tight, little body. My heart had never stopped loving Holly, had never stopped wanting her, and probably never would. We'd had something good for a long time. I missed us, too. I knew that I could have chosen to just forgive and forget and go back to the way we'd been, but my fucking pride wouldn't let me.

Her moan brought me out of my head and back to the present. How could I forget that my finger was swiping between her soaked pussy lips? I thumped her clit, feeling the deep shudder run through her body, and then, unable to help myself, I sank my finger inside her hot sheath. At the same time I lifted my hips so that my dick rubbed against her body, trying to lessen the ache. We both let out a sound that indicated the depth of our arousal.

I wasn't going to fuck her.

But I'd never wanted anything more.

Instead I continued to dry hump against her belly while fingering her cunt. I added another finger, curling them to search out that hard to find sweet spot. The second I found it I knew. Holly couldn't control her body's reaction as it clenched around my fingers and she let out a cry. I heard her mumble, "God, yes," breathlessly, and decided to focus on the patch of nerves to send her flying while I continued to grind myself against her.

Her whimpers and moans and the sound of her breathing turning harsh revealed that she was getting close. The ache in my balls, the way they tightened, warned me that I could easily come. I added a third finger and began to fuck her fast and hard, using my thumb to rub and press against her swollen clit. Christ, she was wet and hot, her body squeezing my fingers tightly. Her hips moved, seeking my thrusts. Needing more friction against my dick, I pressed down on her back until I thought I was going to break my fucking dick off.

The feeling was worth the pain.

Our breathing sounded loud and uncontrolled in the room as we chased orgasms that promised to be intense and gratifying. The telltale tingle at the base of my spine, the swelling of my dick, and I knew I was going to blow. I pinched Holly's clit and curled my fingers once more into those sensitive nerves. "Come for me, Baby!" I demanded in loud pants. "Now!"

I grunted, and then groaned as my dick erupted and I filled my pants with cum. Holly cried out seconds later, convulsing around my fingers and soaking them with her cream. We were both a mess, riding out the overwhelming wave of ecstasy that kept fire in our blood. My whole fucking body felt like a live wire with my release, and my heart was pounding hard.

Fuck, I'd needed that, but I needed more. We'd been fighting the fucking Knights every night for a week, and I'd not found any relief the way that my brothers had. They'd given me a hard time about it, too, noticing that I hadn't taken up with any of the club girls. Holly and I were in a bad place right now, but if I fucked one of the girls I'd have to admit that it was really over.

I wasn't ready to do that yet.

As I felt Holly's body relax against me, I withdrew my fingers. Her soft moan indicated that she was still sensitive. "Don't fall asleep," I teased.

"I won't."

Fuck, was she crying? I withdrew my hand from between her legs and pulled her into a sitting position on my lap. Her hair was in her face, and I brushed it aside so I could see her. Diamonds sparkled in her eyes. Some had fallen down her cheeks. My eyes were drawn to the trembling of her mouth. She must have been chewing on it, because her bottom lip was swollen. My gut clenched. Was this because of that fucking job? I couldn't understand why it was affecting her so strongly. Sure, it sucked that she'd lost it, but it was just a job. "I'll find the asshole who called Crickets."

She shook her head vigorously. "No, Sax, it's not just that." She glanced up to look into my eyes. "I'm crying because of everything," she said passionately. "I never thought my selfishness and making one, stupid mistake would turn into such a fucking mess!" She sucked in a broken breath. "I miss...*us!*" she whisper yelled.

I didn't know what to say. Christ, I'd had my fair share of fuck-ups too, and I'd owned them by accepting the consequences and taking the punishment. It seemed that Holly was doing just that, and suffering, too. I wished things could have been different, but making the decision to go off birth control when she'd known how I felt about having kids was a tough pill to swallow, and if Ava turned out to be someone else's I wasn't sure if I could ever forgive her.

One thing I did know—reminding her that she'd been the one to break if off between us wouldn't accomplish anything. We both knew why she'd done it now. If she'd talked to me in the beginning things might have been different, but I could understand why she'd been afraid to and had run instead. She would have had to admit after the sexual assault that she'd gone off the pill. At least she hadn't decided to never say anything and try to pawn off someone else's kid on me.

"Do you think you can ever forgive me?"

"Forgive, in time, yeah. Trust?" That was a whole other issue. "Not sure. I'm being honest with you, Holly. You were the one person I trusted above everyone else."

"You'll never know how sorry I am." Holly slipped off my lap and pulled up her shorts.

I had an idea. "Enough with the 'sorry,'" I said, releasing a loud breath and standing up. "Now we deal with the fallout and move on, yeah?"

Our gazes clung for a minute. I was so close to grabbing her to me and offering her the comfort that I sensed she needed that I moved quickly to get a pair of clean pants out of my dresser and then disappeared into the bathroom.

When I returned, I was surprised to see Holly standing in the same spot I'd left her. She'd straightened up her clothes and she still had that flushed, just-fucked-look on her face, even though we hadn't actually fucked. I gave her a questioning look, sensing that she had something to say.

She took a deep breath. "I know I don't have any business asking, but has there been anyone else since . . . since we broke up?"

It was none of her business, she was right. But I had the impression that if I didn't answer her, she would crumble. I glared at her for a long minute, trying to decide if I wanted to be honest or leave her with doubts. But I couldn't willingly hurt her. When renewed tears began to fill her eyes, I realized that she'd taken my hesitation as a "yes."

"No," I said sharply.

The relief on her face was instant, and she began to breathe again. Her bottom lip quivered, and when she drew it into her mouth, I knew that it was her way of holding back the tears. I resisted the urge to go to her and take her into my arms to give her the comfort I sensed she needed. I couldn't give her what she wanted right then, the wound was still too raw, the anger still too deep.

We had shit to work out.

I turned and walked to the door.

"Sax."

With my hand on the doorknob, I stopped and glanced back at her. Holly looked almost shy as she offered, "If you need a place to sleep, this bed is big enough for the two of us to share."

So many thoughts filled my head with her words. My dick obviously liked the idea if the tingling was any indication, but I knew that Holly wasn't offering sex. With the clubhouse full, it left me with little options to lay my head. I'd been using Goldie's room while she shared with another brother or one of the club girls.

Goldie was another problem that I had to take care of. She was wearing my patience thin.

"Not sure that'd be a good idea."

I left it at that, then opened the door and walked out.

Chapter 24

H olly

Later, after I'd showered and pulled myself together, I decided that I needed to seek Demon out. I knew that he'd be expecting it. I braced myself for the critical looks I would get as I headed down the stairs, but most who were still around ignored me, other than a few brief glances. It was as if the whole incident had never happened. Thank God, because I didn't think I could take the smirks or snide remarks that usually followed a confrontation involving one of the members. I had to wonder if Sax had said something. I searched the room, but didn't see him. I didn't see Demon either.

My gaze lit on the cluster of old ladies that I hung around with. As I walked their way, I received looks mixed with encouragement, understanding, and amusement. I couldn't help smiling as I neared them.

"Are you walking a little funny?" Raven giggled, her eyes dancing.

At first I thought she'd guessed that Sax had given me an orgasm, but then I realized that she was referring to the spanking. I reached back and smoothed my hand over one cheek. "Not my finest moment," I breathed, referring to my outburst. "Sax has never, um, spanked me before."

Laughter burst out from Bobbie and Ellie, but it was JoJo who practically shouted, "You've never been spanked?!"

Several heads turned our way. I gave JoJo a glare. "Would you hold it down, please?" I scolded, slightly embarrassed. "And yes, I've been spanked, just not in anger."

"Sax didn't look so angry when he came down the stairs. In fact, he looked kind of satisfied."

I rolled my eyes at Bobbie's comment, not about to respond one way or the other.

"Are you okay, honey?"

I gave Annie an appreciative smile and nodded. "Yeah." I took a breath. "I just need for lockdown to be over." I wanted to get on with my life.

"We all want that," Raven sighed.

I sank to the floor and pulled Ava into my arms. She smelled so good, and I couldn't resist the desire to bury my nose into the little rolls around her neck and nuzzle her, breathing in deep. When I expelled a breath she giggled and buried her hands into my hair as if to hold me there. "Were you a good girl, honey?"

"She's teething," JoJo remarked.

I nodded. "Yeah, I know. Isn't it kind of early?"

JoJo glanced to Ellie for an answer. Ellie shrugged. "Don't look at me. How would I know when babies are supposed to start getting teeth? Izzy was about eight-months-old when she got her first one. I think when it's time, it's time."

JoJo frowned. "Has she been keeping you up at night?"

"No, but she's been whinny and drooling a lot. Maybe I should get her in to the doctor." I put Ava over my shoulder and began to pat her back.

"Honey, if anything was wrong with her, she'd be a screaming banshee and would probably have a temperature."

Raven burst out laughing at Ellie's comment. "This coming from someone who took her baby to the emergency room for an ear infection that turned out to be baby powder?!"

Ellie shot Raven a scowl. "The inside of her ears were white!" she snapped in her defense. "Wait until you're a first time mother."

"Calm down, honey," JoJo hushed in a smooth tone. "The first time I ran Samuel to the doctor was when his umbilical cord fell. I was worried too much had come off. Turns out he has an innie, not an outie like me and Oz."

"You both have outies?" Bobbie asked with surprise. "Outies are rare."

"What? No way!" Annie laughed, waving Bobbie off. "How would you know that?"

"I'm more than just a pretty face," Bobbie joked. "Besides, in high school I had to do an essay in biology for extra credit because I was failing. My teacher said she wanted me to choose a unique topic, so I picked innie vs outie bellybuttons."

"Boy, that must have been a riveting paper." I smirked. "Did you pass?"

SAX

Bobbie's mouth turned down at the corners. "Apparently an essay is more than a hundred words." Everyone laughed. "But she gave me another chance, so yes, I passed with a high D." This resulted in more laughter all around.

Ava seemed content on my shoulder. Every so often I inhaled her scent deeply into my lungs, and the world was right again. I caught Raven watching me with a big smile on her face, her hand rubbing her baby bump. She was positively glowing in her pregnancy. I remembered those days. Despite everything else that was happening in my life at the time, being pregnant had been the happiest time of my life.

"So, I take it the job with Crickets fell through?"

I gave Bobbie a nod. "Yeah. Someone called representing me and told them I was no longer interested."

"And they said their name was Sax?" JoJo inquired, arranging some blocks with Samuel. "Talk about a coincidence! Two men called Sax in the same city." Her tone was skeptical.

"Yeah. He swears it wasn't him. He's going to find out who it was."

"Sounds like someone who doesn't like you, honey, someone who wants to cause you grief." I couldn't disagree with Annie.

"Have you pissed off anyone lately?"

"Not on purpose," I snorted. "But..." I cut myself off, unwilling to put my suspicions into words. I didn't want to cause any more trouble.

"But?" Raven encouraged.

I set Ava down in front of me, holding her hands to help her balance sitting up. "I'm afraid to say. I don't have any proof. And it's just a feeling."

"What is it, honey?"

I chewed on my bottom lip. I could hear the concern in Raven's voice. It matched the worry in her eyes. I really didn't want to start anything, especially if it turned out that my suspicions were wrong. I let go of Ava's hands and watched her wobble to keep from falling.

"If it's someone in the club, we should know about it."

I laughed at Bobbie's attempt to get me to open up. "You're just nosey bitches," I joked. I looked around to see who might be listening, but it seemed like everyone was minding their own business. I shrugged and spoke low. "It's just a feeling, but when I was going off on Sax, I noticed a, um, *look*

159

on Goldie's face that seemed a little, I don't know, suspicious to me. As if she was pleased with herself over something."

Annie leaned in as if she didn't want anyone outside of the group to overhear. "You think she had someone call Crickets posing as Sax?"

Before I could answer Bobbie hissed, "I wouldn't put anything past that bitch. She's been sleeping her way through the guys, and it doesn't matter if they're taken or not. I caught her coming on to Demon the other day and tore her a new one. Made it clear that she needed to keep her fucking hands off my man."

"I don't know," JoJo said in a thoughtful tone. "She's been clinging to Sax like a leech. If she wanted you out of the way, she wouldn't do something to keep you around."

That was true. But doubt still lingered.

"Did you mention this to Sax?" Raven questioned.

I shook my head, remembering that Sax had told me that said he hadn't been with anyone else since we'd broken up. "Like I said, it was just a thought, and he's going to look into it."

"Speak of the devil—I mean 'bitch.'"

I turned in the direction of Ellie's gaze and saw Goldie coming down the stairs with Loco. She was clinging to him, which seemed to be her MO, as if they were a loving couple instead of a club girl with a satisfied customer. I shook my head with disgust. Loco chose that time to catch my eye and grinned, shooting me a wink. He was such a man-whore, but I couldn't help but return his smile.

"Who's doing dinner tonight?" It was getting close to that time again.

"The club girls are doing the honors tonight." Ellie gently ran her fingers through her daughter's soft curls while the toddler slept, splayed out on her folded legs.

"If I know Lulu, she'll most of the work. The others don't put any effort into anything but fucking." There was bitterness in JoJo's tone.

"I wish Lulu would see that she's way too good to be a club slut," Raven murmured. "She's so sweet and giving, and she would make a great old lady."

"Too late for that." This came from Bobbie. "You know these men won't make anyone who's slept with his brothers an old lady."

SAX

No one mentioned the fact that Bobbie had come to the club as a club girl, but Demon had taken a liking to her from the start, so none of his brothers would sleep with her. Demon hadn't known that at the time. It had turned into a big mess, but it all worked out in the end.

"I think she was in a bad place when she first came here," JoJo quipped.

"Well, it's their loss," Ellie spoke up. "I bet if she were to leave here or find someone outside the club that one of these jerks would be sorry they didn't make a move on her."

I nodded, believing the same thing. But which brother would it be? Certainly not Loco, he liked variety, and swore he'd never be pinned down. Chewy didn't seem to give her a second thought, unless he was in the mood. Snake? Spider? Dancer? For a while she'd been fond of LD, but that hadn't worked out.

Raven sighed. "Guess time will tell."

I saw Cherry, Mitzi, and Lulu heading toward the kitchen, minus Goldie. I searched the bar and found her rubbing all over Snake. Did she think by keeping herself busy with the men that she was going to get out of helping with the food? It wasn't my place to speak up.

"Huh!" Once JoJo got everyone's attention, she nodded toward the table where Goldie and Snake were making out. "Guess she thinks she's too good to help the others with dinner." Disgust was thick in her voice.

Bobbie immediately stood up.

"Where are you going?" Ellie asked, her eyes growing wide.

"To remind that bitch that she's here for more than sucking dick."

As the president's old lady, Bobbie had every right to say something to Goldie. In fact, all the old ladies did, but they rarely used their power. Bobbie stormed over to the table and put her hands on her hips. Whatever she said broke Goldie and Snake up. I wished I could hear what was going on, but I smiled anyway, knowing that Bobbie wouldn't hold back. Judging from Goldie's expression, she wasn't intimidated by whatever Bobbie was saying and looked ready to mouth off to her, until the door opened and Demon walked in. It was as if someone had flipped a light switch, and suddenly her expression softened and became more receptive to Bobbie's interruption.

Demon, seeing his old lady confronting a club girl, pivoted in their direction. He put his arm over Bobbie's shoulder but remained silent, letting

Bobbie handle the situation. Within seconds Goldie scooted off Snake's lap and disappeared into the kitchen. Demon whispered something down at Bobbie, and gave her ass a hard slap before walking away.

"I'm not sure I want to eat anything she's had a hand in," Raven murmured worriedly.

"That was epic!" Annie whisper yelled when Bobbie returned. "Even though we couldn't hear what was being said."

Bobbie sat down, a satisfied smirk on her beautiful face. "That one's trouble."

"I think we can all agree on that." Ava was giving me signs that she was getting hungry by trying to stuff her fist into her mouth. "I think I'll take Ava upstairs and feed her, give her a bath."

"You'll be back down for dinner?"

I nodded at Raven. "I have nowhere else to go." I got to my feet, pulling Ava up with me, and sighed. "Can't wait for lockdown to be over."

Three days later, I got my wish. By the time Tuesday rolled around, lockdown was over and I was on my way home.

Sax hadn't taken up my offer to share his bed, and the knowledge that he was pulling away from me was crushing. But what had I expected? He was a prideful, alpha male who'd been wronged by someone that he'd trusted. He'd been gone from the club more than he was there, as were most of his brothers, and if any of the old ladies knew what they'd been up to, they'd kept it to themselves. I only knew how the men looked when they returned, their eyes dead their faces haggard.

They hadn't been out there having fun.

I carried Ava through the front door of our little house, took one look, and then released a breath of relief. Apart from for the dust, everything looked the same, as if we'd left long enough to go shopping and had come right back home. I set her down in the playpen and returned to the car to retrieve our bags. As I went to close the trunk I happened to glance across the road, and nearly had heart failure.

There on the shoulder was a man leaning casually against his bike, arms crossed, and legs crossed at the angles. He was watching me, a slight smile on his clean-shaven jaw.

Who was he?

SAX

How had I not heard his approach?

Had he been there all along, and I just hadn't seen him when I'd pulled in?

My gaze flickered over his attire. His cut revealed that he was in a club, but I wasn't close enough to make out which one. For the first time I felt the isolation of where I lived, the fear of being all alone out here. My eyes darted to the door as I wondered if I could outrun him if I had to. So far, he hadn't made a move.

And then he did.

Chapter 25

S ax
    The first thing out of Bull's mouth when I answered my phone was, "Got eyes on Holly, Brother."

A breath of relief escaped me as I realized I wouldn't have to worry about her and Ava now that they'd left the clubhouse. "Thanks, Brother. Who?"

"Frenchie. Been a prospect for a year. Good man."

I didn't like the sound of his name, considering how some of us got our road names. "Frenchie?" I frowned. "Do I want to know?"

Bull snorted. The fucker. "Doubt it."

"You trust him?"

"Wouldn't put him on her if I didn't."

The background noise I heard revealed that he wasn't at the clubhouse. "Where the fuck are you?"

"Morning Glory. My uncle's nursing home."

"Thought he was in Wells."

Bull snorted. "I moved him to Vegas when I became enforcer for LD, Brother."

That made sense. I knew his uncle was the only family that Bull had. The man had been in poor health for years. Heart problems, if memory served me correctly. I had to give Bull credit for seeing to his care.

"How's he doing?"

"Good. Now. Had a heart attack a few months ago, almost lost him. Was in intensive care for a week. Hates being in a wheelchair, but it doesn't keep him from getting around and hitting on all the nurses." There was a smile in his voice.

I'd never met his uncle, but I could picture the old coot riding up and down the hallways with a leering grin on his whiskered face, bothering anyone he came across just because he was cantankerous and lonely.

"Glad to hear it, Brother."

"Frenchie will be on Holly days. Jolly and Morton nights."

I frowned. "Why two?"

"Hell, you been out to her place? It's isolated as shit, and pitch black out there at night. Don't want a brother falling asleep, so LD suggested two."

If LD had ordered it I wasn't going to question it. He knew what Holly meant to me. Now that he had an old lady, something none of us had ever expected would happen, he was in a more understanding place with regard to brothers and their women. He was protective as fuck over Jolene.

"How long you and Holly gonna keep this shit up?"

"'Till it's over, Brother." I kept my answer short, my tone making it clear that I really didn't want to discuss it. Hell, we could talk all day about fighting, fucking, and killing, but none of us wanted to talk about our personal feelings involving our women.

Bull snorted, but was smart enough to let it drop. "What are we telling her when she asks why she has a prospect on her?"

"Nothing. She's been with the club long enough to figure shit out on her own. She knows we've been involved in some shit lately, big enough to go on lockdown. She'll figure out that there are still loose ends that need taking care of."

"Loose ends," meaning Radar, the last remaining Dunlap brother who was a club member and still out there. We knew that we hadn't taken out all the fucking Knights, but all of the key players making the decisions were gone. After the shit that had gone down with Toledo, the Knights had fallen like dominoes. Between Vegas Watchdogs and us, we'd ambushed two more meetings they'd set up with their suppliers in flesh and weapons, letting their contacts live with the warning that they they would be consequences if they chose to do any more business with the Knights.

Word in our world spread fast.

"Got church, Bro. I'll check in with Frenchie later to make sure introductions went smoothly."

"Thanks." I slipped my phone back in my pocket and followed my brothers as we headed toward the meeting room for our own church.

Demon was already at the head of the table with a huge ass cup of coffee sitting in front of him. Our president looked strained and dog-tired. Long nights and longer days had taken a toll on all of us, but at least now we could breathe a little better knowing that our sacrifices had not been for nothing. Unfortunately, we'd lost three soldiers during the shootouts that had occurred, but every single one of us understood that we could forfeit our lives on any given day.

We took our places at the table, and the last brother into the room closed the door. Someone let out a long groan. Mental exhaustion was just as draining as physical, and it was obvious from the expressions on some of my brothers' faces that they'd been pushed to their limit. I felt it too, but none of us would complain. We'd done what we had to to take care of our MC and our families.

Demon cut right to the chase, swinging his eyes to where Cole was sitting beside him. "Anything on Radar?"

Cole's mouth took on an unpleasant twist as he shook his head. "Nothing."

"Fuck!" Demon swore, pounding the table with his fist. "I want that fucker found!"

"Know it, Prez," Cole growled back. "Got eyes on the house now."

"Fuck, we all want to find Radar!" I reminded Demon, drawing his eyes to me. He glared at me for a minute, and I could tell that he was about to explode with frustration. "Want this shit done with."

"Anyone tried talking to the mother?"

"We killed four of her sons, dumbass," Loco said matter-of-factly, earning him the finger from Chewy. "Not there to talk, there to watch."

"We'll keep tails on our old ladies until he's found and put in the ground." My mind immediately went to Holly and Ava.

"Have all the girls we rescued been taken back to their homes?" Oz questioned in a serious tone.

Over the course of a week, we'd found seven more women being held for auction. Destroying the Knights' porn studio hadn't stopped them from grabbing girls off the street or from producing more videos. We'd found proof of that in one of the houses we'd raided.

"All except one, Brother."

That was one good thing that had come out of all this—those innocent girls had gone home. At my response, Oz raised a brow inquisitively. "One of the girls is an orphan and just turned eighteen. She had nowhere to go, so she's staying here until we can figure out something."

I half-expected someone, particularly Loco, to make a crack about her becoming a club whore, but the circumstances of her situation caused him to keep his mouth shut, and no one else had anything to say.

"What about all the damage caused by those drive-bys? Are the repairs done?" Demon inquired, before taking a sip of his coffee.

Oz opened up his ledger. "The bullet holes have all been plugged, if that's what you mean."

Demon's growl warned him that he wasn't in the mood.

Oz read over the page in front of him with a slight smirk on his lips. "Had to replace windows and a mirror, some liquor. Bought a new tattoo machine. Good news is everything was covered by insurance."

"Construction site damage too?" I asked.

He nodded. "Covered under vandalism."

"Why a new tattoo machine?" Demon frowned.

The grin on Oz's face was telling. "Can we help it if that old broken machine we had in the back got struck by a bullet?"

I laughed, as did some of the others.

The look on Demon's face said he was pleased. We had top of the line equipment in our tattoo shop, so it would have been an expensive replacement. "What else?"

"Coffers are full. Still raking in the money from Crystal's Palace and Naughty Secrets. The packages and extra services we added a while back have really paid off."

"Hey, do the brothers get a discount for a night with one of the girls?"

"Loco, man, you ask this fucking question all the time. Why pay for pussy at a brothel when you can get it here free?" Snake uttered with irritation.

Loco grinned like a lecher, his eyebrows dancing. "Tired of the same old snatch."

"What about Goldie?" Dancer smirked, his blue eyes meeting Loco's across the table. "She's a tight little bitch." He spoke like a brother who knew firsthand.

Loco grimaced in humor. "Careful, Brother. I think she has an agenda."

So did I. "We're not here to discuss pussy."

Cole's eyes flashed my way. "Ya know, Brother, since you became VP you're not as fun as you used to be."

I gave him a grin and the finger. He slapped his hand over his heart as if I'd wounded him. There were a few chuckles, but it was obvious that there wasn't much energy behind them.

"Okay, okay," Demon interrupted, leaning forward and steepling his fingers. "Sax is right. Let's get back on track." He yawned. "Shit. Getting too fucking old for all these late nights. Let's hope things stay quiet for a while. Keep your eyes and ears open for signs of Radar and anyone still wearing their colors."

Heads nodded in response.

"Proud of you brothers. Now get the fuck out of here. I'm going home to my woman, gonna sleep for a fucking week."

He was lucky to be going home to Bobbie. Shit, I'd once had that with Holly. Going home to her had made the day's shit that I'd faced worth it. Now I just went to my room here and kicked back.

As everyone but Cole and I got to their feet and headed toward the door, I leaned back in my chair and stretched. I'd heard from Holly after she'd gone home that the DNA kit had arrived in the mail. I wanted to get that test done yesterday.

Demon looked us over. "Church is over, Brothers."

Nodding, I said, "I'm going to take a ride to Vegas. Holly has the DNA kit. Need to go give her a sample."

"You want Ava to be yours?"

I wasn't surprised by Demon's question, only that it had taken him this long to finally ask. My gaze flicked to Cole. The man was happy as a pig in shit that his old lady was going to have his baby, but I couldn't dredge up the same enthusiasm over the possibility of being a father. Unwelcome flashbacks had haunted me lately, ever since I'd come back and found out that Holly had a kid. I wasn't sure how I was going to react when I finally found out the truth, because I was fucking scared.

Scared that Ava was mine.

Scared that she wasn't.

"Don't know how I'm supposed to feel, Prez."

"A baby shouldn't come between you and Holly." His tone was respectful.

I took a deep breath and released it slowly. "She's the one who let it, instead of facing me with the truth."

"You gonna ever forgive her?" Cole asked in a hard tone.

My head snapped his way. "Would you?"

"I love Raven, Brother. More than I've ever loved anyone. Would lay my life down for her without blinking an eye. She makes me whole. Gives me a reason for breathing. So yeah, I would forgive her. Life's too fucking short."

I clenched my teeth and looked at Demon. His expression revealed that he agreed with Cole.

"You going with him?" Demon asked Cole.

"Yeah. Figured I'd go for the ride."

"Good. Better to have backup." He rose to his feet, yawning loudly.

Cole chuckled. "Should we follow you home, old man? Make sure you get there?"

Demon's face split into a wide grin. "Fuck you, Brother. Worry about your own ass." He rubbed the whiskers over his lower jaw. "You going to come back tonight?"

"Planning on it."All I had to do was give Holly a sample, and then I would turn around and come back.

That was the plan.

Chapter 26

H olly
    I'd just put Ava down for the night when I decided it was a good time to call Samson about getting my job back at Grinders. As I waited for someone to pick up, I put my phone on speaker and quickly slipped into my sleep shorts and tank top. The thin material clung to my still-damp body. My long hair was still dripping and clinging to my skin.

"Hello?"

I recognized Candy's cheerful voice. "Hey, Candy, it's me."

"Hey!" she returned with even more enthusiasm. "We've already heard from Demon, honey. You're job is waiting for you. Samson put you back on the schedule starting tomorrow night, if you're ready."

"I'm more than ready," I confessed.

"So what happened with Crickets?" I could tell by her breathing that she was moving around, probably filling drinks.

Being reminded of Crickets pissed me off, but it wasn't Candy's fault. "It fell through. I'll tell you about it tomorrow at work."

"Okay, see you at four."

From the background noise, I could tell that she was busy. "See you then." As we disconnected, I realized that I would need to call Annabelle too. Lord, if she couldn't continue to watch Ava I didn't know what I was going to do.

I found myself in the kitchen. I would have given anything for a glass of wine, but I was still giving Ava breast milk. It wouldn't be long before she was strictly on the bottle, but I could still pump milk for her.

I opened the fridge, my gaze landing on the three full bottles before finding the water I was looking for at the back. I reached for it, changed my mind, and snatched an apple instead.

The house seemed too quiet now that Ava was asleep and the TV wasn't on. It was times like now when I was reminded of how far from it all we lived. I liked the peace and quiet, but the fact that there was a member from Desert

Rebels standing guard across the road made me nervous and hyperaware of the dangers that lurked there.

I pulled back the curtain and looked across the road, taking a bite of my apple. Frenchie had been replaced with Jolly and Morton. Both men were sitting casually on their bikes, smoking, and I had to wonder how they were going to get through the night like that. At least Frenchie had gotten a break during the day when he'd followed me to the park with Ava.

Jolly noticed me watching them from my window and waved. Smiling, I waved back, and then let the curtain fall back into place and moved away. No sooner had I turned around when I heard the sound of a motorcycle coming down the road. Frowning, I peeked out the window again.

It was Sax.

Finally! I'd texted him three days before to let him know that I had the DNA kit and needed his sample. He had said he would come later that day but had been a no-show. Not even a call to let me know that he wasn't coming. I went to the door and opened it before he had a chance to knock.

His eyes raked over me with familiarity, bringing an instant rush of heat to my core. It wasn't just a look, it was a visual caress that my entire body felt and responded to in a big way. I took a bite of my apple to hide my reaction from him.

"Sorry I'm late." He moved past me into the house. "Something came up the other day."

I closed the door. "I figured that. Still, it would have been nice if you'd called."

He turned to me, and his eyes dropped to my mouth as he watched me chew for a minute. My tongue came out to catch the sweet juice at the corner of my lip. The next thing I knew, Sax grabbed the apple out of my hand and took a bite.

"Haven't eaten today."

"It's seven o'clock."

"Know what time it is." He seemed grumpy. "Been busy." He took another bite, chewing with a slight frown between his eyes. "You walk around like that when my brothers are parked outside?"

I glanced down at myself. I was wearing a lot more clothing than I would have at the beach. My tank stopped below my breasts, revealing a strip of flesh to where my boy shorts covered up my lower half. It amused me that Sax was worried that I was giving his brothers a show. "I didn't know they had x-ray vision," I said smartly.

He grunted. "Where's Ava?"

"Down for the night." My gaze ran over him. He looked as if he'd been on the road a few days. Dirty. Tired. In a mood that said, "don't fuck with me." "You need a shower," I said, noticing that his usually pleasant scent of worn leather, smoke, and the outdoors was spiked with the sweat of a man who'd worked some long, hard hours.

"You offering?"

I blinked for a few seconds. Was he serious? He'd only come to give me a sample, but suddenly I wanted to turn it into something more. I'd missed him, even though things had been strained between us lately. Seeing him like this reminded me of all the times he'd come home in the same way he was now, needing the comfort and attention that I'd gladly given him. But in those days he would walk through the door, sweep me up into his arms for a long, hard kiss, cop a feel, and then head off to the bathroom.

"I don't mind if you want to get a shower, Sax. I can toss your clothes into the washer so you don't have to put dirty clothes back on."

I wondered what he was thinking as he stood silently staring at me. God, I wanted to see his face soften towards me like it used to. Maybe he just wanted to do what he'd come there to do and then leave. Damn. I felt the sting behind my eyes that warned me I was getting emotional.

"You got something I can put on?"

I thought about the old pair of sweats of his that I'd claimed and couldn't bear to part with. "Yes." I turned to walk away. "Leave your dirty clothes outside the bathroom door."

By the time I'd dug out the sweats and reached the bathroom door, Sax's clothes were on the floor where I'd asked him to leave them. I could hear the shower running, and I opened the door just enough to slip the sweats in and leave them on the counter by the sink. The tiny room was already steamed up with the scent of my feminine body wash, causing a smile to spread across my face.

I backed out and scooped up his clothes. I set his cut on the washer and put his clothes inside before heading to the kitchen to make him something to eat. Just like old times, and I had to admit that it felt good. I took out the hamburger that I'd defrosted for spaghetti sauce that I planned to make the next day, and made him two huge burgers. The frozen buns wouldn't take long to defrost in the microwave. By the time I'd topped his burgers off with mustard—he didn't like ketchup—lettuce, cheese, and tomato, he walked into the room, bringing with him the fresh scent of rose and vanilla.

I set his plate down on the table. "Eat."

"You didn't have to go to the trouble, but thanks. I'm starved."

We made eye contact briefly when I turned to go back to the kitchen to get him a beer. God, he was sexy, standing there in nothing but low-hanging sweats, his muscular chest and washboard abs beckoning me to reach out and touch him. My eyes followed the enticing v-shaped muscle to where it disappeared in his pelvic region, bringing attention to the prominent bulge of his cock. I didn't even try to pretend that Sax didn't affect me. His rugged handsomeness would turn any woman on, and we had too much history, Years of learning each other's bodies and giving in to the intense, mutual attraction.

By the time I set a beer down next to his plate, he'd almost finished one of the burgers. I smiled and went to the front door, opening it. "Would either of you like coffee?" I called out, loud enough so the guys across the road could hear me.

"Thanks, that'd be great!" Jolly yelled back.

"You're poking the bear, Baby."

I glanced back to see Sax's smoldering gaze run down the length of me. I rolled my eyes and returned to the kitchen to put on a pot.

"They're here to keep you and Ava safe, not for you to wait on them," Sax said before taking a drink of his beer. "Or show them your tits and ass."

That last part was said so low, I'd barely heard him. "I'm decent enough." I pulled down two cups, keeping my back to him, grinning when I felt my shorts pull up to expose more of my butt. His growl told me that he'd noticed. "And it's just coffee, Sax, it'll help keep them awake."

He didn't say anything after that, instead focusing on his second burger. I knew the minute he was done, because he released a noisy, contented sigh and sat back in his chair, a look of satisfaction on his face. His hand rubbed up and down his full belly.

"That was good."

Smiling at the domestic picture he made, I poured the coffee. "Would you like another beer?" As soon as I asked I remembered that he would have to ride back to the clubhouse, but I knew that two beers wouldn't be enough to inebriate him.

I heard his chair scoot back. "I'll get it."

Suddenly we were both in my too-small kitchen. I felt the heat of his presence behind me as I placed the two cups of coffee onto a small baking tray. I closed my eyes, his scent and warmth flooding me with the memories of how good we'd been together, while leaving me with a feeling of immense loss. I tensed when I felt his hand at the hair behind my ear. He moved it aside, and then I felt his lips against my ear.

"Seems just like old times."

I shivered as his warm breath ran over me. "I'm—"

He growled low in a threatening tone, "You say you're sorry one more time, I'm going to lose it, Baby."

I clamped my mouth shut tight and stood quivering at his closeness. Somehow I found the courage to ask, "Are you going to spank me again?"

A grunt was his response. "Check my clothes while I take the coffee out to my brothers."

I didn't even think to bitch at him for being so bossy. "Okay."

He stepped away from me and reached for the tray. Once he left the kitchen I went to put his clothes into the dryer. I stood there for a minute, gripping the corner edges of the dryer, and tried to calm the arousal rolling through me. It felt like a tidal wave that threatened to suck me under and never let me up. I wanted Sax, and not just for sex, but at this point I would take him any way that I could get him. But he'd have to make the first move. The crippling fear of rejection would keep me from acting on my desires.

I heard the door close, and then the telltale click of the lock. When the sound of Sax setting the tray down on the kitchen counter carried to me, I was finally able to move. I turned the corner to see him clearing his plate off the table and taking it to the sink. He must have sensed me there, because he turned and leaned against the sink and crossed his arms. His eyes dropped lazily down to my breasts, and I knew that he could see my nipples hardening. I knew it because I could feel the sharp tingle of them as they peaked against my thin tank.

He looked up and released a harsh breath. "Let's get this DNA shit done."

"The kit is right behind you."

He pivoted and reached for the box.

"You'll need to take four swabs of the inside of your cheek and put them in one of the sample envelopes. I've already done Ava's."

I knew that Sax had heard me, even though he was reading the box. I knew that I'd chosen a reliable kit because I'd called the doctor's office for a recommendation, and we'd have the results within a week.

Once Sax seemed satisfied with what he'd read, he swabbed the inside of his cheeks four times and placed the swabs in an envelope. As he sealed it closed, his eyes came to me.

"I'll let you know when the results come in." I smiled even though I didn't feel like it. "So, um, is all the trouble done at the club?"

"Still have loose ends to tie up. Until then, you and Ava will be watched." He crossed his arms.

"Pff, there's always loose ends. Can I ask you something?" The briefest nod of his head was my response. "What happens if—" I caught myself, afraid to put my thoughts into words, even more afraid of what his answer would be. I'd had the last four days to think about what I could expect after the test results came back. I knew that Sax was angry, maybe even hated me a little, but now that he'd showered and eaten, he appeared more approachable, easier to talk to.

Did I want to ruin the mood?

"That's a pretty open-ended question," he finally said when the silence grew between us. "You've never been afraid to speak your mind before."

The corners of my lips turned up, but it could hardly be considered a smile. "That was before, when I knew where I stood with you." I swallowed. "When I knew what I could expect."

"Just spit it out, Holly." When he said my name like that, I knew he was getting annoyed. "What's the worst that could happen, huh? Have I ever hurt you?"

I knew he didn't mean physically. Although..."You did spank me the other day."

Amusement gleamed in his eyes as he snorted loudly. "You deserved that." He paused for a second. "And it turned you on more than pissed you off."

It had turned him on, too. I felt my cheeks heat as I recalled what had followed. We'd both gotten something out of it.

"Ask your question, Baby."

What's the worst that could happen, other than hearing the truth? I sucked in a deep breath and spit it out in one breath. "What's going to happen if we find out that Ava is yours?"

There, it was out. The humor disappeared from Sax's eyes, replaced with a deep intensity that reached all the way to my soul.

He finally exhaled a heavy breath and lowered his arms. "Are you asking for Ava, or are you asking for you?"

"For both of us," I answered truthfully.

He shrugged. "Told you I'd take care of any kid of mine."

Yes, he had, financially, but not emotionally. I knew something had happened to Sax when he was a child, something terrible, something so traumatizing that he couldn't, or *wouldn't*, talk about it. He'd never alluded to anything, it was just a strong feeling that I had. It wasn't just that he didn't want children—he was *scared* of having them. And to see a man like Sax scared of something was frightening in itself.

As we stood there, eyes locked, I could see the fear in his now. Even his big, strong body, his bad ass biker persona, couldn't disguise the raw emotion of pain. I knew him too well. His silent suffering broke my heart. I wanted to help him, but in the past, he'd shut me out any time that we'd discussed having children.

The kitchen island was between us. I moved closer to it, closer to him. So far Sax hadn't moved from where he was casually leaning against the sink, looking relaxed, when I knew he was anything but.

"What exactly does that mean, Sax?" I wanted to hear the words. "If Ava's your daughter, are you going to be around for her? Are you going to be part of her life?"

A muscle twitched in his jaw. His eyes narrowed on me, and I knew he wasn't happy being backed into a corner. "Not going to discuss this now when it could be for nothing."

SAX

His cold response made me so angry. And sad. *He* didn't want to talk about it? Tears filled my eyes when I thought about my precious daughter asleep in her crib. "Maybe it would be better if it turns out that Ava isn't yours," I mumbled without thinking. Sax's mouth tightened a fraction more, showing his displeasure. I watched the play of emotions move over his face, instantly sorry for what I'd said.

"I didn't mean that," I said sincerely.

He surprised me by saying, "I know."

Chapter 27

Sax

I was afraid to move from my spot against the sink. Holly looked so damned sexy in her tiny sleep shorts and tank, all of her curves on display, and my hands itched to touch her. If that happened, it wouldn't take long for me to have her beneath me. I might have been pissed off for the shit she'd put us through, but I couldn't seem to stop wanting her. *Needing her.* I was torn, because I wanted to fuck her as much as I wanted to punish her.

I could tell from the look in her watchful eyes that she still wanted me. I wondered if she would still feel the same if I told her the truth. The difference between my secret and hers was that mine wouldn't hurt anyone. It was all mine. I'd lived it, I'd survived it. And it wasn't lost on me that I'd let it fester like a cancer inside that wouldn't go away.

"Would you like anything else?"

A loaded question. There was a nervous little smile on her face. And was that an invitation in her eyes? Fuck, yeah. She was aroused and fighting it. Her little nipples were hard as pebbles and pointed in my direction, taunting me to taste them. I was willing to bet that she was wet, too. My dick reacted to that enticing thought. I'd never had to work hard at making Holly wet for me. I wished I were strong enough to walk away, but fuck if I didn't want to slide between her legs and lose myself in her sweet pussy.

The dryer buzzer went off, and Holly used that to make her escape. She spun around and disappeared around the corner. I ground my back teeth and closed my eyes, begging the powers that be for strength to ignore the sharp pull between us, but the hunger only grew. I needed to get dressed and get the hell out of there.

"God, give me strength!" I muttered in a harsh whisper, and then I pounded my fist against the cupboard door with frustration. My dick was in full fuck mode now and demanding that I do something about it. I moved briskly through the kitchen and rounded the corner in time to see Holly folding my pants. When our eyes met there was no stopping me, and I could tell that she didn't want me to. She didn't move as I moved up behind her and boxed her in with my arms.

I pressed my aching dick into her fleshy bottom with a savage groan. "God, help me, I can't stop wanting you."

A little moan escaped her as she rubbed her ass against my throbbing cock. "I want you, too, Sax." Her breathy words were full of barely suppressed emotion. I could feel her trembling against me. "I—"

"No talking." I mouthed the words against her ear. I wanted to wrap myself around her tight little body and lose myself in the feeling, make the last year disappear and have things go back to where they'd been before. I wrapped my arm around her waist and held her tightly against me, letting her feel the strength of my arousal. I groaned low, my thighs quivering as I dry humped her, knowing that it would never be enough.

Her whimpers revealed her pleasure at what I was doing to her. Her tantalizing scent was like a drug to me, and I ran my tongue up the side of her neck until I could take her ear into my mouth. I ran my mouth over it, nibbling behind the lobe, where I knew she was sensitive. Her gasp caused me to smile as I moved her hair and continued to the back of her neck. Not enough skin. I needed more. I took the material of her tank in my hands and ripped it open down the back.

"Sax!" she whisper yelled, trembling.

But I knew it turned her on when I lost control.

I pulled the ruined tank off her completely, easily keeping her pinned against the dryer where I wanted her. Then I kissed my way over her shoulders and down her back to the sexy as fuck dimples where her pelvis and spine met above her ass. Her shorts were next to go with a single tug. I took a moment to appreciate the full, mouthwatering globes of her ass. Taking them in my hands, I squeezed them roughly, drawing a loud moan out of her.

Grinning with satisfaction, I bit each cheek, hearing her breath catch. She jerked forward, but there was nowhere for Holly to go, pinned against the dryer. I loved her ass, but right now I needed her juicy cunt. I flipped her around, which put her bare mound right in front of my face. Hands on her hips, my eyes flew up to hers. She was panting and watching me closely, and the minute I snaked my tongue out to touch her clit, she rolled her head back and groaned and went into a full-bodied shudder.

Christ, she was soaked with her juices. The sweet taste of her exploded on my tongue and I lost control. I clenched my hands into the cheeks of her ass and ground her pussy against my mouth, using my tongue, lips, and teeth to drive her wild. I parted her folds, licked her labia, and speared her deep with my tongue, slurping up her thick nectar.

"Yes, Sax!" Holly panted. Her hands fell upon my shoulders as her hips gyrated into my administrations. The harder I fucked her with my mouth, the louder her breathing became, and then her hands were in my hair, her nails raking over my scalp. "Oh!"

I growled, sinking two fingers in her as I worked her swollen clit. Locating her sweet spot, I curled my fingers against it mercilessly, holding Holly up when her legs started to buckle. "You like that, Baby?" I asked roughly, already knowing the answer.

"God, yes! Don't stop!"

The thought never crossed my mind. "You want to come on my tongue?"

She whimpered breathlessly. "Yes!" Her hands clenched in my hair. "So close!"

"Soon as you come on my tongue, I'm going to give you another orgasm on my dick," I grated, my breath seesawing. My dick and balls were so full they hurt. I could feel pre-cum running out of my slit. "Can't wait to get my dick inside your tight pussy, Baby."

Holly cried out her release, but quickly bit down on her bottom lip to cut the sound off. Her hips thrust convulsively, pounding her swollen cunt in my face. I fucked her through her orgasm, wanting to get every fucking drop of her sweet cream.

"Oh, God..."

I barely gave her time to come down before I stood and pulled my sweats down below my dick and balls. My dick bobbed up strongly between us, slapping against Holly's thighs. When I lifted her she automatically wrapped her legs around me. I pushed her against the opposite wall and reached for my dick. "This is going to be fast," I grated, lining it up and slamming home.

We both sounded out our pleasure as I bottomed out inside her. "Like coming home," I rasped against her ear. I took a moment to enjoy the feel of her body squeezing me, the hot wetness surrounding my aching flesh. "So fucking tight." I pulled out to the tip and thrust back in again. "So fucking hot." I repeated the action, plowing in so deep that I hit her cervix. Holly took in a ragged breath and bit down on my shoulder.

I grunted and kept going, aiming for her cervix each time. We had discovered a long time ago that Holly was able to experience a full-bodied, intense orgasm by stimulating her cervix with deep penetration. She didn't achieve it every time but, when she did it all but knocked her the fuck out. Either way, I was going to pound her into a climax. Using the wall for support, I ran my hands up and down her body, settling on her spectacular tits. I leaned back enough to take one into my mouth, sucking and nipping at it until my whiskers chafed her flesh red and her nipple was swollen. Holly's hands were twisted in my hair, holding me against her as she offered up her other tit for the same attention.

I willingly moved on to the next fleshy delicacy, and dropped my hand to her pussy, zeroing in on her clit. I picked up my pace, pistoning into her fast and hard. Her swollen folds squeezed me tight. My balls were full and tight, and I was ready to blow my load. The tickle at the base of my spine and my tensing muscles warned me that I'd reached the point of no return.

"Sax..." The desperation in her husky tone revealed that Holly was getting close, too. Her panting was climbing and choppy, her tits heaving against me.

I slipped my hands under her bottom and squeezed, urging her to let go. At the same time I made sure our loins were grinding and creating the friction that would heighten the experience for both of us. "Open your eyes," I demanded. I wanted to watch her come apart. "I want you to see who's fucking you," I said between breaths. "I want you to come on my dick and know it's my cum filling you."

Her eyes were wide in her flushed face, puffs of air escaped between her parted lips. A steamy sweat covered us both. The air that surrounded us was heavy with the thick fog of sex. Fuck, I didn't want to stop. It felt too fucking good, but the signs were there, reminding me of how fucking good it felt to come undone inside Holly, feeling her body squeeze mine until she'd milked my balls dry.

"Fuck, Baby." I slammed into her again and again. "Come."

Her breathing increased and then she crashed with sweet release. I cut her scream off with my mouth and followed right behind her, my dick erupting full force deep inside her. Every clench of her body around my cock dragged a rugged grunt from me. My hands tightened on her hips. It would be a miracle if I didn't leave bruises.

"Oh, God...oh, God...oh, God..." Holly chanted, still twitching uncontrollably against me.

I swung her away from the wall and headed toward the only other door in the house. Her bedroom was dark except for the night light next to the crib on the opposite side of the room. I aimed for the bed, following her down as I gently lowered her onto it. My dick was still twitching inside her. My weight fell against her damp body, weakness overtaking my limbs. As I struggled for air I was aware of her hands smoothing down my backside in a gesture that soothed much more than my spent body.

"Shit, Babe," I rasped when I was able to speak again. "I needed that." I felt Holly's smile against my shoulder. "As much as I want to hate you, I just can't. I love you too fucking much."

We both seemed to realize the gravity of what I'd just admitted at the same time. We stiffened against each other, as if afraid to breathe or move. Afraid to believe the words. I hadn't meant to say them, but I wouldn't take them back now. It was how I felt, and as I slowly cooled down and my dick softened, it hit me like a brick. I was tired of denying myself what I really wanted. Tired of being without her.

Holly had broken us apart, but I was going to bring us back together.

She sniffled beneath me, and I knew that she was crying. I pulled back to meet her eyes and brushed the wet hair out of her face. "Don't cry, Baby. We'll work it out." No truer words had I ever spoken. For my sanity we had to.

"How?" she asked hoarsely. "Because of me it'll never be the same between us." She wasn't seeking forgiveness from me, just stating a fact.

"Not the same," I agreed, kissing her softly. "Better." God, it had to be. "Not going to happen overnight, Baby. It's going to take time and work. I have some issues to work through."

She nodded up at me, her lashes sparkling with tears. When she tugged her bottom lip into her mouth, I leaned down and kissed where her teeth were cutting into it. An unexpected feeling of peace came over me. Maybe this is what I'd needed all along—to make a decision about where we were going. I wasn't ready to forgive Holly, but I wasn't going to let my pride and stubbornness keep us apart any longer.

"What about Ava?"

I let out a resigned breath. "She's part of you." I couldn't say much more than that.

I wasn't sure Holly was ready for the truth.

Chapter 28

H olly
    It was dark when I opened my eyes, but I sensed that it was early morning. Something had awakened me, some sound. It didn't surprise me that I was completely naked. Sax and I had made love several times during the night until we'd depleted our energy and fallen into a sex-induced sleep, wrapped around each other. At some point he must have pulled the covers over us, but I didn't remember moving once I was out.

I lay there for a minute, staring up at the ceiling and taking stock of the delicious aches in my body. My breasts and nipples were tender where Sax had rubbed his whiskers over them and were dotted with love bites. I touched my still swollen pussy, smiling when it felt bruised and well used. I was so wet and sticky down there, some of our mixed bodily fluids dried on the inside of my thighs. It crossed my mind that if Sax was going to continue to fuck me without using protection I needed to get back on birth control. Hopefully it wasn't already too late.

I didn't know what his reaction would be if I turned up pregnant again. I wouldn't have minded having another baby, but I knew that another pregnancy right now would jeopardize our fragile relationship. We needed time.

For the first time in a long time, I felt as if things between us were going to be okay. Sax had admitted that he loved me and wanted to work things out, but I'd heard the caution in his voice. He had doubts, and I could understand that. I wasn't going to rush anything. I had a lot of making up to do to build his trust in me again.

A sucking sound brought me out of my musings. Frowning, I instinctively glanced in the direction of the crib. My heart almost stopped at the sight of Sax rocking Ava while giving her a bottle. It was the last thing I had expected to see, and I couldn't take my eyes off them. Sax looked like a natural. Ava was bundled up in a blanket in his arms against his naked chest, staring up at him without fear or confusion as she sucked down her first bottle of the day.

My heart swelled with a strange mixture of love and worry. I was afraid to move, afraid to break the spell. What had made him decide to get up and take care of her? If she'd made any sounds, I hadn't even heard her, which just went to show how worn out I'd been. I waited to see what Sax was going to do after Ava finished drinking. Would he know enough to burp her?

He set her bottle down on the floor and surprised me when he placed Ava over his shoulder. He must have watched JoJo or Ellie do that with their babies. I kept a receiving blanket draped over the crib for spit-up emergencies and should have warned him to put it over his shoulder, but I remained silent. Some things he had to learn for himself.

"Burp it up, little girl." He patted Ava gently on her back, bringing a smile to my face.

She was usually a good burper, and in no time a big gurgle exploded from her little mouth. Recognizing the signs that she was about to spit up, I quickly said, "Sax—" but it was already too late. Ava spewed milk all down his back, and I had a second of regret for not suggesting the blanket earlier.

"Shit!" he said on a surprised laugh, jumping to his feet.

Giggling, I quickly left the bed and went to them. "I give you credit for not throwing her," I joked. I took Ava from him, grabbed the receiving blanket, and wiped her mouth. "Turn around."

"Did I do something wrong?"

Using the same blanket, I wiped his shoulder and back down. "Not at all. She does that sometimes, especially if she gobbled her milk down too fast."

He turned back around to me, a slight grimace on his face.

"Shit smells," he grumbled. "You slept through her crying." There was no censure in his tone, just fact.

"Guess I wore your ass out," he said with a cocky grin.

He'd slipped back into his sweats. I gazed downward where his cock was nestled behind the soft material and showing signs of hardening. A mild pulsing between my thighs was my body's natural response. With Ava in between falling asleep and being awake, I decided it would be best to ignore what our libidos wanted until she made up her mind about what she was going to do.

There was nothing worse than starting something and not being able to finish.

I was curious. "How did you know that she wanted a bottle?"

He shrugged. "She was sucking on her fist when I came over to check on her. Figured at this age she either eats, poops, or sleeps." He turned his head and took a deep whiff of his shoulder, and then made a face.

"You'll probably want to get a shower," I laughed. "Or you'll smell like sour milk all day." It looked as if Ava was going to keep to her schedule of sleeping another hour after her morning bottle. As her eyes closed, I placed her back in her crib.

When I turned from laying her down I caught my breath at the arousal blazing in Sax's watchful eyes. I'd forgotten that I was naked, and suddenly all of my senses were heightened with awareness of him. He looked as if he wanted to devour me, and the next thing I knew he wrapped an arm around my waist and pulled me sharply against him. I gasped, dropping my hands against his warm chest.

"Are you too sore for my dick?" he growled down at me with a thrust of his hips.

I was sore, but it was a pleasant ache. "Never," I whispered. I brought my arms up and circled his neck, all the invitation Sax needed to cover my lips with his.

His kiss started out slow and tender but quickly turned rough and hungry, sending spirals of ecstasy through me. My core clenched with need and I eagerly opened my mouth, and then we were using teeth, tongue, and lips to probe and nibble and taste the burning passion that always lay beneath the surface. By the time he was done ravishing my mouth, my heart was pounding wildly and I was breathless.

His hand traveled to my hair and pulled my head back, and then his mouth was against the arch of my throat, dragging a moan out of me. I grew wet and tingly between my legs, grinding my pussy against the hardness of his cloth-covered cock, needing the friction. "Sax!" I whispered sharply, overwhelmed with the need swelling through me.

"We'd better take this to another room," he grated, breathing hard.

Thank God he was in control of his senses enough to realize where we were. Ava was sleeping, but she wouldn't be for long if we continued making love next to her crib. Neither of us was exactly quiet when we were having sex.

Without warning, Sax lifted me. I wrapped my legs around him, and as he walked us to the bathroom, sucked and kissed the side of his neck.

He set me on my feet next to the shower, then reached in and turned it on. I used the break to roll his sweats down so that he could step out of them. I couldn't resist pausing long enough to give his bobbing cock a lick from the tip, where pre-cum was leaking, all the way to where his sizable shaft was rooted to his balls. A savage groan filled the bathroom, and I looked up to see intense arousal on Sax's face, a satisfied gleam smoldering in his eyes.

"Get up here, woman."

He pulled me to my feet and pushed me into the shower, following me. As soon as he had the door closed, he turned me around and pushed me against the wall. The cold tile bit into my nipples and caused me to suck in my breath.

"Spread those legs and pop that ass out," Sax demanded, his big hands grasping my hips.

I did as he asked, shaking as anticipation thrummed through my blood. My clit pulsed, and I was so turned on that I wouldn't have been surprised if I'd come from a single touch. "Fuck me, Sax!" I demanded in a loud whisper. "God, fuck me!"

I was so ready, shamelessly wagging my ass in his face to entice him to get on with it. I heard his masculine chuckle right before he ran the head of his cock up and down my slit. Damn him, he was teasing me.

"Please! I need you!" I didn't care if I sounded desperate.

I was desperate!

The head of his cock separated my folds, and then he slid into me, filling me. I released a small cry, the sound magnified in the enclosed shower. Stinging water beat down on us, surrounding us with steam. Neither of us seemed to care, too caught up in the pleasure we were giving each other.

"This what you want?"

"Yes," I grunted, each plunge of his cock slamming me up against the smooth tile. There wasn't much I could do in this position but meet his every thrust with shameless eagerness. "More!" I demanded, arching my back.

Sax grunted, his hands squeezing my hips as his speed picked up. "So tight, Baby."

I reached behind me and grabbed his balls, giving them a squeeze.

"Oh, fuck!" he shuddered. "Play with your clit."

I did as he demanded, moaning loudly at the first touch of my fingers. My clit was swollen, slick, and sensitive. It wasn't going to take me long to come, the feeling was already there, building up to what would be a climactic freefall.

"You want my cum inside you?"

His words caused a shiver to run down my spine. "God, yes!"

"Your mine, Holly. No one touches you. No one's cum but mine fills your pussy."

I could barely catch my breath, he was shoving his cock in me so fast and hard. "Yes!" I managed to get out.

"You'll have so much fucking cum inside you that every man who comes near you will know who you belong to," he rasped gutturally. "My scent will be all over you."

He scraped his teeth down my neck, over my collarbone, and stopped at my shoulder, where he added enough pressure to cause a little sting. But it was his filthy words, spoken in a growly threat, that sent me flying over the edge, hard and possessive, leaving no doubt that Sax owned me completely. Shock waves surged all through my body and I exploded in rapture, crying out with the force.

"Fuck!" Sax grunted next to my ear.

His cock swelled even more inside me. I clamped down, and then he was coming, filling me like he'd promised. The pressure of his cock head against my cervix created a pleasant ache that produced another orgasm, and another, until I was a trembling mess barely able to stay on my feet. I closed my eyes and gasped for breath, listening to Sax's manly grunts and groans as he emptied his balls into me. We remained connected and convulsed against each other for a long time.

Sax's hands relaxed on my hips and smoothed up my sides to cup my breasts, massaging the mounds briefly, he gently pulled me back away from the tiled wall.

His mouth was against my ear. "Christ, Babe, I've missed this."

I knew that he wasn't just talking about the sex. Sax and I had actually enjoyed our life together, had loved being with each other. We liked the closeness and the domestic routine that we'd developed over the years. Some of it had become comfortable over time, as most relationships did, but we'd managed to keep certain aspects of it spontaneous and fresh. Our sex life had never become a habit or unexciting.

His soft cock slipped from between my legs and he turned me around to face him. His kiss was simple and tender, and the way his warm eyes moved over my face caused a flutter in my belly.

"I love you, Sax. Never doubt that." Emotion choked me into clamping my mouth shut,

He inhaled deeply and released the breath, brushing the wet hair out of my eyes. "I know, Babe."

It hurt that he didn't say it back, but I understood why. He wasn't ready. I was just thankful that he was willing to give us a chance. "We'd better shower. Ava will be up soon."

We spent the next few minutes doing just that. Sax finished before me and stepped out of the shower while I was rinsing my hair. By the time I'd dried off and dressed in shorts and a t-shirt, Ava was awake and ready to begin her day. I didn't see Sax anywhere around, but smells coming from the kitchen revealed that he was fixing breakfast.

I picked up my daughter and gave her cheek a loud smooch. "Good morning, baby girl."

She giggled excitedly, drool running out of the corner of her mouth. I reached into her mouth with a finger and ran it along her gum line. The protrusion that I felt indicated that she had a tooth coming in. Ave closed her mouth tightly and gummed my finger. I was glad that I'd picked up some teething rings the last time I'd gone shopping and that I'd had the foresight to place them in the freezer.

"Breakfast in five, Babe!"

"Just need to change Ava and I'll be right there!"

I wondered what he was fixing. Sax was a good cook. I quickly changed Ava's diaper and slipped a tee with a colorful butterfly on the front over her head. We headed out to the living room. Sax was at the stove, scooping scrambled eggs from a skillet onto two plates. Next to the eggs were toast, sausage links, and orange sections.

Normally for breakfast I would have fruit and yogurt, and maybe toast, but Sax needed more to start the day, and when he cooked he made enough for both of us. Seeing him looking so comfortable at the stove flooded me with warm memories. I didn't fool myself into thinking that we were going to forget about the last year and just take up where we'd left off, too much had happened, but I couldn't stop myself from wishing for it.

Sax hadn't said so, but I knew that we needed to talk.

Chapter 29

S ax

While Holly was busy with Ava, I stepped outside the house to take care of some business. The first thing I saw was Frenchie sitting on his bike across the road, doing something on his fucking phone. Bull had vouched for him, but finding him distracted while he was on duty pissed me off. Before I went over and ripped him a new one, Demon answered his phone with his usual gruff greeting, blasting in my ear.

"Yeah?"

"What's up?"

Demon snorted. "You're the one who fucking called me, Brother."

I grinned. "Anything I need to be there for today?"

"Shit, it's early. Who the fuck knows what will come up? You okay?" I could hear the slight concern in his voice just before he took a sip of something.

"Got some personal shit I need to deal with."

There was a brief pause. "You still at Holly's?"

"Yeah." I didn't really want to go into it with him. What I had to tell Holly was something I'd never told another living soul, but it was time that I shared my past with her. It would help her to see things a little clearer, differently. It might even make her fear me. There was nothing I could do about that. All I could do was hope that with those emotions came understanding. I knew that she could also pity me, and if I saw that in her eyes it would destroy me. But if we were going to have a chance at making us work, she had to know the truth.

"Make it work, Brother. You two belong together."

As if I didn't already know that. I snorted but remained silent.

"She makes you a better man."

I couldn't argue with that. Holly had taken to club life as if she'd been born into it. From the start, she'd accepted and understood the way we lived,

191

had embraced the freedom and the challenges that came with keeping it. She had understood that I wasn't good with talking about feelings and emotions and shit.

I decided to change the subject. "Any word on Radar?" We'd had eyes on his mother's house for days with no sign of him. Cole, Sax, and I had spent a few days in Boulder City looking for his ass after he'd been sighted there. That had been the reason why I'd been a no-show for Holly when I'd originally planned to provide the DNA sample.

A grunt came over the line. "Fucker's a ghost."

"The Dunlap brothers underestimated us. Thought their numbers would defeat experience." Most of his club had been made up of rejects and gang members, other clubs that hadn't made it. If we hadn't stopped the weapons sale with Toledo and another no-name arms dealer, things could have ended differently. "Bastard's scared and on the run now."

Demon laughed. "We'll find him. And we'll find the rest of his holding places and free those girls, too."

That was turning out to be a big fucking win for our club's reputation, as one of the captives had turned out to be the sister of a Texas politician. It never hurt to have one who owed us a favor in our back pocket, and he'd been very grateful that we'd found his sister and returned her home alive—grateful enough to tell Demon that if we ever needed anything to contact him.

It was like a get out of jail free card.

"Don't worry about today. I'm hoping shit remains quiet. Can use a little R and R."

After the last week we'd had, we all could.

"Oh, shit, Brother, almost forgot—got an interesting call last night. Had to do with Holly and that job that fell through."

I perked up. It would be nice to have one thing on my fucking list that I didn't have to worry about. Not that her losing the job at Crickets was that big of a concern to me, but whoever was throwing around my name was. "What?"

"Guy was too fucking chicken-shit to face me or give me his name. Confessed that he'd called Crickets saying he was you."

"The fuck?" There had to be more to the story.

"Yeah. Said he'd been at the clubhouse the weekend before, hooked up with one of the club sluts. She got him good and drunk and convinced him to make the call, said it was a harmless prank. When he got sober and realized what he'd done, he thought he'd better fess up."

I didn't give a fuck who the guy was, I wanted to know which club slut got him to do her dirty work. "Who's the bitch?"

"That's where it gets questionable, Brother—said her name was Lulu."

Lulu?! My gut reaction was to defend her. Lulu had been with us for years, and she'd proved herself to be loyal and honest. All the brothers loved her, and so did the old ladies. She was sweet and caring and a good listener. She'd become more than a club girl to most of us, she'd become a friend.

"Don't believe it, Prez."

Demon grumbled low. "She wouldn't be the first club whore to cause trouble within the club. But I'm with you. Gonna get to the fucking bottom of it."

That meant that Cole would be doing some interrogating. My thoughts drifted to Goldie, and I wondered if she'd had anything to do with this. I hoped not. I'd brought her into the clubhouse thinking that she would make a good replacement for Tamara, but so far she hadn't impressed me.

"Got any way of tracking down the asshole who made the call?"

"Oz is working on it. We think it has to be a new hang around, someone who isn't familiar enough with the club girls to know if he was given the right name."

That made sense. "Got it. You know where I'll be if you need me."

As soon as we hung up I hollered across to Frenchie. He was paying attention now, but that didn't excuse his earlier behavior. "Might as well take off. I'm sticking around. And the next time I see your fucking nose in your phone when you're on guard duty, you'll feel my fist at the end of it."

He opened his mouth to defend himself, and then thought better of it. He may have been in LD's clubhouse, but he answered to any officer that outranked him. He was older than most prospects. I'd found out that he'd done a stretch in prison for assault with a deadly weapon, and he'd been a sniper in the army. Bull knew him from way back, and was backing him to become a member.

He acknowledged me with a chin lift and started his bike. It was a good sign that he could take orders without bitching about it. I turned to go back inside the house. My gaze lit on Holly as soon as I walked through the door. She was just coming out of the bedroom with her phone in her hands.

"I need to call Annabelle to see if she can sit for me tonight."

I raised a questioning brow.

"I work at Grinders."

Oh. If she'd already told me that, I'd forgotten. I had other things on my mind, specifically the talk we needed to have. I'd gone back and forth about wanting to tell her, but had made a decision. "Wait and call her later. Sit down, Babe."

Immediate worry filled her eyes as the sound of my voice sent warning bells through her. When she started to pull out one of the chairs situated around the small dining table, I shook my head and motioned toward the living area.

"Get comfortable." This wasn't going to be a five-minute talk.

"What's wrong?" There was no disguising the slight panic in her voice. She sank down onto the sofa. "You're scaring me." Her lips trembled with a small, nervous smile.

I sat opposite her in the chair, close to the edge with my knees spread and my clasped hands between them. I took a deep breath. Where the hell did I begin? Because once the words left my mouth, I wouldn't be able to take them back, and Holly would know my humiliation. I thought about Ava, sleeping in her crib. This was for her, too.

"Sax, what is it?"

God, I loved this woman. I needed to be strong for her, yet my gut was churning with the acidic bile that wanted to come up my throat. I could tell that Holly wanted to say more, but something stopped her. Maybe she sensed that I needed time.

I took another deep breath and released it.

"I'm going to tell you a story." I clenched my jaw, searching for the strength I'd need to get through it. "All I ask is that you remain silent until I'm done, or I won't be able to finish."

She nodded, and I could see her throat work as she swallowed.

I decided to begin by ripping off the Band-Aid.

"The first time my father raped me I was seven."

Holly gasped sharply, her beautiful face morphing into a mask of absolute disbelief and horror. When her mouth dropped, I shook my head to warn her not to speak. I'd get up and leave the room if she did that. She snapped her mouth shut, but I could tell that what I'd said was tearing her apart. Tears came instantly to her eyes, but she didn't let them fall.

I looked down to the floor, so many fucking emotions running through me. Shame. Anger. Disgust. I swallowed hard, determined to go on.

"I had a baby sister, Stephanie. She was a couple of years younger than me. She was Daddy's little girl. He adored her. Even at my young age, I knew that he had a different kind of love for her than he did for me. He treated her differently. Always brought her toys home from work, spent more time with her, loved her more. It was obvious, but it didn't matter to me. I loved her just as much. I thought that was the way all daddies were with their little girls, because something made them special.

"He'd treated me differently, even before Stephanie came along. He was cold with me, rigid, said I had to be raised with a tough hand if I wanted to grow up to become a man. He rarely sought me out when he came home from work or touched me affectionately. He pushed me away, and punished me for the same things he let Stephanie get away with. I asked my mom one day why he didn't love me as much as Stephanie, and she laughed it off and said that he did, he just didn't know how to show it. To a little boy, that didn't make any sense. But after a while, I got used to his indifference. Stopped seeking his attention and affection. I started school and made friends there."

I paused and took a deep breath.

I couldn't look at Holly.

"I was in second grade when Stephanie drowned."

I heard Holly's shocked gasp.

"We were at a birthday party for one of my friends. They lived on a lake. Parents were there, there were kids all over the place. No one realized Stephanie was gone until it was too late." I finally glanced up at Holly to see that she was silently falling apart. "That night was the first time he raped me. Said it was punishment for causing Stephanie's death. He'd told me to look out for her, and I'd failed. He was beside himself with grief when they found her body. Inconsolable. And then later, when we were at home and it was dark, he came to my bedroom crying and said it should have been me that drowned."

With a cry, Holly left the sofa and fell to her knees in front of me, laying her cheek against my knee. I hadn't realized that I was shaking until then. That my eyes were wet. I put my hand on her hair, smoothing over the softness.

"Every birthday, every anniversary of her death, every kid's holiday, he'd come to my room drunk and beat me with his belt. It always ended the same way." I breathed in deep for control. "There were times he'd just come to my room, drunk and crying over her. Said I was never going to forget it was my fault that she was dead. That if there was a god, one day I would learn how it felt."

I stopped, leaned back in the chair, and closed my eyes on a long sigh. I felt sick to my stomach, and could feel my heart pounding. The attacks hadn't stopped until I got big enough to protect myself. I'd nearly killed him the last time he'd come to my room, drunk and stumbling, with his belt in his hands and his pants already opened. I'd packed up my shit and left shortly after that, and had never returned.

"Your mom—"

"Never knew." I'd made sure of that. Even after she and my old man had divorced, I'd never told her what he'd done to me. What good would it have done?

"Oh, Sax," Holly sobbed brokenly. I was relieved there was no pity in her tone, just teary sadness for a little boy that had been dealt a shitty hand. "I'm so sorry you went through that! I wish I could undo it all for you."

"Don't," I said sharply.

"I hurt for you. I feel sad for the little boy who only wanted acceptance and love from his father." Her tears left a wet spot on my pants leg where she rested her cheek. "This is why you don't want kids? Because of what your father did?"

I looked down to see Holly gazing up at me, her face ravished by tears. "I used to think so," I admitted. Being beaten and abused by my own father for years had cemented the idea that I would turn into a monster just like him. Fear, disgust, shame were powerful tools in shaping someone's moral fiber. After a while, I'd convinced myself that I would do the same thing to my children that he had done to me. But as I'd grown older and wiser, I'd realized that I wasn't my father. That I could never be like him.

My sister's death was another matter. If I'd been watching her like my father had told me to do, she wouldn't have wandered down to the lake and drowned. I'd been selfish, and had been more engrossed in having fun with my friends than watching Stephanie. The guilt over her death had been like an anchor around my neck for all these years. The phobia of being a failure to any children I might have had grown into a fear that I couldn't seem to overcome.

The solution had seemed simple.

You can't fail what you never had.

Now there was Ava, and regardless of what the DNA results said, she was my daughter. I knew that if I wanted Holly in my life, I was going to have to accept her daughter.

"You believe something that you did caused your sister's death, but it didn't, Sax. You were a little boy. It wasn't your job to take care of Stephanie. Your father should have never put that burden on you, he was wrong, it was his responsibility to take care of her and keep her safe, and what he did to you..." She paused and dragged in an uneven breath. "He blamed you for his failures and took it out on you. Did he pay for what he did to you?"

I shook my head. "You're the only one I've told this to, Babe. And that's the way it's going to stay." The last thing I wanted was for my brothers or anyone else to look at me with pity.

"You're afraid that if you have your own children that you'll fail them in some way."

If there was a god, one day I would learn how it felt.

To lose a child, though he hadn't said the actual words.

Holly's assumption was half-right. "For a long time I was afraid that I'd turn out like him. Like father, like son. The thought of treating my own child..." Fuck, I couldn't put it into words.

"You won't, Sax! You're not like your father! You're a good man. Do you think I wouldn't know it? Wouldn't feel it? What your father did was his choice, Sax. It's not something in your blood, not something you inherit. He was sick. His obsession with your sister, his indifference towards you, wasn't natural. Parents are supposed to love all their children. I'm sure if you were to look back you'd recognize that there were signs he was a monster."

Maybe so, but I'd never seen anything that would have warned me of what was to come. Other than his lack of interest towards me, he'd worked hard and had provided for us. The relationship between my parents had seemed normal, but what the fuck did I know? My mom had seemed oblivious most of the time. Maybe that was her way of dealing with what was right in front of her nose. I'd never blamed her, though.

I'd blamed myself for all of it. There had been something wrong with me.

"Are your parents still alive?"

I shrugged. "Don't know. After they divorced he disappeared, mom went to live with her sister in Utah. Haven't talked to her in about ten years." I let Holly take my hand when she reached for it. "I told you this so that you'd understand why I didn't want kids. I didn't want you to think that I was just being a controlling asshole."

Regret flashed across her face. I wondered what she was thinking. If I had to guess, she was probably questioning her decision to stop taking her birth control. But then she wouldn't have Ava, and I couldn't change that.

"We both screwed up, Babe."

Her eyes drifted back to mine.

"No sense in dwelling over what we can't change."

Hope blossomed in her glistening eyes. I wiped the wetness away with the pad of my thumb, and then dragged my thumb down to her luscious bottom lip. "I don't know if I can ever forgive you for what you did, but what I do know is that I don't want to face a future without you."

"What does that mean?"

"It means we take it one day at a time."

Chapter 30

H olly
We take it one day at a time.

Even a week later, Sax's words resonated with me and gave me hope that we were going to be okay. The day that he'd told me about his horrible childhood had ended on a good note. We'd spent the day getting reacquainted; filling in the year we'd been apart while Ava had done everything she could to keep our interest focused on her. Sax hadn't seemed to mind the times that she'd demanded my attention, and I'd watched him carefully to see if there was any hint of resentment or annoyance toward her. But he'd been patient and understanding.

His interaction with her had been telling, and I knew that I had nothing to worry about.

That night, after Ava was sleeping soundly in her crib, we'd made love for hours. Just like old times. I couldn't say how many orgasms Sax had wrung out of me until I'd fallen asleep in blissful exhaustion with his body wrapped around me. I'd awakened that morning to an empty bed, and Frenchie back outside standing guard. Soon after I'd found Sax's brief note next to the coffee maker, with just two words.

Club business.

Just like old times.

That had been a week ago, and other than a few texts and one phone call, we'd had no communication. He hadn't shared with me what was going on with the club, and I hadn't expected him to. Trust was everything, and I had a long way to go to earn his back. It was enough to know that he wanted me.

"Are you sleeping?"

I kept my eyes closed, but I was sure my smile gave me away. It was Monday and we—meaning the girls—were all at Demon and Bobbie's. Well, those of us who had been able to make it. Annabelle and Jolene had to work. Jolene had said that she might be able to show up later, after Danny came in for his shift. She'd told us that one of the perks of Annabelle and Danny being together was that he showed up for work on time.

"I see your smile," Bobbie laughed.

"I guess I'm drifting in and out," I fibbed. Truthfully, I'd been content to just listen to the kids squealing with glee while they played in the pool. Raven had taken Ava over, wanting to get in some practice. She looked so cute in her bathing suit with her rounded little belly, and she was really good with Ava. She was going to make a great mom.

I opened my eyes and peered in the direction of where all the noise was coming from and saw Ellie, JoJo, and Raven clustered in the shallow end of the pool. Annie was out of the sun and napping inside the cabana.

"She's good," Bobbie said, guessing my concerns.

"She loves the water," I said.

"Don't we all at these temperatures?"

I nodded my agreement. I looked over at Bobbie, noticing how her gaze lingered on the girls and the babies. It wasn't the first time I'd seen a wistful look on her face. "So, when are you going to join the ranks of motherhood?"

She laughed softly, pulling her eyes back to me. "I'd like a baby, it just hasn't happened yet."

"You guys are trying?"

Bobbie nodded and smiled. "*All* the time."

"Obviously not enough if you're not in there napping with Annie." We both laughed. "It'll happen, honey. Just be patient."

I tried not to think about the possibility that I could be pregnant again. Sax and I hadn't been using protection, and I wasn't on anything. We'd skirted around the issue the first time we'd hooked up, but it didn't seem to be a concern of his now. I knew I should probably bring it up.

"Yeah, I'm not stressing over it. You want to come in and help me with snacks?

"Sure."

We rose from our loungers. Bobbie reached for a sexy mesh cover up and slipped into it while I grabbed my short floral wrap and brought it around my hips.

"We're going to fix some snacks," she announced when we neared the shallow end of the pool. "Any requests?"

"Fruit." Raven grinned up at us. She was being extra careful with what she ate these days.

"Cheese," Ellie said. "And alcohol of some kind."

Everyone laughed at that.

"Do you have anything sweet?" Samuel was floating on his back, and JoJo slowly removed her hands from beneath him where she'd been supporting his little body.

"I made a dump cake, will that do?"

Raven gushed. "I love dump cake!"

"And it has fruit in it," Bobbie laughed as we continued into the house and to the kitchen. "What about you, honey?" She headed to the fridge.

"I'm good with all of it," I joked. "What do you want me to do?"

Bobbie stopped and thought for a moment. "I think we'll just set it up buffet style and everyone can come in and help themselves. It's too hot to take it outside. Why don't you hunt for the paper plates, napkins, and silverware. There are some plastic forks in the drawer next to the dishwasher."

She turned back to the fridge, opened the door, and started digging around for stuff. Since I knew where Bobbie kept everything, it didn't take me very long to set up the things we needed.

"What are you doing this coming Saturday?" She'd taken out a package of Brie and smoked Gouda and set them onto a paper plate.

I thought for a moment. "Just work that night. Why?"

"We're throwing Raven a baby shower in the afternoon."

"What time?"

"Two." She arranged some crackers around the cheese. "She doesn't know."

"I could come for about an hour. What do you want me to do to help?"

Bobbie set the dump cake down and my mouth immediately started to salivate. "Oh, God, that looks yummy!"

Bobbie laughed. "Thanks. If you can come around twelve you can help us set up. Cole is going to keep Raven away until it's time, then make up some excuse to get her to the clubhouse."

"Sounds like a plan." I was already thinking about what I could get her for a gift. Something practical or something fun? Since they were waiting until the baby arrived to find out the sex, it would have to be something unisex.

"You want to let them know snacks are ready?" Bobbie set out a bowl of fruit and an assortment of White Claw beverages.

"I call dibs on the mango. I've wanted to try that flavor."

A chuckle sounded from Bobbie. "I've got more. I've got to go to the bathroom."

As I called the girls into the house, I received a text from Jolene.

havin fun?

loads

u off fri?

yea

dont u ever work? off today off fri

lol, an wed

lol

why r u buggin me?

girls nite fri spread the word

where

grinders 9

I frowned. We usually went to a club for girls' night. It was odd that the plan was to go to a place owned by the club when the whole idea of girls' night was to get away from the men for a while.

explain

LD wants us 2 stay close says we'll b safer at a place owned by the club

Hmm. I knew that security at Grinders had been beefed up since the trouble had gone down, and all the women had someone from the club watching them. Until our men were done dealing with whatever was going on, our options for going out were limited. I didn't necessarily want to go out to a place where I worked, but I felt safe there and could use a night out.

hope i can find a sitter

ask lulu

she'll most likely watch izzy an samuel

There was a short pause before Jolene came back with, *there's a club girl at LD's i'd trust, she an lulu could team up an watch them all*

idk... I wasn't eager to let a stranger look after my daughter.

hon i promise u carmen is lulu's doppelganger in character

I smiled and reminded myself that Jolene would never steer me wrong.

my house is small but they could all go there
work it out, c u fri 9

"Who are you texting?" JoJo was trying to fix a plate of food while holding her squirming son in her arms.

"Jolene. Girls' night this Friday, nine o'clock at Grinders."

"Figured the alpha assholes wouldn't let us hit a real club," Bobbie snorted, entering the kitchen at the tail end of our conversation. She picked up a plate. "They're so protective." It sounded like a complaint, but I knew better.

"Who's going to watch our little monsters?" Ellie set Izzy down and reached for the dump cake.

"That's for dessert," Raven pointed out.

Ellie winked. "I'll have a piece for dessert, too."

"I'll watch the kids. I can't drink anyway."

I reached for a small slice of Gouda and popped it into my mouth. "No, Raven, you're going, too. Jolene suggested we get Lulu and some woman she knows named Carmen to watch them together." I noticed that Raven was having a hard time fixing her plate and holding Ava at the same time. "Here—" I moved around the island. "Let me take Ava." Ava's little arms reached out for me when I got close. I gave her a sloppy kiss, or rather, she gave me one as I cuddled her close. "Ya'll are coming to my house."

"Who's Carmen?"

I couldn't blame JoJo for the suspicious tone, which matched the frown on her face. "Someone Jolene swears is Lulu's doppelganger."

"I trust Jolene's opinion," Ellie quipped. "I'm cool with that." She stuffed a forkful of cake into her mouth.

"Um, are you planning on feeding Izzy anything?"

We laughed as Ellie glanced down toward the floor to her daughter. When she looked up her face was red with embarrassment, and it was clear that she had forgotten Izzy was there.

She swallowed. "Oops!" She reached for a banana, broke it in half, peeled it, and handed it down to Izzy.

"Well, I guess we know cake is your weakness!"

Bobbie's comment drew a laugh from all of us, a reference to the last movie that we'd watched while on lockdown, Jumanji. In it, cake had been one of Kevin Hart's weaknesses.

Annie chose that moment to walk in from outside. "Ya'll bitches totally forgot me."

I couldn't help but laugh at the sleep line running down her left cheek. "Have a nice nap?" I teased.

She nodded. "Colton and I are trying to get pregnant, and I swear that man has the stamina of a twenty-year-old. Keeps me up all night. When I do get pregnant it'll probably be with triplets."

"Careful you don't jinx it, honey. My best friend, Bailey, has triplets. I helped out with them in the beginning, and they were a handful."

"Is that why she doesn't hang out with us? Too busy?" Bobbie opened one of the White Claws and took a drink.

"Well, she is busy, and she's actually pregnant with number five right now."

It suddenly occurred to me that Bailey hadn't been included in a lot of the club events, and I had assumed that it was because Moody didn't belong to any club.

"Five kids, holy crap!" Annie whisper yelled.

"That doesn't matter," JoJo said. "We need to start asking her to join us."

The conversation led me to think of someone else in the club who had been left out. "While we're on the subject, how about we ask Kathy, too? I like her."

"She's another one who might be too busy, but it's always nice to be included."

"I agree with Ellie. And the more, the merrier. "Raven smiled, munching on an apple."Ava looks like she's about to go down for the count."

I agreed. When she laid her head on my shoulder, it was always a clear sign that she was getting tired. I was surprised that she wasn't whining for a bottle, until I remembered that Raven had given her one about an hour before. "I better change her and lay her down."

"Can I do it?" Annie asked. "Raven practiced with her all morning, it's my turn."

"You're not even pregnant yet," Raven pouted.

"After last night I could be." Annie came over and carefully took Ava from me. "Is her bag in the bedroom?"

I nodded. "It's the pink one with lambs." I watched her disappear toward the guest bedroom before turning back to the girls. "You know, before I came home I didn't have anyone to help me with Ava."

"That's what family is for," Bobbie responded, cutting herself a piece of cake. "When will you get the DNA results back?"

I'd been waiting for that question, and I released a deep sigh. "I already did." It got quiet as all eyes fell on me expectantly.

"They came in the mail yesterday."

Chapter 31

S^{ax} Fuck, I was tired. Seven straight days of being on the road, looking for that asshole Radar, and still no fucking sign of him. Someone had to be hiding his ass. We knew that he was still in the area because he'd been sighted. Three separate groups of us had gone out to look for him, and none of us had had any success. Until we put the bastard in the ground, there would be a concern that some kind of shit could happen. He could just be biding his time to strike.

Between nights spent in shitty hotels and at the clubhouse, I hadn't made it back to Holly. Our texts and phone conversation had done little to take the edge off of my need to be with her. Our last night together had been spent fucking our brains out, and I'd rubbed one off a couple of times from the memory. All I'd had to do was close my eyes and think about the sight of her riding my dick while I played with her bouncing tits.

We still had some things to work out. I wanted us to live together again, but I wasn't sure her little house was big enough, considering that there was only one bedroom. Ava needed her own room. So would any future children...Christ, I wasn't sure how I felt about the idea of more children. Telling Holly about my fucked-up childhood had alleviated any remaining doubts that I'd had that I might turn out to be just like my sperm donor. I knew in my gut that I wasn't like him, that I could never abuse a child.

My father's words had done a lot of damage to my seven-year-old self that Holly had spent hours trying to undo, but no matter how many times or how many ways she'd tried to say that my father had been irrational and cruel, it didn't erase the fact that Stephanie was dead. Because of that, I'd spent a lot of years convincing myself that I didn't want to bring any kids into the world that I would be responsible for.

You can't protect them all the time, Sax. Things will happen. That's life. No one goes through it without being hurt, physically or mentally. It's how we grow,

206

how we learn. All we can do is nurture and love them the best we can. Be there for them. And God forbid if anything happens outside of our control, we'll deal with it then. Together. Your dad was sick. He was a monster for putting the thought in your head that you killed your sister.

Holly was right, and maybe I'd been wrong for keeping that shit to myself all these years, letting it fester and eat away at me like a cancer, so that his words became so cemented in my brain that, even as an adult, I hadn't been able to recognize the lie. Nothing would ever take away the hurt of losing Stephanie in my heart, though.

Nor the hatred I felt for *him*.

I opened the bathroom door. The light behind me allowed me the perfect view of my woman in bed, asleep. I grinned at the sight of her ass hanging out of her tiny sleep shorts, and cursed the blanket tucked intimately between her legs. That was my spot. By the time I walked to the bed I was sporting sizable wood. I stood staring down at her for a minute, giving my dick a few tugs. I'd just gotten out of the shower and was till damp, but I didn't give a fuck. I needed Holly like I needed my next breath.

I took a quick look over at the crib, satisfied that Ava was sleeping soundly, and then I proceeded to crawl up Holly's warm, soft body beneath the blanket. I made it all the way to her tits before she stirred slightly.

"Mmm..." She sighed breathlessly when I moved her tank aside and latched on to a nipple. "I thought I was dreaming."

I sucked hard until her nipple puckered. "No, Baby." I moved on to the other one and did the same thing. Her body shuddered beneath me.

"How did you get in?"

"Through the window." It was a lie. My brothers had a spare key in case there was an emergency that required them to get inside the house to Holly and Ava.

"And they didn't shoot you?" I could hear the smile in her voice. "I'm going to have to issue a complaint." Her hands traveled up to my hair. "I missed you."

"I missed you more, Babe." I moved aside her sleep shorts, baring her mound, then took my dick in my hand and ran the head up and down between her slit. "I'm so fucking hard for you," I groaned, feeling how wet she already was. I couldn't wait. Easily I pushed my dick past her soaked folds and into her pussy as far as it would go.

We both groaned loudly and stilled for a moment to soak it in. Seated deep inside Holly, my dick throbbed on its own, swallowed up by her tight body. "I could go to sleep just like this."

Her husky laugh came against my throat. "In your dreams." I could tell by the strength of her tone that she was fully awake now. "Maybe after I've had a few orgasms and you've filled my pussy with cum once or twice, *then* you can think about sleep."

"Is that so?" I grinned as her warm mouth traveled over my neck and shoulders. "Sounds awful demanding to me."

She began kissing her way down my chest. "I think I'm being reasonable." She tongued one of my nipples, causing my dick to jerk and a deep groan to escape me. "You have a week to make up for."

I pulled back and thrust back in.

"Oh God, Sax!" Holly shuddered. "That feels so good."

I did it again, and again, relishing in her breathless moans and the way her body tightened around my dick. "Jesus, Baby, this first time is going to be fast." It wouldn't take much to send me over the edge.

She whimpered, giving my nipple a hard bite as her nails dug into my sides. "Do it, Sax," Holly demanded, squeezing my dick. "Fuck me fast. Fuck me hard."

"I aim to please my woman," I growled. I was too fucking horny, too far gone to try and rein in my lust. I pulled up one of Holly's legs over my hip, grinding my pelvis down on hers at the end of every thrust. Giving her fast and hard was no problem. I'd gone seven days without her pussy, and sinking inside her hot juices felt too fucking good.

I pistoned into her over and over again, my jaw clenched as I breathed loudly through my nose. Every time I bottomed out I felt her body clamp down on my dick. She was determined to milk me dry, and she would, but first I was going to give her those orgasms she wanted. Somewhere I found the strength to pull out right before I came, and ignored her sound of protest as I scooted down her body. I ripped her shorts off her, took her ass in my hands, and pulled her up sharply, locking my mouth over her cunt.

Her sharp cry was abruptly cut off, and when I looked up I saw that she had brought a pillow over her face. It didn't take much effort before her first orgasm exploded through her body onto my tongue. The sounds of my slurping as I greedily sucked up all her sweet cream drowned out her muted cries as she convulsed uncontrollably. I barely gave her time to catch her breath before I started all over again.

I fucked her with my tongue. I sucked and nibbled carefully at her swollen clit. I used my fingers to reach the elusive sweet spot, flicking it until Holly was quivering and jerking and scraping my scalp sharply with her nails. Her fingers tangled in my hair, at first holding me to her, and then tugging me away before urging me back again. When I sensed that she was close, I flipped her over and pulled her to her knees, needing to be inside her. I wanted to feel her body lose control around me.

Before I could say anything, Holly arched her back and thrust her ass out, opening herself to me. I slammed forward, going deep enough to hit her cervix. She moaned loudly and buried her face into her pillow. The instant my balls slapped up against her clit she came like a fucking geyser, screaming into her pillow. The feel of her body clenching around my dick was all it took for me to come so fucking hard I thought my head was going to explode.

With a grunt I fell over her bent body and unloaded everything I had in my balls.

"Fucking hell, woman, you drain me dry," I rasped against her ear, panting for air. Holly had turned her face away from the pillow and was sucking in air, too. Her wild hair was wet and sticking to her. I reached up to move it out of her face, kissing her shoulder as we sank fully against the bed.

"I needed that," she whispered tiredly.

I grinned as I reluctantly pulled away from her and rolled to the side. She turned her face toward me, but made no other effort to move. A lazy smile tilted her lips up. I could tell by her half-lidded eyes that she was ready to go back to sleep.

"You didn't even kiss me hello."

"I didn't?" I thought about it for a minute. She was right. I leaned in and kissed her. "Hello."

"Hi."

I pulled the covers over her. "Go back to sleep, Babe."

"You won't leave me?" she mumbled.

"No."

She drifted off almost immediately with a smile softening her face. I was tired too, and felt my eyes get heavy as I lay listening to the soothing sound of Holly's breathing. Just as I felt myself about to go under, a small noise coming from Ava's crib jerked me awake again. I listened for a minute, realizing that she was awake and moving around.

I quickly rolled from bed before she could wake Holly and slipped on a pair of clean sweats from the drawer. By the time I made my way to Ava she was making little sucking noises. It didn't surprise me to find her trying to cram her fist into her mouth. When she noticed me staring down at her she giggled and threw her little arms and legs with excitement.

"Shh," I whispered as I picked her up. "We don't want to wake up Mommy." I wasn't uncomfortable talking to her—I talked to Samuel and Izzy all the time. I grabbed the small, thin blanket that Holly kept draped over the crib, a diaper and wipes off the changing table, and took her out to the living room.

I'd changed her a couple of times with Holly watching, and knew that I could handle it. I figured the floor was the safest place for her, so I threw the blanket down and set Ava down on it. It took me a while to get her out of her onsie, and as I reached for the tabs to the diaper, I prayed that I was only going to find pee inside. I slowly pulled the diaper away from her squirming body and peeked, as if it would make a difference. I was going to change her regardless.

I smiled. "Good girl!" I cooed. Then the smile left my face when I realized that I was cooing. If my brothers had heard me, I would never live it down. Ava's little face twisted into a pout, and the smile quickly returned to my face. "It's okay, little darlin', didn't mean to scare you. Soon as we get you changed, I'll give you a bottle. I hope Mommy left one in the fridge, because you're not going to get any milk from my nipples." I stopped the inane prattle and shook my head. What the fuck was I saying?

After putting the clean diaper on Ava I sat back, feeling pretty proud of myself. I dreaded putting the onsie back on her, but Holly liked Ava to sleep in them since she didn't cover her up. Thank fuck her bones were still soft as I contorted her limbs and finally got the garment back on her. By the time I was done I was breathing hard and sweating. Ava, on the other hand, was all smiles and giggles.

"Be right back with your bottle, darlin'." Her little eyes followed me when I got up to leave.

Please let there be a bottle, please let there be a bottle, I chanted all the way to the fridge. I wanted to do this for Holly, she looked so tired. And she should be. I hadn't been very gentle with her.

You would have thought I'd hit the fucking lottery when I opened the door and found two bottles right in front. I grabbed one, removed the nipple, and popped it into the microwave for a few seconds. While I was waiting, I noticed an envelope on the counter and frowned to myself. I picked it up, noticing the name at the top. It was from a lab, and instantly I realized that it was the DNA results. Why hadn't Holly opened it? I set it down when the microwave dinged.

The milk was warm enough, so I replaced the nipple and went back to Ava. "You hungry, darlin'?" When she saw what was in my hand she reached for it with excited impatience. I gave her the bottle, and she began to suck it down like it was good whiskey. I laughed at the comparison and watched as Ava drank the bottle noisily.

As I watched Ava, my mind drifted back to the envelope. Maybe Holly hadn't opened it because she was afraid of what was inside. Hell, I was afraid too, but I wanted to know.

But first I needed to tell Holly something.

Chapter 32

H olly
I was surprised, and a little disappointed, when I rolled over and found that Sax had gone. His side of the bed was cool to the touch. I seemed to remember that he'd told me he wouldn't be leaving. My gaze shot to the crib and found that Ava was gone, too. The scary thing is that I'd known nothing once I'd fallen back to sleep. It had been deep and worry-free knowing that Sax was around.

I slipped from bed naked from the waist down and deliciously achy all over. Sex with Sax had always been intense and satisfying, but it seemed different now, in a good way. He held nothing back, and there was more passion. It made me wonder if he'd been holding back before, afraid to reveal exactly how much he wanted me. But that was silly, right? I mean, we'd been together a long time.

I grabbed a pair of clean shorts from the drawer and slipped them on before going out to the other room, where I expected to find Sax sitting in a chair or on the floor with Ava. What I saw took my breath away, and gave me real hope. Sax was stretched out on the couch with Ava lying on top of him, both asleep. His hand rested against her back, looking so big and strong. The sight caused my heart to swell with emotion. The two people I loved most in the world, together, and looking so natural together.

As I smiled down at them, Sax's eyes popped open. "Just woke up, didn't want to disturb her."

"I'm a crappy mother," I said softly. "I didn't hear anything once I fell asleep again."

His sexy grin warmed me. "I wore your ass out, Babe."

He certainly had. "Coffee?"

"How about I make it while you take Ava?"

I carefully slipped my hands beneath her and lifted her, turning her into my body as I straightened up. She made an attempt to wake up as I arranged

212

her against my shoulder, but quickly settled down again. She wouldn't stay sleeping for much longer, but I put her back in her crib anyway.

Before rejoining Sax I went to the bathroom, took care of business, and brushed my teeth. I stood for a minute in front of the mirror, not impressed with the image reflected back at me. My hair was a scary mess. I ran a brush through it and pinned it up in a sloppy bun, making my way out to the kitchen.

Sax was leaning against the counter, waiting for the coffee to finish brewing. My steps faltered when I saw the envelope in his hand. He was staring down at it, and I could tell that his mind was elsewhere. When his eyes blinked and came up to meet mine, I felt my stomach churn with dread. What if he wasn't Ava's father? I swallowed hard as I made my way toward him.

"You didn't open it." His expression was hard to read.

"I thought we should do it together."

Could he see how nervous I was?

"Come here."

I walked around the island to where he was standing. I stopped in front of him, but I suppose not close enough because he wrapped an arm around my waist and pulled me against him. As my head snapped back he swooped down and took my mouth. Instant arousal curled in my core and I moaned loudly, opening my mouth to the rough demands of his. Our tongues clashed in a sloppy, wet kiss, and I was glad that I'd taken the time to brush my teeth. All I tasted was the refreshing mint of my toothpaste and the warmth of Sax's mouth.

He began to massage my breast through my tank, squeezing and rubbing it until it was swollen and my nipple had puckered. Soon, my kitchen was filled with our mutual sounds of pleasure. When Sax spread his legs I instinctively stepped between them and arched against his hard-on. I was on board for a little morning sex, but too quickly he pulled back, breaking our heated kiss.

"Before we open that envelope I need you to understand something," he rasped out of control. I could feel the strong beating of his heart against me.

I sensed the importance of what he was about to say, and stepped back to give him space. As our eyes clung I saw the fierce resolve reflected in his, as if he'd made up his mind about something and nothing was going to make him change it. I slowly took in air to calm myself down, noticing that he was struggling, too.

"Maybe you shouldn't have kissed me," I teased with a knowing smile.

His smirk set me at ease. "The kiss isn't the problem, it's what happens after that fucking ruins me." He reached down and adjusted his cock.

I felt it was a good sign that he was kidding around. "So, ah, what did you need to tell me?"

He took a deep breath. "I've had plenty of time to think, Babe. Telling you about my past helped me more than you know. Made me accept other perspectives I hadn't been willing to see. Before you, I was content to just go through life alone, with just my brothers and my club and easy pussy. But you came into my life and made me start to want other things. For the first time, I could see a future with a good woman." He looked down at the floor, but not before I saw the regret in his eyes. "Deep down, I always thought it wouldn't last. I waited for the day to come when we were over."

"And then it happened," I said quietly.

"Yeah." He sucked in a deep breath and looked up at me again. "It didn't exactly end the way I'd imagined it would. It wasn't over a stupid fight, or someone else getting in between us."

That wasn't exactly true, but I kept quiet.

"The reason you kicked me to the curb—I never saw that coming. I was too fucking stupid to think it was anything I could have done. I convinced myself that it was because of the assault, that you couldn't stand to have me touch you, and that you just needed time."

"Sax—"

"Let me get this out, woman." He ran a hand through his hair with a sound of annoyance, but I didn't think it was directed at me. "Jesus, I'm taking the long way round." He closed his eyes and rolled his head back on his shoulders, taking a minute before pinning those dark eyes on me again. "All I really wanted to say is that no matter what that fucking test shows, Ava is mine. You get me? I'm her daddy. We're going to be a family, Baby. We're going to find a bigger place for anything or anyone that comes along in our future, and do this together like we should have from the beginning."

As the meaning of Sax's words sunk in, my eyes grew big, and happiness blossomed inside me.

"I want you both in my life, Holly."

Well, it didn't get any more straight-forward that that. I couldn't contain the big smile on my face. He didn't need to hold out his arms for me to go to him and wrap my arms around his waist. We hugged each other tightly, my face crushed against his bare chest. "I love you, Sax. I'll never stop loving you."

"Love you, too, Babe. Now let's open that envelope before you go get our daughter up." Ava was making noises that revealed that she was awake and ready to begin her day.

I turned to the envelope, praying harder than I'd ever prayed in my life that the results were what we both wanted. I wasn't surprised to find my hands shaking when I picked it up and handed it to Sax. "I'm too scared," I admitted in a whisper.

"Nothing to be scared of."

He took the envelope and tore into it. Before he opened the folded paper he held out an arm for me to come to him. He turned me so that my backside was against his front and we were both facing the paper. I held my breath as he unfolded it.

"Ready?" he asked in a slightly nervous tone, before unfolding the bottom portion that listed the results.

I could only nod.

We silently read over the explanation leading up to the final DNA results.

"Thank fuck," came his husky murmur.

Ava was his.

Epilogue

Six months later...
 Sax

"Congrats again, Brother."

The sound of Cole's voice drew my eyes up to where he was just stepping around the empty lawn chair next to me. He patted my knee right before sitting down.

"Thanks, man," I grinned, accepting the beer he handed out to me. "I have a lot to be thankful for."

I scanned the activity in my back yard. My brothers' kids were running around and screaming as they played a game of tag. Several old ladies had spread out blankets in the grass and were sitting with the smaller children. As with any new baby, Cole's infant son, Mathew, was the center of attention. The kid had weighed in at ten pounds and measured twenty-two inches long when he'd been born, so he was already an armful.

My gaze sought out my old lady and now wife, Holly. She looked like a princess in her wedding gown, sitting and laughing among her subjects as our daughter used her as a prop so she could stand up. Her princess-style gown hid her swollen belly. Daughter number two was due in four months, and I couldn't be happier.

Thanks to Holly, I'd conquered my demons.

Her best friend, Bailey, was sitting with her, and her brood were among the children running around. She'd suffered a miscarriage a few months before, and I could see that there was deep sadness behind her smile that didn't quite reach her eyes, which lacked their usual sparkle. Moody had said that she was struggling with the loss, which had occurred in her second trimester. He'd been deeply affected as well, the pain was obvious in his eyes, but he was remaining strong for Bailey. It had to be hell to lose a baby.

As I looked around, I realized that a good number of brothers were missing. "Where are the others?" I asked Cole.

"Some are out front smoking. LD, Demon, Moody, and Loco took off for a ride. Heard Colton in the bathroom gagging." We both laughed at that.

"I wonder if there's any truth to what he's claiming."

Cole shrugged. "Anything is possible. All I know is that since Annie announced she was pregnant he's been suffering morning sickness right alongside her."

"He just wants the attention. Thank fuck none of the rest of us are going through it."

"Gotta be something in the fucking water, Brother." Cole laughed, taking a sip of his beer. "There's more pregnant old ladies than not."

His observation wasn't too far off. Kathy, one of the old lady's who'd started hanging out with our women, was ready to pop any day now. Bobbie—yes, Demon had finally knocked her up—and Annie were both due around the same time in summer, and JoJo had just announced that she was three months along.

"Christ, Brother, this time next year the clubhouse is going to be full of screaming babies."

In spite of Cole's comment, there was a grin on his face, and I knew what he was feeling. Having children changed a man—maybe not always for the better, but for my brothers it made us feel like fucking kings.

The next generation of Desert Rebels was well under way.

So were the new club princesses.

"You think the peace is going to last?"

I wondered what made Cole ask the question, if he had concerns about whether the currently smooth waters would last. His gaze was focused on his woman and son. "For a little while I hope."

The last few months had been quiet, too quiet. Radar was still out there. We hadn't given up on looking for him, but it was as if he'd dropped off the face of the earth. We had other MCs we were friendly with keeping their eyes and ears open. We also had prospects watching his mother's house, but she'd surprised us all by packing up and moving away to another state.

The warehouse that the Knights had been using for their bogus beauty supply business had been abandoned. We'd expected to find a shitload of empty boxes, but what we'd found instead had been weapons and drugs, which had been confiscated by the Feds once someone tipped them off. We hadn't wanted that shit laying around for gangs or nosey kids to get their hands on. We'd taken their computer to the office so Oz could hack into their accounts to see what other shit they'd been up to.

Bull came around the corner of the house and headed straight for us. I couldn't read from his expression if he had good or bad news for me. "Is it done?"

He nodded and sat down on the ground. "Put her ass on a bus. Told her if she didn't stay gone this time, she wouldn't like the consequences."

I released a loud breath of disgust. Good riddance. Goldie had stuck her nose into shit that wasn't any of her business, and had caused trouble between the club members and their women, so we'd cut her loose. Found out that she'd been the one who'd given Lulu's name to the asshole she got to impersonate me on the call to Crickets. We'd given her enough warnings, but she'd thought that because the guys liked what she could do for them she was exempt from the rules. She was a liar and a manipulator, and we didn't need another Tamara in the club. It was good that we'd discovered who she really was early on.

Cole snorted. "She's like a bad penny, Brother." There was a note in his tone that suggested that he didn't think we'd seen the last of Goldie.

"Yup." I grinned when Holly got to her feet with a helping hand from Jolene. "No more talk about that bitch on my wedding day."

Holly grabbed Ava by the hand and walked my way.

There was a big smile on her beautiful face. "Our daughter needs to be changed."

Her words, and the rank smell that wafted from Ava's diaper, wiped the smile right off my face.

"I don't want to take a chance and get poop on my gown."

"That's a weak excuse, Babe," I mockingly grumbled. Ava let go of her mother's hand and grabbed my knee. She was looking more and more like Holly every day, but I saw some of me in her facial expressions, especially when she was being stubborn. But when she peered up at me with that little smile on her cherub face, I couldn't resist her. Like her mother, she already had me wrapped around her little finger, and she knew it.

"Dada."

That's all it took. My heart swelled. I glared at Holly, because she knew it. Her eyes sparkled triumphantly.

"See? She wants her dada to change her."

I let my eyes drift down to her large tits, and then her baby bump. Her changing body turned me on, and I wanted to fuck her all the time. When we'd signed the papers for the house we'd bought, we'd christened every fucking room and surface. I wanted to pull her down onto my lap now, but that would be hard to do with Ava clinging to my leg.

"Here, let me take the little munchkin." I hadn't even noticed Jolene approaching us. "Come to Aunt Jolene, honey bun." She lifted Ava, wrinkling her nose. "Whew!"

"She needs to be changed," Holly said, stating the obvious.

"You think?"

"I was going to put her down for a nap, too."

"I can do that. Do I need to give her a bottle or anything?"

"There's a bottle in the fridge, and you might have to rock her for a minute or two."

"I think I can manage that, huh, baby girl?" Jolene turned and disappeared into the house.

As soon as Jolene was gone, I grabbed Holly by the hand and pulled her down on my lap. "Thank fuck for aunts," I said against her neck. God, she smelled good.

Holly shivered beneath my lips, a husky laugh escaping her. "Sooner or later you're going to have to change a shitty diaper." Her fingers tangled in my trimmed hair.

I pulled back to meet her smiling eyes. "I've changed shitty diapers!"

She grunted. "When?"

I hesitated as I tried to decide if it was in my best interest to change the subject. "Are we really going to discuss shitty diapers right now?" I nuzzled her neck again.

"What would you like to do, husband?" Fuck, I liked the sound of that. "Go for it right here in this chair and give our guests a show?"

"Well, it is our wedding day." I couldn't resist her mouth another second, and covered it with mine. Our kiss quickly turned rough and deep, bringing up moans of pleasure. My dick was already getting hard beneath her ass, and Holly ground against it, using the full skirt of her wedding dress to camouflage what she was doing. "You're playing with fire, woman."

She giggled. "I thought I was playing with your cock."

Someone cleared their throat. Bull was still on the ground, watching us with unashamed interest. Cole was pretending to be interested in something across the yard.

"Just thought I should remind you that I'm here," Bull quipped humorously. "So you won't do anything to make my eyes fall out."

Bull was not the only one—the entire club and their families were there.

Holly laughed, but that didn't stop her grinding, and it wasn't long before my dick was at its hardest. Two could play at her game, and I snuck my hand under her skirt. When she felt my hand on her leg she turned her head to give me a look. I raised a brow, as if daring her to say something. I let my fingers climb up between her silken thighs.

She leaned into my ear. "Don't you dare."

I grunted when her teeth bit down on me. "Oh, but it's okay for you to grind that sweet ass against my dick?"

Someone cleared their throat, and we both looked at Bull. "Um, I hear everything you're saying, and just wanted to point out that it's having an effect on me." The cute, endearing smile he tried to pull off didn't work with his size and bulk.

"Then get your own woman, Brother," I growled, flicking my fingers over the silk covering Holly's wet pussy. I knew she was wet, because her panties were soaked.

"None of the club girls were invited," he pouted.

"Not talking about club girls. You need to find yourself a woman you can have this with. Someone who will put up with your bullshit outlaw ways." I gave Holly a brief kiss. "Someone who loves you unconditionally." My lips landed on her again. "Someone who will make you a better man, Brother. You need a good woman."

"Okay, okay!" Bull said, getting to his feet. "You've just ruined the mood!" He stomped off like a disillusioned child.

One day Bull was going to fall, and it was going to be epic.

Holly and I shared a laugh. "He doesn't know what he's missing, Baby." I easily fingered her panties aside and sank my finger inside her. She quivered wildly, moaned, and spread her thighs to give me more room.

I looked out across our yard. No one was paying us any mind, and if they were to happen to look over, all they would see was a man holding his bride on his lap while she wrapped her arms around his neck and held on. The layers of her skirt easily hid my hand and most of my arm.

"Sax..." she mumbled breathlessly against my neck.

Soon her tongue was licking my skin and sending electrical shocks straight down to my dick. I thrust my hips up in a slow, subtle movement, grinding my aching cock against her bottom. Her sigh went straight through me, and I added another finger. "Fuck, Baby, I can't believe I'm going to make you come right here on my lap."

She shivered wildly, her body clamping down on my fingers as slick cream surrounded them. Little puffs of her hot breath bathed my neck as she held back her normal response when she came.

"You're fucking beautiful when you come." With her pussy convulsing around my fingers, I kissed her roughly and thrust my tongue against hers, showing her what she did to me. "I'm barely holding on here, Babe."

She smiled as a last tremble shook her. "We haven't christened the garage yet," she suggested in a husky voice.

She looked like an angel, her expression soft. The dreaminess in her eyes had little to do with being tired. My gaze lingered on her swollen mouth. Damn, I wanted those lips around my dick. But more than that, I wanted my dick swallowed by another pair of succulent lips. I slowly pulled my fingers from her swollen pussy, satisfied by her low moan of protest.

"I like how you think, Babe."

"Go ahead. I'll make excuses if anyone comes looking for you."

"Oh, God!" Holly whisper yelled at the sound of Cole's amused voice. She buried her face against my neck in embarrassment.

I met my brother's eyes with a contented smirk. I'd forgotten he was there. He clearly had witnessed what had just transpired and made no apologies for it. I couldn't have cared less. We'd been brothers a long time, had been through a lot together, and had seen a lot. I got up with Holly in my arms.

"You do that, asshole."

His laughter followed us all the way to the garage.

THE END

THANK YOU FOR READING my book, SAX. A review where you purchased the book would be greatly appreciated.

Below are blurbs for the first three books in the series as well as a blurb and excerpt for Taken by the Outlaw. Check out my other MC series like Phantom Riders MC and Nomad Outlaws Trilogy.

DESERT REBELS MC SERIES
Cole
Demon
LD
Sax
Bull - coming the end of 2020

BOOK 1, COLE
As enforcer of the Desert Rebels Cole's job is to protect his MC. As a favor to a friend they take in a young woman who they think is trying to escape a crazy ex. But she's lying. When the truth comes out, so does trouble to the club. Cole wants Raven, but will their explosive attraction to one another be enough to overcome the deception, and give them both a chance at happiness?

Book 2, DEMON
Demon - He's a known womanizer and a man with secrets, but he runs Desert Rebels with an iron fist. He had an old lady once, and he doesn't want another one. A spirited little club girl catches his eye, but fear of commitment forces him to push her away. Trouble and betrayal in the MC brings them back together, leaving him with a decision to make—either trust her and claim her, or send her away for good.

Bobbie - She's a club girl whose purpose is to satisfy the men, but there's only one man she wants—the president of Desert Rebels. He avoids her until the pain of seeing him with every other woman causes her to leave. But leaving doesn't keep her from getting into trouble with the club, and soon she's right back where she started. Distrust and betrayal comes between them, but Bobbie's determined to prove to Demon that she can be the old lady that he needs.

Book 3, LD

Jolene was a fucking goddess, the kind that men would go to their death willingly just for a taste of her. To see if the reality lived up to the fantasy. But I wasn't a man. I was a fucking monster. And her interest in me was going to be her ruin. The only thing I gave a damn about was my club, and my brothers. And I was going to show her just how fucking dangerous I could become.

TAKEN BY THE OUTLAW

WOULD YOU GIVE YOURSELF to a stranger? Gwendolyn Myers never thought about it until she runs into Marcus 'Bowie' Ford at the Pink Pussy. A run-down hotel at the edge of town. She's on the run, but one taste of the sexy biker convinces Gwen that her running days might be over!

Excerpt

I watched his hand slowly descend but before it reached my cheek another hand shot out, out of nowhere, clamped around the drunk's thick wrist, and stopped his arm in mid air. Heat radiated off a presence behind me and I slowly turned, catching my breath. My eyes locked onto the narrowed, fear-provoking gaze of my savior, the hunky biker. His warm, whiskey laced breath bathed my forehead, and my gaze fell to his mouth, which was way too close. For a crazy second I wondered what kissing those sensuous lips would taste like.

Realizing that I was staring I glanced up at him.

"Run little girl, things are about to get fucking ugly."

I shook my head. "I don't want to cause any trouble."

"Then you should have heeded to my warning." His tone said he was annoyed that I hadn't. "Now get the fuck out of here."

I opened my mouth to speak but his expression darkened even more. I shivered from the intensity, realizing that his anger was directed at me as much as the drunk. I didn't know this man, and it occurred to me that I didn't want to. He might be hot as hell, but danger dripped from every pore.

He looked determined, and dangerous.

I don't know why I listened to him, but suddenly my arm was released, and I was heading toward the door. On my way there I dodged other bikers who were quickly heading toward the bar. I heard a loud commotion start but didn't turn around. Once I hit the door and was outside, I took a deep breath, not realizing until then that I'd been holding my breath.

Fuck! My heart was racing a mile a minute. That was...intense, and had happened so fast. I couldn't recall ever striking anyone before. My reaction to the biker's command pissed me off because Greg had always told me what to do. I didn't need some stranger taking his place, even if it was my fault for jumping when he said jump. If I was going to make it on my own then I needed to exert myself.

I checked for traffic before crossing the road to the hotel. I made it all the way to my door before remembering that I'd forgotten my damn sandwich. Crap! Well, I wasn't going back. The cheese and crackers I'd picked up at a convenience store earlier would have to do until morning. I unlocked my door, and headed straight to the bathroom, thinking about a nice long soak in the tub.

Don't miss out!

Visit the website below and you can sign up to receive emails whenever Tory Richards publishes a new book. There's no charge and no obligation.

https://books2read.com/r/B-A-WTJ-NBXFB

BOOKS 2 READ

Connecting independent readers to independent writers.

Did you love *Sax*? Then you should read *Ace*[1] by Tory Richards!

The Sentinels continues with ACE.Standalone MC romances!A road side bombing left Ace disfigured and dead inside. He faces the world with silent bitterness and a damaged ego. Then a quiet beauty comes into his life cracking the shell around his wounded heart and healing his soul.

Read more at www.toryrichards.com.

1. https://books2read.com/u/mZPWZl

2. https://books2read.com/u/mZPWZl

Also by Tory Richards

Desert Rebels MC
Cole
Demon
LD
Sax

Nomad Outlaws Trilogy
Ruthless
Dangerous
Furious

Phantom Riders MC Trilogy
Phantom Riders MC - Hawk
No Mercy
What He Wants

The Evans Brothers Trilogy
A Perfect Fit
Surrender to Desire
Burning Hunger

Standalone
Up in Flames
Bishop's Angel
The Mating Ritual
Out of Control
Wicked Desire
Someone to Love Me
Wild Marauders MC
Big, Black and Beautiful
Carnal Hunger
Dark Menace MC - Stone
His Possession
No Escape
The Evans Brothers Trilogy
The Sentinels
Hands-On
Kiss Me!
Obsession
Wild Surrender
All the Right Moves
Hers to Claim
Nothing But Trouble
One Night Only
Serve and Submit Series
The Cowboy Way
Ace
The Alpha Wolf's Mate
A Soldier's Promise
Taken by the Outlaw

Watch for more at www.toryrichards.com.

About the Author

Tory Richards is a fun-loving grandma who writes smut with a plot. Born in 1955 in the small town of Milo, Maine, she's lived most of her life in Florida where she went to school, married and raised a daughter.

Penning stories by hand at ten, and then on manual typewriter at the age of thirteen, Tory was a closet writer until the encouragement of her family prompted her into submitting to a publisher. She's been published since 2005, and has since retired from Disney to focus on family, friends, traveling, and writing.

Read more at www.toryrichards.com.

CPSIA information can be obtained
at www.ICGtesting.com
Printed in the USA
BVHW081047170522
637233BV00006B/196

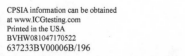